D1624797

PRAISE FOR

Keep My Heart in San Francisco

"An absolute charmer of a book. . . . Delightful!"
—**JENN BENNETT,**
author of *Alex, Approximately* and *Starry Eyes*

"This rich and delightful debut kept our hearts from page one."
—**EMILY WIBBERLEY AND AUSTIN SIEGEMUND-BROKA,**
authors of *Always Never Yours*

"Intriguing and charming."
—*KIRKUS REVIEWS*

"Sweet and charming. . . . Those who enjoy Jenn
Bennett's works or Rachel Lynn Solomon's *Today
Tonight Tomorrow* will find much to love."
—*SLJ*

Also by Amelia Diane Coombs

Keep My Heart in San Francisco

Between You, Me, and the Honeybees

AMELIA DIANE COOMBS

SIMON & SCHUSTER BFYR

New York   London   Toronto   Sydney   New Delhi

SIMON & SCHUSTER BFYR

An imprint of Simon & Schuster Children's Publishing Division
1230 Avenue of the Americas, New York, New York 10020

Text © 2021 by Amelia Diane Coombs
Jacket illustration © 2021 by Kat Goodloe
Jacket design by Tiara Iandiorio © 2021 by Simon & Schuster, Inc.

For information about special discounts for bulk purchases, please contact Simon & Schuster Special Sales at 1-866-506-1949 or business@simonandschuster.com.
The Simon & Schuster Speakers Bureau can bring authors to your live event. For more information or to book an event, contact the Simon & Schuster Speakers Bureau at 1-866-248-3049 or visit our website at www.simonspeakers.com.
Interior design by Tiara Iandiorio
The text for this book was set in Adobe Caslon Pro.
Manufactured in the United States of America
First Edition
10 9 8 7 6 5 4 3 2 1
CIP data for this book is available from the Library of Congress.
ISBN 9781534453005
ISBN 9781534453029 (eBook)

To Steve, I couldn't write love stories
until I met you

"No need to hurry. No need to sparkle.
No need to be anybody but oneself."
—Virginia Woolf

Chapter One

LITTLE-KNOWN FACT: HONEYBEES are nature's first feminists.

I hold the hive frame up to my face, and scan the layer of fuzzy bees that cover the wax comb. After I track down the laying queen—the key indicator of a healthy colony—I set the frames back into the hive body. I give them a puff from the smoker to clear any bees off the tops of the frames, then lower the copper lid into place. A few girls fly onto the landing strip, their back legs swollen with pollen. They look like colorful balloon pants—white, red, yellow, purple, and gray blues.

Over the years I've learned everything about the eco-system of the beehive. For instance, any honeybee out in the wild, climbing over flower petals collecting pollen or nectar, is female. I could go on about them for hours, but if you have to know one thing about honeybees (other than we'd die without them), know this: Male bees are drones, and drones either (a) die *while* mating with another hive's queen or (b) get kicked out of the hive when winter comes. Sometimes the females chew off their wings so they can't fly or return to the hive.

They're an advanced society.

I step beneath the vine-covered archway and dump the smoker onto the bench, popping off the lid with my thumb. Dark tendrils curl into the air, the charred remains of twigs and fire-starter fibers turning to ash in the wind. My phone buzzes, but since it's tucked into the back pocket of my shorts, I don't bother to check it. My nitrile gloves don't work on touch screens. Not like I need to look at the text to know it's Nan prodding me with reminders.

Like I'd forget my own high school graduation.

Bail on it, play hooky? Sure. But my head's not too far into the clouds to forget the actual ceremony. I snap off the gloves, sticky with strings of honey, and toss them in a sealed garbage bin beneath the table. Exhaling, I drag my fingers through my damp hair. Even without a protective bee suit, sweat rolls down my back, collecting in the waistband of my shorts. I lean against the workbench and take a moment.

Breathe. Listen to the slow, steady pound of my heart.

Out in the apiary, the worries of daily life fall away. I'm

able to forget everything and focus on being present. Since my anxiety disorder isn't going away anytime soon, I spend most of my free time out with the bees. More so when I'm stressing out about life, my future.

My phone buzzes again.

I push away from the workbench and force myself back toward our two-story renovated farmhouse. I slide my phone from my pocket and unlock the screen, scanning the text message.

NAN: Be there in fifteen!

ME: Okay, okay! Meet you out front

I tuck my phone back into my pocket and try to shake off the creeping unease clinging to my shoulders. My beekeeping-induced calm is slipping away, lessening with each step I take closer to the house.

"Josie!" Mom leans out the back patio door, waving me inside. "Isn't Nan picking you up any minute?"

"Sorry, lost track of time," I lie as I hop up the patio stairs. Before entering the house, I pat down my body, making sure a bee isn't hitching a ride with me inside. All clear. I scoot past Mom and step over Ford, our ancient French bulldog who's curled up at the base of the stairs, and run up to my bathroom.

No time to shower, so I roll on deodorant—real deodorant, not the hippie crystal stuff Mom stocks in my bathroom—swap my damp tank top for my *Destroy the Patriarchy, Not the Planet* tee, and attack my curls with a brush. Then frown and twist them back into a bun, securing the whole mess with an alligator clip. My graduation gown hangs from the second-story banister outside my bedroom, and I grab it on my way down.

"Text me if you forget anything." Mom pulls me in for a hug, and I inhale her natural scent. We rarely wear perfume, since it attracts bees, so she smells like I do. Of clean smoke, of honey, of nature. "And I'll see you there! Exciting!"

I force a smile and hoist my bag over one shoulder, the graduation gown dangling from my other hand. "Super exciting," I say, infusing some enthusiasm into my words.

Mom smushes my face between her cheeks and rests her forehead on mine. "Proud of you, Bug."

For a moment I squeeze my eyes shut and savor this. Pretend like I'm someone Mom would actually be proud of. Then a car horn blares outside and that brief moment of yearning shatters.

"Go, go," Mom says with glassy eyes, shooing me out the door. "Don't be late!"

"Bye!" I kiss her on the cheek and jog down the front porch steps to Nan's waiting Mini Cooper, idling in our dirt-dusted parking circle. Music blasts from the rolled-down windows and I duck inside, instantly assaulted by

Nan's French perfume and twangy country-pop lyrics.

"Hey!" Nan squeals, and leans across the center console to hug me. Then she pulls back with a disapproving frown. "*That's* what you're wearing?"

"We're all wearing these ugly-ass gowns. Does it matter what's underneath?" I ask, dumping my stuff in her back seat. The car lurches as she shifts it into drive, and we're off.

"Well." Nan turns down the music a notch. "You could've at least done something with your hair. This is our *high school graduation*, Josie."

"Exactly. I'm not there to impress anyone. And, I'll have you know, I brushed my hair," I say defensively, flattening my bangs with my palm. "I was out in the apiary. Lost track of time." I don't like lying to my mom or Nan, but they wouldn't understand. Graduation—the ceremony, the implication of it all—makes me dizzy with anxiety, and beekeeping helps calm me down.

Nan's sigh speaks volumes. "Getting out of this shit town will be the best thing that's ever happened to you, Jos," she says, her blinker clicking as we wait to turn left into Volana High School's parking lot. "Trust me."

I bristle. Then I wilt.

I've never been all that talented at standing up to Nan Johansen.

We park and Nan turns to me, a brilliant smile lighting up her face. Silken hair parted down the center, not a strand out of place. Sometimes my best friend is blinding, like the sun.

So golden, so essential to my daily life and survival. But that doesn't mean she can't burn.

Despite it all, I love Nan. Every friendship has a balance, and Nan's always had the bigger personality. She's the more outspoken, divisive one. But I've never minded living in Nan's shadow; it's safe here.

"This is it," Nan says, grasping my hands with hers. "Graduation. Then Los Angeles."

"This is it," I repeat, a lump forming in my throat. Tiny flecks of guilt collect like buildup on my heart. Clearing my throat, I smile. "Let's go get ourselves graduated."

◇ ◇ ◇

School officially let out during the last week of May, and in the week since, the administration outfitted the quad with rows and rows of folding chairs and one of those portable stages. Families and students crowd the seats. There are balloons anchored to chair legs and dozens of floral arrangements turning the air sweet. It doesn't resemble the school I dragged myself to five days a week for the past four years.

Good riddance.

The graduating class sits together in the front rows. To my left is Olivia, one of my closest school friends. Olivia's the type of friend you don't invite for a sleepover because you're not *that* close, but who you're always relieved to see at school. Nan's to my right, holding her pink note cards so close to her face I'm surprised she can even read them. Like the rest of us, she's wearing an ugly navy graduation gown, but a golden sash cuts across her chest: VALEDICTORIAN.

"Did your mom do this?" Olivia asks, tapping the top of my head. She smacks gum nervously between her molars and keeps readjusting her dyed-blue curls. I don't know what she's so worried about. In the fall, she's off to New York City to earn her bachelor of music and major in the violin. Following her dreams.

Since we keep our mortarboards, most graduates decorate them in some quippy or personal way. Mom decorated mine with a gigantic bedazzled honeybee. Olivia's has a miniature violin glued to the base, and Nan's simply states, in pink gemstones, BOSS BITCH.

I fiddle with the bobby pins precariously holding the mortarboard in place. "Yeah, she stole my cap last night," I say, grinning. Not many things make sense in my life, but honeybees always do. My one constant.

"I love it," Olivia says, and I kind of regret not making more of an effort with our friendship. But Nan was always quick to point out three's a crowd whenever I suggested we invite Olivia to hang out with us.

"Don't encourage her." Nan shuffles her note cards together and tucks them into the pocket of her gown. "When we're in Los Angeles, Josie isn't going to have time for beekeeping."

Olivia frowns, but our principal walks up the stage,

tapping her forefinger to the mic. A screech of feedback resonates, and she adjusts the mic, beaming out at our class.

"Hello, graduates," Principal Pedersen says, "and welcome, family and friends! This afternoon . . ."

I tune her out. Tune the entire graduation out. Because something barbed and panicked fills my chest. Not just the fact I'll have to walk across the stage in front of everyone, although that *does* make me nauseous. No, it's all the unknowns. The end of the first chapter of my life. The beginning of one still shrouded in mystery.

Nan squeezes my arm as she passes, headed to the stage to deliver her speech as Volana High School's valedictorian. My best friend climbs the stairs and stands behind the podium. Despite everything, I'm proud of Nan. During our high school career, I've seen all the pain Nan's endured to earn her title. Not like I'd ever dare ask her, but I can't imagine it was worth it.

Resting her hands on the podium, Nan searches the crowd until our eyes lock. I give her a thumbs-up. She takes another deep breath and begins her speech. A speech she's recited in front of me so many times I have it memorized. Fiery, full of Nan's passion, with a few choice and clichéd Robert Frost quotes.

Except Nan never takes the road less traveled.

Standing up there, Nan is so happy, so confident, and excited about her one-size-fits-all future.

Our future.

Two best friends on their own in Los Angeles.

Nan wants me to be more excited about all the unknowns ahead of us—me at Golden State University, her at UCLA. She has our entire next four years mapped out in her mind *and* on a shared Pinterest board. It's a beautiful future. One of endless summers, palm trees, and delicate tan lines, of sun-bleached hair and boys with strong jawlines and salt water on their lips.

Except there's one problem.

I'm not going.

Chapter Two

EVEN THOUGH NAN'S headed to Europe at the end of the month for her graduation present, she still tried to convince me that we needed to celebrate *tonight*. But after graduation, I'm officially peopled-out for the day. Mom had to run after the ceremony to work the closing shift at Waxing Poetic, our shop in downtown Volana, and I promised I'd meet up with her. Plus, we're supposed to FaceTime with my gran in Florida after dinner. An annoyed Nan drops me off on her way to a house party up in the foothills, and I approach the storefront alone.

I pause outside the door, which is decorated with etched flowers and the store name on frosted glass, and my anxious bones relax. Graduation is over. High school is done. I'll tell

Mom about Golden State University soon. Not tonight, but soon. Then I'll finally start living the life *I* want to live.

Believe it or not, I never wanted to lie to everyone. Long-term deception wasn't my goal.

But I'm stubborn. Probably to a fault, but at least I know what I want from life.

Hazeldine Honey has been in my family for three generations, and I'm next in line. I always figured it'd be the natural progression of things, my mom taking me under her wing when I turned eighteen, as her mother had done for her. Except my mom wants my sights set on college, not the honey business.

"If you don't apply to college," Mom said last November, "then you can't work at Hazeldine Honey."

So I did the thing. I applied to a handful of colleges and crossed my fingers none would accept me. But one small college did, and when Nan heard Golden State University wanted me next fall, that was it. A done deal, her plan in motion. GSU isn't far from the prestigious UCLA campus.

Mom was so excited—so proud—when I received the acceptance. And I get it, I really do. She wants me to have the life she missed out on. Mom always wanted to go to college, but a mixture of finances and responsibilities at Hazeldine Honey kept her Volana-bound.

In May, when I had to accept or decline my acceptance, I turned it down. It wasn't a rash decision—I'd humored the idea ever since that acceptance e-mail pinged my inbox. After all, Mom said I had to apply to college.

She didn't say a thing about me actually going.

I haven't told anyone what I did. Avoidance, anxiety, and guilt have been the main themes of my life for the last month. Nan will be mad. Mom will be disappointed. I'm just waiting for the right moment to break it to them. To explain that it's not like I want to ditch college and bum around. I want to *work*.

I finally push open the door, the bell above it jangling.

Waxing Poetic was my mom's own extension of Hazeldine Honey, the impact she made on our ongoing legacy, when she took over for Gran. It's an unusual, quirky store with pricy jars of raw honey, royal jelly, and real beeswax candles. We get enough cross traffic from the touristy wine country to sell our products. A bee spends her entire lifetime producing one teaspoon of honey—roughly seven drops—and the high price tag is warranted.

Mom expanded the store to include a small book section when I was in elementary school. The shelves are stuffed with poetry, new releases, nonfiction, obscure used tomes, and special orders from our customers. The entire store smells warm of beeswax and used books: musty and real.

It's a long, narrow store laid out in an L shape, and I work my way between the wine barrels laden with various bee products to the register at the other end. Music plays from the record player, and I can hear my mom's voice distinctly rise in pitch as I round the corner.

"We are not selling funny honey," Mom snaps, bracing both hands on the counter.

On the other side, with his back to me, is Mr. Blumstein. "I'm not making any accusations. Just telling you what I've heard around town. Don't shoot the messenger."

Mom's pale cheeks are flushed. "Right," she snorts. "Like you're *not* the one telling everyone in town."

The Blumsteins have lived in town longer than my family, and they're—I'm not being facetious—my mom's *nemeses*. Rather than insert myself in their argument, I hang back behind a display tower of locally made greeting cards and shamelessly eavesdrop.

Mr. Blumstein is as old as time, an unapologetic asshole who hasn't gotten any nicer as the years have gone on. His wife is no peach either. Mrs. Blumstein is always giving me these *looks*, like I'm a slut for wearing jean shorts or a tank top when it's ninety degrees, or that one time she caught me making out with James Funderburk, my ex-boyfriend, in the town square. The rivalry has gone on since the mid-1900s. It's long-standing.

"You have no proof of that." Mr. Blumstein sniffs loudly, then snatches up a nearby jar of blackberry coastal honey from Mom's display and holds it up to the light.

Tensions are particularly high this year because the Blumsteins stand to lose their record-breaking winning streak at the Northern California Honey Show this July. Before Gran and my mom began entering, Blumstein Farms won Best of Show twenty-five consecutive years. To honor their winning streak, they were given an award—the Royal Jelly—and are still honored every year with a commemorative slide show. It drives my mom up the wall.

If we win this summer, we'll finally catch up with the Blumstein family. Ribbon number twenty-five. And the Royal Jelly—with its modest cash prize—will be ours.

"Put that down," Mom snaps, eyeing Mr. Blumstein as he inspects the jar of honey, "unless you plan on buying it."

"I wouldn't buy this crap if it were the last honey on earth."

I can't help it—I *laugh*—and my mom and Mr. Blumstein turn in my direction.

"Hey," I say casually, like I wasn't just eavesdropping, and step out from behind the card tower. I point to the jar of honey in Mr. Blumstein's hand. "The blackberry coastal is really delicious this year."

Mr. Blumstein's beady eyes sweep over me. Returning the jar of honey to its display, he harrumphs, then strolls past me without another word. The bell jingles as he exits the store.

"Sorry about that," Mom says, the color in her cheeks slowly fading.

"Mr. B. is back on his bullshit, I see." I stand next to the air-conditioning unit while Mom wraps up closing the store. It was a high of ninety-five today and graduation turned me into a sweaty, sticky mess. I lift the back of my shirt to cool off.

"Yep." She locks the register and grabs her purse from the office. "He also said this year's the year."

"That he's going to keel over?"

"Josie!" Mom admonishes, nudging me with her elbow as we walk out. "Be nice."

"What? He's old. And mean."

Mom gives me a *behave* look and locks the storefront door, but her lips twitch as she fails to hide her smile. "I was thinking Magic Noodle for dinner. Are you sure you don't want to go out tonight with Nan?"

"No way." I lean against the brick building, smiling at my mother. "I want to celebrate with you. And Magic Noodle sounds delicious." She loops her arm through mine, and we start off across the grassy town square to our favorite Chinese restaurant. "So. What else did Mr. Blumstein say?"

"Apparently Penelope's moved back to town." Mom's voice is edged.

"Penelope?"

"Their daughter. She was down south and worked at an apiary. Won some awards." Mom pulls her braid over one shoulder and starts worrying the split ends. She's always been so youthful compared to other people's parents, and the gesture makes her look younger than her forty years. Even if she talks the big talk, she's nervous and awful at hiding it when it comes to the honey show. "Mr. Blumstein was bragging about her. He thinks she might help them nab the win in July."

"They think they can beat us because their daughter came to town?" I ask, and we duck inside Magic Noodle. The restaurant is old and doesn't have air-conditioning, but the food is cheap and delicious. We've been coming here for years and snag our favorite table in the back.

Mom purses her lips to one side as she adjusts her chair. "They're confident about their harvest, and Penelope brought some fancy new extraction equipment up with her. Makes him think they might have the advantage. But I'm not buying it. He's trying to psych me out."

"Not gonna happen," I say, my determination palpable.

Mom grins as if she's proud of the cutthroat little monster she birthed. "That's the spirit. This is our year, Bug. I can feel it." To say my mom is competitive is putting it lightly. "But he must be nervous to spread such a ridiculous rumor, right?"

"Definitely," I agree, but the conversation is cut short by our waiter.

I love this. Chinese food and talking shit about the Blumsteins. All I want is *this*, forever.

"I have something for you," Mom says, and digs into the tote bag she brought with her from Waxing Poetic. She brandishes a medium-size gift bag across the table. "Herman's was having a blowout sale."

Money's pretty tight around here, and she already gave me a graduation gift this morning—the honeybee pendant necklace currently resting against my collarbone was from her and Gran—but I take the bag curiously. Peek inside.

And do my best to pick my heart up from the floor.

"Oh wow," I say, all forcefulness, as I pull out a shower caddy kit. Beneath it are a pair of shower sandals. "Thanks, Mom."

"I keep saying it, but I'm so proud of you." She rests her chin in her upturned palm, those green eyes watery. "College . . . this is huge. I love you."

My smile is wobbly on my lips. "Love you too."

◇ ◇ ◇

By the time we stuff ourselves full of Chinese food and walk home beneath the fading June sun, the guilt that plagued me during dinner has lessened—slightly. Mom will be disappointed, maybe even pissed off, when I tell her the truth about college, but she'll have to accept my decision without nudging me forcefully in the opposite direction. More than anything, though, I need her to realize that Hazeldine Honey is my place too. The silly feud, the honey show, the passion—all of it.

Our two-story house is backlit by the dropping sun as we walk up the porch steps to the electric-blue front door. Inside, I slide onto the wooden floor to greet Ford while Mom grabs her iPad from her bedroom. The old dog clambers into my lap, reaching up to lick my chin. I nuzzle my face to his and press my eyes shut.

"I'm not a bad person, right, Ford?" I whisper to the dog, who just slurps his tongue along my jaw.

Mom's footsteps pound the staircase as she jogs back downstairs.

"When's Gran calling?" I ask, resting my chin on Ford's balding head.

She glances at the Betty Boop wall clock above the fireplace mantel. "Ten minutes. Where's your mortarboard?"

I groan, struggling to my feet. *"Mom."*

Mom quirks her brow. "It's for Gran," she reminds me.

Really, that's the *only* thing she could've said to make me willingly put on the ugly gown—which I need to return to the school by Friday—and plop the mortarboard onto my head.

Up until four years ago, Gran was here, and an active member of the local "beek" community. But she has advanced Parkinson's disease, and you can't handle fragile frames of honey and brood cells with shaking hands. Instead of staying local, she moved to where all old folks go: Florida.

Gran leaving California right as I started high school was devastating in its own way. For so long, it'd been the three of us. Well, four if you count Ford. And then she was gone. As if that wasn't bad enough, two years later her Parkinson's got worse and the dementia set in. Mom tried getting her to come home, but it was too hard for Gran to be around what she loved and could no longer do. She's also incredibly stubborn. It must be genetic.

"What is wrong with this thing," Mom mutters with a frown, struggling to power on the iPad. She's not technologically savvy. I reach my hand out and she relents, and I navigate to FaceTime. The Instagram app, with its dozen unread badge notifications, catches my eye, but they can wait until later.

Since Mom shuns computers and technology, handling Hazeldine Honey's social media accounts is my biggest—and sole—responsibility. She avoids giving me too much work so I can "enjoy my teenage years." But if you ask me, the best way for me to enjoy my teenage years would be working full-time at Hazeldine Honey. I don't mind the social media part, though. Beekeeping is a male-dominated field and the average age of a beekeeper is *fifty-seven*. But with the right content and online reach, maybe we can engage younger audiences.

That's my goal, at least.

Once FaceTime is set up, I lean the iPad against the vase on our coffee table and sit on the couch. And not a second too soon because *GRAN CALLING* flashes on the screen. I hit accept. After a second, the resolution loads, and Gran's happy—yet confused—face becomes clear.

Watching Gran fade, the cornerstones of her personality disappearing, has been painful. She used to be her own brand of vivacious. Gran was sharp-tongued and smart, and wielded a lip-liner pencil like no other.

"Hi, Gran," I say, feeling a little foolish in my graduation getup.

Gran's normally auburn hair has faded to gray; her caretaker, Rosa, hasn't dyed it recently. Her skin is loose, sunken around her cheeks, and her face is naked. Behind her is a seafoam-green wall and a small window. An orange tree sways outside the pane.

The last time I FaceTimed with Gran was more than a month ago. She usually calls us with Rosa's help every weekend, and while I'd noticed her speech was wobbly and she was more forgetful than normal, it was different seeing it.

Tonight, Gran's a colorless, wrung-out version of herself. The only thing reminiscent of the grandmother I once knew is her fuzzy zebra-print sweater.

Gran's motions are jerky, but it isn't the internet connection. "Emmaline?" she says, confused as she peers at me. Mom frowns and settles beside me on the couch.

Rosa comes into view. "Sorry. Annalyse is having a rough day. The nights aren't easy for her." She murmurs something to Gran, and I catch a few words. Rosa reminding my gran about my graduation. Reminding her who I am. I dig my fingernails into my thighs and pretend like it doesn't hurt.

"Mom," my mom says loudly, "Josie had her graduation today. Remember?"

Gran nods, and the embarrassment in her eyes makes me look away.

"Of course," Gran says, but her words aren't certain. They're slow and unsure, stuttery due to the Parkinson's. "Of course, I remember."

Mom launches into a detailed play-by-play of my graduation while I forcefully smile, even though the conversation is one-sided. She tells Gran about Nan's valedictorian speech.

That one unfortunate kid who tripped and fell on their face. How scholarly I was onstage, with my diploma in hand.

"I'll send you the video, okay, Mom?" my mom says, enunciating her words carefully, loudly. Like she's talking to a child.

Rosa ducks back into view. "Oh, that'll be lovely, won't it, Annalyse?"

Gran nods, her eyes meeting mine. "Proud of you, Josephine."

My chest tightens, but my smile is real for the first time since I got on the call. "Thanks, Gran. I miss you."

"Miss you, too," she says, and Rosa turns the camera to face her.

"Congrats, Josie," Rosa says, then looks to my mom. "Emma, can we touch base tomorrow?"

Mom's smile falters. "Sure. Give me a call in the morning, okay?"

Rosa nods and we all say goodbye. Then the screen goes dark.

"Mom," I say, sliding the mortarboard off my head, "Gran's getting worse, isn't she?"

Mom releases a long sigh and pushes up from the couch. "Yes. But let's wait to hear what Rosa says tomorrow before jumping to any conclusions. Parkinson's is . . . complicated. And you heard what Rosa said. Nights are harder for her."

I glance at the clock as I remove my gown and mortarboard. Seven our time. Ten in Florida, probably past Gran's usual bedtime, but Mom told me Gran wanted to see me on graduation day. If Mom wasn't such a mess with technology, she could've FaceTimed my whole graduation, but filming it was enough of a challenge for her.

I don't see what the big deal is. Graduation isn't a *thing* for me. I'd much rather Gran see me excel out in the apiary. But we all have our own versions of what's important in this family.

Mom pops into the kitchen and returns with bowls of ice cream, settling beside me on the couch.

"So." She unfolds one of Gran's quilts over our legs. "Are we doing so-bad-it's-good or bad-movies-people-think-are-good movie night?"

Shuffling all my hurt over Gran into the back of my brain, I tap my chin in faux thought. Force myself to be present with my mom, because she deserves that at the very least. "The latter." While the categories might sound similar, they're two very different calibers of film.

As Mom cues up *American Beauty*, I snuggle into the couch, resting my cheek on her shoulder. Comfort her without words. Because if I hurt this much over Gran, what she feels must be ten times worse.

Mom's my person. Nan only lives ten minutes away and Olivia's always asking me on day trips into the city, but there's no one I'm closer to than my own mother. Maybe it's because she had me young, at twenty-two. Or because we're so similar. Small-framed with narrow shoulders and bony wrists, green eyes, and pale skin that burns within minutes without sunscreen. Our biggest difference is our hair: Mom's a brunette, and mine is coppery orange.

That's why it hurt so much when she pushed me toward college. If that's what my mom thinks I need from life, then how well does she actually understand me?

When the credits roll, it's not even ten, but Mom yawns so big her bright green eyes begin watering.

"I'm headed to bed, Bug." Mom wraps the quilt around her shoulders like a cape. "Need anything else before I go to sleep?"

"Nope," I say, and offer up a tentative smile. "See you in the morning. I can help with the hive inspections before it gets too hot?"

"We'll see. Might want your help at the store." After giving me a smacking kiss on the cheek, Mom disappears upstairs.

Ford lets out a stubby-nosed snore from his pile of blankets in the corner.

The house is suddenly too big, too lonely. I turn my phone around in my hands. Nan's off getting drunk. Olivia's out with her girlfriend. Leaving me alone on graduation night. I didn't expect this would hurt, the hidden loneliness. After all, I was totally over human interaction earlier today. But now I'm antsy. Filled with energy over worrying about Gran.

I take the empty ice cream bowls into the kitchen and set them in the sink. The window above the sill overlooks our backyard. I pull the sleeves of my cardigan over my hands and lean my forearms against the counter, staring outside.

The land slopes down to the apiary and it's too dark to see the Langstroth hives, but it's comforting knowing they're out there.

I've always wanted to be a beek like my mom, Gran, and my great-grandmother.

Hazeldine Honey was birthed during the Great Depression; my great-grandmother Millicent started it all when she moved to the lush wine country in the 1930s. Millicent died before I was born, and her daughter, my gran, took over Hazeldine Honey. Millicent raised Gran to follow in her footsteps, and my mom kept the tradition alive. We're not the biggest apiary in the area, but we have the sweetest honey. And twenty-four blue ribbons from the Northern California Honey Show to prove it. Soon to be twenty-five ribbons.

I want to leave my own imprint, my own *legacy*, on this business.

I want this. More than anything.

Chapter Three

I **NEED TO** channel my restless energy, so I fish Ford's leash out of the basket by the front door. He waddles in circles around me, thumping his nonexistent tail. The dog's ancient, half-blind, and a total love. Before Gran left us for Florida, he was her shadow. Since she left, I've done my best to take care of him. Including multiple daily walks and sending cute pictures of him to Rosa to show Gran.

I clip the leash to Ford's collar and rub his stubbly little head. Making sure the leash is secure, I lead him out the front door and down the street into the moody darkness. There's only one place open in Volana past eight: LaLa's Diner. And I could definitely go for some of their famous blackberry cobbler. Celebratory cobbler, because I am officially, finally done with high school.

"Wanna go to LaLa's?" I ask Ford as we pause on the street corner, then wince at how utterly pathetic this is.

The old-man dog wags his nubby tail at me.

With a sigh, I tug on his leash and we cross the street. "Let's go, buddy."

As we walk, I fumble with the buttons on my sweater. The cool air nips at my bare legs and the oversize cardigan hangs loose near my knees, but I wouldn't trade my middle-of-nowhere-California goose bumps for anything.

Soon enough, we enter downtown Volana. LaLa's is kitschy and sacred. Open 24-7 with cracked vinyl booths, perpetually sticky countertops, low lighting, and consistently good food. There's a heated outdoor section with flimsy plastic screen walls. Ford and I cross the grassy town square to reach the diner.

Since Ford's my plus-one tonight, the hostess seats me outside and fetches the doggo a bowl of water. I don't mind sitting on the patio because LaLa's is *packed*. Families, friends, balloons, and gifts crowd the tables. Faces I recognize but names I don't know and never bothered to learn. This is where a typical recent high school graduate might be walloped with a huge dose of nostalgia. But not me. All that flutters in my chest is an antsiness to finally start living *my* life.

"Hi, Josie," Carol greets as she walks over with her pad. "How was graduation?"

"Not bad, but I'm glad it's over," I say truthfully. I come

here a lot, and Carol's worked at LaLa's for as long as I can remember. My mom and I have a game where we try to guess Carol's age, because she is truly *ageless*. Seriously, we have no idea. She could be thirty or sixty. Her big blond curls are coiffed in perfected rockabilly form, and she has doves tattooed on each of her collarbones.

"School or the ceremony?"

"Both. Definitely both." I grin, then hand over my menu. "Any chance I can get some blackberry cobbler?"

Carol winks her eyelash extensions. "Sure thing. We technically ran out, but"—she lowers her voice—"I always set a few aside for my best customers."

"You're a lifesaver."

Carol beams, kneeling to pet Ford. "Can I get you anything else, sugar?"

I put in an order for chamomile tea, and Carol bustles away.

Relaxing a bit, I pull the sleeves of my cardigan down over my fists and glance around the patio. One big group—a graduation celebration for a girl I vaguely recognize—took over the largest outdoor table, a cutesy couple cuddles together on one of the two-person booth seats, and a few tourists busy up the place. Tourist season kicks off in the late spring and now it's full tilt.

Carol pushes the patio door open with her hip, juggling my cobbler and tea. "Here you are." She slides the plate and mug down in front of me. "Holler if you need anything else, okay?"

"Thanks, Carol." I give her a smile, and she hurries back inside.

The cobbler is sweet and crumbly, and actually does a decent job of lifting my spirits. Seeing Gran earlier pushed my already precarious mood into full-blown sadness. My only alternative to spending my evening alone was going out with Nan, and partying in the foothills sounds like torture, but a distraction would've been nice. Even if my anxiety skyrockets in social situations and I often end up the default designated driver.

I work through Hazeldine Honey's Instagram notifications with one hand, the other scraping cobbler onto my fork, and occasionally people-watch. Growing up in a small tourist town is weird. There're always a handful of people you see around town—and have seen since you were a toddler—then hundreds you'll never see again. It's an odd combination.

The tea gets to me, and I slide out of my chair to use the bathroom, but Ford tries to follow me. The leash tying him to the table goes taut, and he whines. The dog has serious abandonment issues. Maybe because Gran left him here when she moved to Florida.

"I'll be right back, you weirdo," I mutter, scratching him behind the ears. LaLa's won't let him inside with me. I've tried. Not turning around, I back away from Ford, who begins whining even louder. Loud enough that a few people turn to find the source of the noise.

My cheeks warm—*freaking dog*—and I turn to the nearest booth. Just one lone guy reading by himself. He's an unfamiliar face, around my age. Probably a tourist, and a good-enough dog sitter if I've ever seen one.

I untie Ford's leash and tap the guy on the shoulder. "Hi, this is embarrassing, but can you watch my dog while I use the bathroom?" As I talk, I try to figure out what he's reading because it's a graphic novel and I'm a snoop. "Pet him or something so it doesn't sound like he's being tortured?"

"Sure," the guy says, and glances up.

I open my mouth to thank him, but my brain comes to a full stop. Because the guy I asked to watch my dog is cute. Very cute. Rich brown eyes, complemented by wavy tawny-brown hair. Freckles softening sharp cheekbones. Nice, wide shoulders. An uneven smile tugs at his lips.

Without responding, I shove the leash into his hands, turn on my heel, and hurry to the bathroom, silently cursing myself for being unable to hold a conversation like a normal person. Nope, it's like the second I noticed him, my brain shut down. But the guy is cute and our pool of guys at Volana High School was *extremely* small. And after I broke up with James Funderburk last summer, I had zero interest in the male species.

Still don't, I mentally correct myself, and duck into the single-stall bathroom to pee, then wash my hands. The mirror above the sink is small, and I hate the extra second I take to clean up. Not like it'll do much good. For one, I'm dressed like a hobbit. Nan attacked my face with some of her makeup before graduation, but it's mostly been sweated off by now. Baggy cardigan sweater. Jean shorts. Jelly sandals. Truly, this is *not* my best look.

Not like it matters.

Not like I care.

I switch off the bathroom light, and as I work my way through the crowded restaurant, someone calls my name. Olivia and her girlfriend, Moira, are first in line by the pickup register at the main entrance.

I glance out the large picture windows to my left. The cute guy is sitting with Ford curled up in his lap. Ford's a sweet dog, don't get me wrong, but he's also fourteen, has liver spots, and is perpetually letting out one long dog fart. I mean, I rarely let him sit on *my* lap. But since they look comfy, I head toward my friends.

Olivia and Moira are dressed up and comically out of place inside LaLa's. Olivia's pretty blue hair is down around her brown shoulders, and she shivers in her bodycon dress. Moira's only a bit more subdued in a pink jumpsuit, her platinum-blond bob styled in big waves. They look *amazing*, and I bristle with self-consciousness over my outfit.

"Hey," I say when I reach them. "What're you two doing here?"

"Pit stop on our way into the city," Olivia says, lifting up a bag of to-go food. She tilts her head to one side. "Are you here by yourself?"

I nod and smile as if to show I'm totally okay with my sad-sack plans. "Yeah."

"You want to come with us? There's room in my car," Moira offers, her doe eyes hopeful. If Moira is anything, it's painfully sincere. All the time. She's, like, the nicest person I've ever met.

"Nah, I'll pass." I'm a solid *no*, considering they're going to a rave. In San Francisco. At, like, ten at night. "I'm probably going to head home soon anyways."

Olivia purses her lips to one side, as if debating her next words. "Hey, so, James is here."

"James?" I repeat, because I really hope I heard her wrong. But Olivia nods sympathetically. My anxiety flares—the tightening of my shoulders, the uptick of my heart rate—as if reminding me this is what I get for leaving the comfort of my house. "Where?"

Olivia motions toward the patio. "A booth outside. He and his cousin came in after us."

I release a low groan. "Thanks for the warning."

I haven't seen or talked to James Funderburk since last September. I was hopeful that'd be the very last time I *ever* saw my ex-boyfriend, and I definitely don't want to see him tonight. See, people generally don't take it well when you stop replying to their texts. James was no exception.

The cashier hands Moira her receipt, and she stuffs a handful of napkins into the to-go bag. "You sure you don't wanna come with?"

"I'll be fine." I offer up a limp smile. "Have fun."

Olivia and Moira both hug me before walking out, and I'm left alone to devise a way to pay my check, get my dog, and get out of here before James sees me. If Ford *weren't* here, I'd leave and pay Carol tomorrow. She'd understand. Unfortunately, later-daysing out of this situation is impossible.

Ducking my head, I walk outside and head straight toward Ford and his impromptu dog sitter. Too bad it's near impossible to be stealthy with hair brighter than a traffic cone.

"Josie?" James calls as I dash past his table.

Shit, shit, shit.

I pretend not to hear, and practically dive-bomb into the bench opposite Ford and his dog sitter, slouching out of sight.

"Uh"—the guy leans forward and peers down at me—"are you okay?"

I peek over the edge of the table. "Yep. Don't mind me. Just hiding."

His gaze shifts to something over my head. "I take it you don't want to talk to the guy headed our way?"

"Very astute of you."

"Josie?" James sidles up to our table and looks between me—nearly horizontal in my efforts to hide—and the guy sitting across from me, still holding Ford.

Busted. I sit upright and stare to my left, but he's in my peripheral. James is your typical NorCal bro—he even had the lifted truck, which I loathed. At a solid five foot ten, James isn't bad-looking. Sandy-blond hair in an overgrown buzz cut, a Superman dimpled chin, and nice blue eyes. But all the Superman chins in the world can't make up for his utter lack of a personality.

I turn and give a forced smile. "Oh . . . hey, James. Didn't see you there."

"I tried texting you. Thought we could hang out while I'm in town—"

My smile disappears, because *seriously?* "Um, no. It's just—I'm busy. Really busy, all summer . . ." I ramble, and don't bring up that I blocked James last summer and never got the booty-call texts he likely sent.

"Oh, right. Yeah." James's cheeks flush, and he looks warily at the guy across from me. "So . . . who's this?"

"I'm Ezra," the guy introduces himself, and holds out his hand. "Nice to meet you."

"Uh, hey." James shakes Ezra's hand with a perplexed expression before turning to me. "Jos, if we could just talk—"

Ezra interrupts him and says, "It's obvious she doesn't want to talk to you. Maybe you should listen to her and leave?"

While thankful for Ezra's intervention, the conflict-averse part of me is resisting the urge to duck beneath the table again. The entire exchange is making me cringe, but my desire for James to get the hell away from this booth is worth the anxiety sweats.

"If you really want me to leave, Josie, I'll leave," James says, his cheeks flushing darker. "But I'm not leaving just because this guy thinks I should."

"You know what?" I say, and sit up straighter. "I agree with Ezra. I think you should go."

"I was willing to give you a second chance, but not if you're going to be such a bitch about it." And with that, James stalks back to his booth.

Ezra widens his eyes, like *Can you believe that guy?* and I laugh. How nice of James to show his true colors. It makes me feel even less guilty about disappearing on him last summer.

"Thanks for that," I say, then add jokingly, "Whatever can I do to repay you?"

"You could . . ." He trails off and surveys the patio. "Oh! You could share your blackberry cobbler with me?"

I almost laugh at this random request, but then Ezra turns back to me and smiles. My mouth goes dry. Surely my pupils are dilating, because that's one nice smile. Ezra should trademark that smile.

The least I can do is share my cobbler with him, right?

"A fair trade." I scoot out of the booth, trying to ignore the warming in my cheeks that's no doubt brighter than neon. My fair complexion and fiery hair make for an unfortunate combination: I wear my emotions on my face.

Carol spots me, and winds her way over between the crowded tables with a rag and spray bottle. "Josie, sugar, are you done with your table? Grad night's the worst and we have people waiting."

Before I can even open my mouth, Ezra says, "We can share a table. Unless you have to get going?"

I look from the cobbler to Carol and back to Ezra. Either I stay and share my celebratory cobbler or I pay my bill and walk home with Ford as my only company. My anxiety is not-so-gently nudging me toward the latter, but I'm surprised that I want to resist it. That I want to stay and talk to Ezra.

"Y-yeah, okay. I don't have . . . anywhere to be." Hopefully that's not *too* pathetic. As I collect the cobbler and the rest of my stuff, Carol winks—small towns are the worst sometimes—and begins wiping down the table.

I slide back into the booth seat across from Ezra and place the plate between us. "Sorry there's not much left. It was my celebratory cobbler."

"Celebratory cobbler?" He grabs one of the extra plates stacked by the condiments.

"Yup. Graduation was this afternoon." I divvy the remaining cobbler between our plates. Gran's situation made it impossible to be excited about graduating earlier, but now I feel it in full force. Making me much bolder and talkative than normal. "Hence, celebratory cobbler," I add, motioning to the cobbler with my fork.

Ezra takes a bite of cobbler and nods his approval. "I understand now."

"LaLa's cobbler has won, like, ten awards. All the plaques are up by the register."

"Oh, I saw. That's why I tried to order it. But the waitress said they were out?" He grins teasingly. It's a very boyish grin—I like it.

"Hey," I say defensively, "I've been coming to LaLa's since I could eat solid food. I earned this cobbler."

"That's like . . . cobbler nepotism."

I snort-laugh, and cover my mouth so I don't spew cobbler on him. "What?"

Ezra laughs, and leans forward conspiratorially. "LaLa's is playing favorites! But I guess I can't complain." Then he smiles again, which causes my brain to go completely blank for a solid five seconds.

Can you blame me? I'm pretty sure I saw dimples when he smiled.

"Are you using me for my cobbler access?" I ask once I recover.

He nods gravely. "Sorry you had to find out this way."

A strange and pleasant warmth fills my chest as I laugh.

Between bites of cobbler, Ezra asks, "So, that James guy. Did you break his heart or something?"

"No," I hasten to say. "*Definitely* not."

He lifts a brow, scrubbing Ford on his balding little dog head affectionately as he polishes off the cobbler.

"But I might've ghosted him. A little bit." I narrow the space between my thumb and forefinger to signify the amount. "It was warranted."

James and I had a compatibility problem, which was highlighted when we had sex a few weeks before he left for college. The act was very uncomfortable, slightly painful, and a total letdown. Conversely, James thought the sex was, and I quote, "awesome" and kept texting me to hang out whenever his parents were gone.

Since we'd already decided to break up when he left for college, I just . . . stopped replying to James's texts until he left town. Be it anxiety or just a personality flaw, I really don't like conflict. I swore off guys afterward. That relationship confused and disappointed me. If that's what romance was supposed to be like, then why bother?

"I don't even think he liked me that much," I add, which is the sad truth. We had fun at first, but he quickly tired of my anxiety. "But James is the kind of person who isn't used to being told no."

"Clearly not much has changed," Ezra says, glancing at James's booth. Then his eyes meet mine and he offers another smile that makes my palms sweat.

The conversation stalls, and I chew on my bottom lip. Without the cobbler, without the James Funderburk icebreaker, I'm left anxious and unsure. All my earlier boldness gone. "Thanks again. For Ford *and* running interference."

"Why're you thanking me?" Ezra leans both elbows on the table. "I was well compensated. Worth it."

I glance curiously across the table. Ezra's so . . . calm. So easy to talk to. I'd bet money that he's never felt socially anxious in his life. Just as I open my mouth to say I should head home—tonight's been oddly perfect, and the longer I wait, the more I'm tempting fate to ruin it all—Carol swings by our table.

"Can I get you two anything else?" she asks, and flips open her notepad.

"I'll take a tea," Ezra says. "Herbal, if you have it?"

"Um, yeah. Another chamomile tea," I tell Carol, who beams like that was the correct answer and moves on to her next table. Guess there's no harm in staying a little longer.

Ezra scrapes his spoon against the blackberry-streaked plate for crumbs. "Don't get me wrong," he says, "this cobbler is amazing. But you *graduated*. Why are you hanging out here by yourself?"

"My mom and I celebrated earlier," I explain, not like that makes me sound any less like a dork. "My friends invited me out, but I didn't feel like going out and doing all that . . . I don't know, it's not my scene."

"I get it." Ezra gives me this look like he understands. "I'm glad you didn't."

My face flushes, and I rub my sweaty palms against my thighs. "Me too. Volana is small, though. There's not much to do, even if you want to."

"I haven't been here long, but it has that . . . everything-closes-by-sundown kind of feel."

"You're not far off," I say with a small smile. "You're visiting, then?"

"From Santa Barbara. Kind of a pit stop between home and college . . ." He trails off, and for the first time, his cheerfulness drops for a half second. "Where are you headed next year?"

"Um." I pause, considering my options. No one knows about GSU, but Ezra's another wine country tourist. It's not like I'll ever see him again. And I need to tell *someone.* "Nowhere, actually. I applied and got in, but college isn't for me. I turned my acceptance down."

"Really?" He tilts his head to one side, like he's studying something he doesn't quite recognize. "That's brave."

No one's ever called me brave before, and I twist my sleeves nervously under the heat of his attention. "Thanks."

For some weird reason, I'm overly aware of my heart. Like when I'm anxious—it's an unavoidable beat. Except . . . I'm not anxious. Well, that's not true. Anxiety is my default setting. It's more like, I'm no more anxious than normal. Which is weird.

Ford, who I honestly forgot was sleeping on Ezra's lap, lets out a snuffy snore, and we both laugh—the strange energy between us breaking. Carol brings us our tea, and Ezra makes room by moving the graphic novel he was reading earlier. But I catch a glimpse of the cover: *Gest*, volume five.

"Have you read the latest release?" I ask, my inner nerd freaking out. "Volume seven?"

Gest is an indie graphic novel fantasy series with a steady underground following. I read a lot of comics, but it's by far my favorite. It has everything: kick-ass ladies, star-crossed lovers, warring kingdoms, and simply amazing artwork. I don't know anyone who reads *Gest*. Nan mocks the entire franchise whenever I make the mistake of reading it in front of her, and Olivia prefers poetry anthologies to comic panels.

Ezra's brows crease for a second before he follows my line of sight. Then another smile breaks out across his face. "Yeah! I'm rereading the whole series."

"What do you think about Gregor's decision to abandon his fleet?" I'm way too eager but too excited to care. "Pro or con?"

Ezra doesn't say anything at first—just stares at me with an unreadable expression. "Pro," he says after a moment, nodding resolutely. "Gemina could've died if he hadn't."

"Right? Thank you. I'm on this *Gest* subreddit, and everyone there blames Gemina."

"That's probably because Reddit is the Bad Place," Ezra jokes with a half smile.

"Don't get me wrong, I love Volana, but the people here don't have the best taste in graphic novels. Reddit's the only place I've found other readers."

"Well," Ezra says, and holds my gaze, "until now, right?"

"Right." For some reason, I'm far too aware of my body and breathing and my sweaty hands clasping my mug. Before I can say anything else, my phone chimes from the depths of my purse, and I check the screen.

> **NAN: This is Emery. Can you pick Nan up? She's puking all over my front yard.**

I sigh. *Damn it, Nan.* "Hey, sorry, I need to go."

"Oh," Ezra says. Is it bad that I'm happy he seems disappointed? "Everything okay?"

"Yeah." I scoot out of the booth. "Well, no, I guess not. Nan—my best friend—is apparently drunk and puking all over her host's front yard. I have to go pick her up."

Ezra grimaces. "Yikes."

I pull some money from my wallet and tuck it beneath the saltshaker. Ezra plops a sleepy Ford onto the ground, and I'm left with no excuse to linger. Twisting Ford's leash around my hand, I say, "Hey, it was nice meeting you."

"Likewise." Ezra shifts, crossing his foot over his knee. "Definitely the highlight of my night."

"You need to get out more, then," I joke.

He hesitates, like he wants to say something else. "Uh—"

"Thanks again," I say, accidentally interrupting him, and my cheeks warm. I tug Ford's leash and he clambers onto his feet. "C'mon, pup. Bye, Ezra."

"Good luck with your friend." Ezra gives me a half smile—which fully trips up my heart—and opens his copy of *Gest*.

I force myself out of LaLa's before I change my mind about picking Nan's drunken ass up, turn around, and spend the rest of my night with the cute tourist with the nice smile. Instead I hurry Ford home, grab Mom's keys, and head into the foothills.

My chest is lighter, though, as I drive to fetch Nan. Connecting with Ezra over *Gest* was the most fun I've had in weeks. Spilling my secret felt amazing. And Ezra called me *brave*. *Brave* has never, ever been a word used to describe Josie Hazeldine.

Too bad I'll never see him again.

Chapter Four

MY ALARM GOES off at eight thirty the next morning and I smack it silent. Stare at my bedroom ceiling with its peaked roof and the droopy cobwebs I was supposed to clean last week. I'm not too concerned about getting out of bed just yet, though, since my mind is still solidly reliving last night and Ezra. Replaying that slow bloom of his dimples every time he smiled. One perfect night, even if it was cut short by Nan's binge drinking.

After James Funderburk and his many disappointments, I told myself I was over dating. Not for a lack of interest; I was too disheartened to try again. But last night, I *liked* talking to Ezra, with his cute dimpledness and great taste in graphic novels. I liked how I felt around him. Which is ridiculous. I don't even know the guy.

On one hand, I want to ask Carol to break the law and find out his last name from his credit card information. On the other, never seeing Ezra again is probably for the best.

It's also entirely possible he paid in cash.

My alarm blares again—must've hit the snooze button—and I lean over the edge of my bed to unplug it from the wall. It silences midbeep with finality. I sit upright and rub at my eyes with my fist.

My bedroom used to be my mom's. The posters on the walls are hers and remain for the sake of nostalgia and her dated, yet excellent, taste in music—Radiohead, the Smiths, Nirvana, Foo Fighters—held down by layers of tape and pushpins. A more recent addition to the scene is my best friend, stretched out on an air mattress with one arm thrown over her head.

Sliding out of bed, I step around the air mattress and stare down at Nan for a moment.

Part of me wants to jostle her awake and tell her about last night. But if I keep last night to myself, I can pretend like it was perfect. Pretend that Ezra liked me. Whereas if I told Nan . . .

Well, let's just say Nan has a habit of making most things about her.

With a sigh, I turn on my heel and pad downstairs.

"Good morning." Mom waves, sloshing coffee from her mug onto the kitchen counter.

I beeline straight to the coffeemaker. "Morning."

"Did I hear you leave last night?" she asks, merely curious as she wipes up the spilled coffee with a rag.

Mug in hand, I lean against the counter. "Yeah, sorry, I borrowed the car. Had to pick up Nan."

"Ah, so *that* explains the five-inch heels in the entry hall."

I tap my nose. "Nothing gets past you."

Mom motions to the kitchen table and I sit down across from her. "On a scale of one to ten, how bad will Nan's hangover be?"

I palm my coffee mug with both hands. "A solid eight, if I have to guess."

Mom winces. "There's Advil in my bathroom."

I'm unsure if it's Mom's parenting ideology or just the fact she was a young mom, but no topic is off-limits. When it comes to drinking, drugs, and sex, Mom has an open-door policy. Not like I've ever really had to utilize it. I don't like any major form of inebriation, and my sole sexual encounter was enough to turn me off—pun intended—from ever trying again.

Until recently, I've been the epitome of the perfect daughter. The first and only time Mom punished me is when I drew on her bedroom wall with crayons when I was seven. Which is why I have to be careful, waiting until the perfect moment to tell Mom about GSU. It'll be a shock, but hopefully one she'll understand.

I tuck my leg beneath me and hold the mug to my chest, watching my mom from across the table. Her brow creases, but it's not for Nan's imminent hangover. She looks concerned.

"Is everything okay?" I ask.

"I touched base with Rosa earlier," Mom says, and she stares over my shoulder at something in the distance. "Gran's . . . not doing as well as we hoped. Rosa's been monitoring her and says she's been declining steadily since her fall last month."

"Shit. Really?" I don't want it to be true. The swoopy happiness in my chest, courtesy of last night, is fading fast.

Mom drags her fingers through her hair, disrupting her curls. She worries her bottom lip between her teeth. "Yeah. She, um, got violent with Rosa last night. After our phone call." She shakes her head sadly. "Gran didn't recognize Rosa, started yelling and fighting her. . . . It's not good, Bug."

"Oh, Mom. I'm sorry." My heart aches. I'm caught between sadness and anger. Sad because I can picture Gran, all alone in Florida, slowly losing her mind to a cruel disease. Angry because she should've never moved away in the first place.

Mom reaches across the table, wraps my hand in hers. "It'll be okay. Rosa gave me the information of a neurologist in Orlando. They have an opening next week, on June ninth. Rosa said we got lucky; sometimes the wait lists are much longer."

"What can we do between now and then? Anything?"

Mom lifts one shoulder. "Not much, but I'll be flying out to be with her and talk to the doctors in person."

The weight of those words hits me hard. "You're going to Florida?"

Mom *never* takes vacations during our busy months. Or

really ever. When I was younger, we could leave because Gran was here, but now the only time we're comfortable leaving is fall, after harvest, and the winter. Bees aren't high-maintenance, but they need care. Especially when our livelihood depends on them.

"I found a cheap flight out Sunday morning from Oakland." Mom's gaze finally returns to mine, her green eyes sad. "Think you'll be okay here by yourself?"

"Yeah," I rush to say, still puzzling over her words and what they mean for the apiary. The weight of that responsibility. "You'd be okay with leaving me in charge?"

"Of course. You're going to be eighteen in a few weeks, after all." Mom sips her coffee, the crease between her brows softening. "It'll only be ten days; I booked a return on the sixteenth. But I need to see Gran's situation in person. Don't worry, I'll be home in time for your birthday."

"My birthday," I say, nodding. I turn eighteen in less than three weeks, on June 21, the summer solstice. But right now, I couldn't care less about my birthday. "Right."

Mom keeps talking, but I zone out as I sip my coffee. Gran's situation is shitty, and I wouldn't believe it if I hadn't seen her lost eyes last night. How she confused me for Mom.

I hate that this is happening, but Mom's absence could be the opportunity I've been waiting for. A chance to prove myself. A chance for Mom to finally see all that I'm capable of.

"Bug?" Mom nudges my slipper-covered foot with hers.

"What?" I blink at her.

"You don't mind?" she asks. "I hate asking. It's your last summer before college, after all. But I could really use the help with the apiary."

"Yeah." I sit up straighter in my chair. "I don't mind."

Mom smiles and—*poof*—her concerned brow softens completely. "I'll have Bev check on you, and she's around if you need help." She pauses for a moment. "Thank you."

"Anytime." My heart's warm.

"Can you head over to the store?" Mom asks, scooting back from the kitchen table to set her mug in the sink. "I have to wrap up some bookkeeping and banking if I'm going to be gone a week. Bev'll take over at three until closing."

It's nine. Waxing Poetic opens at ten.

"No problem. Let me get dressed." I down the rest of my coffee, the grounds catching in my teeth, and grab a muffin on my way back upstairs. Mouth full of blueberry streusel, I push open my bedroom door and assess the situation. Nan's still passed out, which is to be expected.

"Nan," I say, shifting my beehive-shaped pencil holder and some pens loudly on my desk, hopeful she'll wake up. *"Nan."*

She groans and rolls onto her side. "Too early."

"I have to work." I walk past the bed, whipping open my blinds.

Nan swears as the sunlight filters in, and sits upright. She rubs her eyes, smearing makeup onto her cheekbones. "You're such an asshole. It's *early*."

I sigh. "I peeled you off Emery's front lawn, so be careful who you're calling an asshole." My closet's a mess, but I find a clean T-shirt and skirt, and grab some underwear from my dresser. Then I duck into my bathroom for a quick shower.

After I'm showered and dressed, Nan's disappeared from my bedroom. I find her downstairs with my mom, nursing a big mug of coffee. Nan's mom has always been distant and cold—the opposite of mine—and she gravitates toward my mom and her soft openness.

Nan's the mostly tightly wound person I've ever met. Competitive, sometimes cruel in her bluntness. She's been my best friend since the sixth grade, but lately I don't know how things ended up so . . . unbalanced between us. As we got older, and Nan became hyperfocused on her academic achievements, the little grooves between us deepened. Because the more Nan pushed herself at school, the more often Nan had to find ways to blow off all that steam, her extroverted side pushing my introversion to its limits.

Nan was always the brighter one in our friendship. The louder, more outspoken one. Most of the time, I liked how she took charge and made all the difficult decisions for me.

Nan always took the lead, and I always followed.

Well. Until recently.

Because I've begun wondering: Why do I pour myself empty for a person who never, ever returns the favor?

Mom offers to drive Nan home on her way to the bank, so I head to Waxing Poetic with Ford in tow. As I walk, I pass the hill leading to Blumstein Farms. We live half a mile from their farm and adjoined property. There are dozens of farms in Volana—they're as common as wineries—but the Blumsteins' might've been the first. Horses, cows, chickens, goats, and their towering boxes of honeybees. Their store, Bee Happy Beekeeping and Farm Supply, is downtown, close enough to Waxing Poetic to anger the hell out of my mom even if they sell beekeeping and farming supplies—the only things we *don't* sell.

Yesterday, Mom was so concerned about Penelope Blumstein coming to town. Their daughter should be around Mom's age, and she must've bolted from Volana post-graduation because I don't remember her at all—only the two elderly people my mom and Gran have loved to hate since my earliest memories.

I tug Ford down the road, leaving Blumstein Farms in my periphery. I can't conjure up a scenario where we lose in July. We'll earn our twenty-fifth ribbon and the Royal Jelly award. It comes with a small cash prize, but the Royal Jelly is more than that. It's status; it's proof that we're truly the best. Mom wants the ribbon and award so bad, and I do too.

I can see it now: finally winning that twenty-fifth ribbon, Mom's happiness, her pride in me and my passion finally shining. The thought is so tangible I can almost grasp it. Sure, sometime between now and then I'll have to out my secret to Mom. But I can only hope my dedication will make up for my lies.

I unlock Waxing Poetic's storefront and turn on the overhead lights.

After brewing a pot of fresh coffee, I flip the CLOSED sign to OPEN and get to work.

While the first hour is slow, a steady stream of customers picks up around eleven. The record player spins in the corner, the music barely audible. Mom buys stacks and stacks of used records from the Salvation Army for our listening pleasure during the drudgery of retail.

The Rolling Stones' *Out of Our Heads* spins and the opening notes of "Play with Fire" fill the store. Dust filters in the light, and I lean my elbows on the countertop, messing around on my phone. For my first official day of summer break, this is surprisingly dull. I'm mildly annoyed Mom asked me to help out here instead of the apiary. Although I'll have plenty of time when she leaves for Florida.

The bell above the door jangles, and I shove my phone in the cubby beneath the counter. I have a second before the customers round the corner, and force on my most cheerful, customer service–friendly smile. But right as I open my mouth to greet them, my mind goes blank. Weaving between the bookshelves and wine barrels laden with bee products is none other than Ezra.

"Hi," I say in surprise, my lips tugging upward with a smile. A confused smile. Did he ask Carol where to find me? Because this can't be a coincidence.

Ezra lifts his hand in a wave, the arc of his brows highlighting his own surprise. "Josie?" Okay, *maybe* it's a coincidence. He pauses beside our display of honey-infused body lotion. "You work here?"

A woman with a brunette pixie cut in oversize overalls rounds the corner behind Ezra and strolls up to the register. She squeezes his arm as she passes.

"Welcome to Waxing Poetic," I say, turning from Ezra to the woman. "Can I help you find something?" As I talk, I gather a fistful of my curls and twist them back from my face.

"You must be Josie!" the woman says, her voice chipper. "Is your mom around?"

"Um." My gaze flickers to Ezra. "I'm sorry, who are you?"

The woman laughs—it's a soft, breathless laugh. "I'm Penelope. Penelope Blumstein-Abramo." As realization dawns, she motions to Ezra. "And this is my son. Ezra."

Ezra and I stare at each other for one long second.

This isn't good. Oh no, this is bad.

I'm internally panicking, but try to appear calm. Ezra's a *Blumstein*! Which is problematic for me in so many ways. Last night, talking with Ezra was one of the better times I've had in far too long. And not only did I divulge my biggest secret, but I divulged it to a Blumstein.

Really, I shouldn't be allowed to talk to strangers. Especially not cute strangers. I overshare. It's a small miracle I didn't give him my SSN.

But what's worse? Telling my biggest secret to a Blumstein?

Or having my first perfect romantic moment in over a year—scratch that, *ever*—with a Blumstein? Mercury must be in retrograde or something, because this is seriously fucked up.

Ezra clears his throat and says, "Josie and I met last night."

"Oh? That's great," Penelope says cheerfully. Then she lifts onto her toes and peers around me, but the office door is closed. "Is your mom here? I was hoping to say hello."

Finding my voice, I say, "Well—"

"I haven't been back to Volana since I was barely out of high school," Penelope chatters on, oblivious to the fact she's holding a one-sided conversation. "Not much has changed, from what I've seen! Then again, we've only been back a week. . . ."

I tune Penelope out, trying not to focus on my feral heartbeat or the sweat moistening my palms. What're the odds Ezra will keep my secret about ditching college? Feuding families or not, we definitely connected last night. Maybe, if I ask nicely, he won't tell anyone? Or I can lie, say it was all a joke? Ugh. It's like the universe is playing some cruel cosmic joke on me. What did I do to deserve this?

Well, you've been lying to your mom and best friend, my conscience supplements, and I want to wilt onto the counter.

Penelope's still talking. ". . . and I'm looking forward to the honey show. You're entering, aren't you?"

I adjust my weight on the stool, my feet slipping on the bottom rung. "Oh, um, yeah. Best of Show for twenty-four years now."

"Fantastic," Penelope says, and her smile is wide and genuine. "I worked on my in-laws' bee yard in Santa Barbara. Won a few ribbons of my own. Abramo Apiary won Best of Show at the Southern California Honey Show for five years when I was running it."

What Penelope's saying almost sounds like intimidation, but the woman is so freaking cheerful and smiley I can't tell if it's a ruse. She honestly seems jazzed to be here in Volana.

I smile tightly, shifting my focus to refilling the receipt paper. "That's great," I tell her, avoiding Ezra's gaze. He keeps trying to catch my eye, and I am *not* going to let that happen. "But my mom isn't here. Is there anything else I can help you with?"

"No, just wanted to say hello. Will your mom be back in later?"

I thread the new roll of receipt paper through the machine. Gotta love busywork; it's an excellent excuse to avoid eye contact in any situation. "She'll be in tomorrow morning."

"Wonderful," Penelope says, and smacks the counter to emphasize her point. "I'll swing by then." After saying goodbye, she heads toward the door.

Ezra hangs back. "I'll be out in a sec," he tells his mom as she exits the store.

Finally I glance up at Ezra. Last night I appreciated his attractiveness. Now I kind of hate it. Daylight Ezra is even more attractive than Nighttime Ezra. His nose is a constellation of exploded freckles, trailing onto the cut of his cheekbones, and his eyes shine, light and lively.

"I come in peace," he jokes, and takes a few steps closer to the counter.

I almost laugh. But I check myself and instead purse my lips. "You really shouldn't be hanging around here." I motion toward the window facing the sidewalk. "Your mom's waiting."

Ezra's smile fades and he digs his hands into the pockets of his unzipped hoodie. "Josie, what's going on? Last night—"

"I didn't know who you were last night," I interrupt. "And I know our families hate each other, but please don't tell my mom—or *anyone*—what I told you last night. About college."

"Why would I tell anyone?" he asks, genuinely lost in this bizarre conversation. "Also, I don't care about this whole . . . feud thing." He adds this casually, like it's funny.

"You don't?"

"You do?" He rests his elbows on the counter and leans forward until we're eye level.

It's silly, but as I stare into Ezra's eyes, my gut tells me I can trust him. Unless I'm confusing my gut for hormones, which has happened before. "My mom cares."

"You didn't answer the question." Ezra's grin is tentative, teasing. Like he senses my wavering resolve.

I lean back and cross my arms. "Yeah, well, it's complicated."

Mom cares deeply about the feud, about beating out the Blumsteins this year, about our legacy. If this is my summer to show her I belong at Hazeldine Honey, fraternizing with the enemy is literally the worst thing I could do.

Especially when all I *want* to do is fraternize with him.

"Does it need to be?" He pushes back from the counter, humming beneath his breath. Before I muster a response to *that* loaded question, he asks, "You do swarm pickups?" He taps an informational flyer by the register that reads: *LIVE BEE REMOVAL.* The flyer also lists the number for town folks to call if they happen across one.

My defensive stance drops slightly as I uncross my arms and lean my elbows on the counter. Why am I not demanding he leave the store this instant? What is wrong with me? Mom could swing by and sniff out his Blumstein DNA in seconds, then glare me into a puddle of shame.

Ezra picks up the flyer and holds my gaze for a second too long. Waiting for an answer.

"Yeah. My mom's the head of the Volana County Bee-keepers Association," I say, reaching for my canteen so I have something to do with my hands. "Wait. You beekeep?"

"I dabble. Hard to escape when your mom drags you to work every weekend as a kid." But he's not annoyed or upset. Instead he's wistful. "Can I sign up for this? Or would your mom turn me away because of my last name?"

"Probably turn you away," I say, my brain still humming over the fact that he beekeeps. The universe and its sick sense of humor is straight-up taunting me. I don't know anyone else my age who does. "But we don't get volunteers for swarm pickup and removal, so . . ."

Believe it or not, most people *don't* volunteer to secure swarms of loose honeybees.

"Fair enough." He tucks the flyer into his pocket. "I've done swarm pickups before, and I know what I'm doing if you ever want any help."

"Right." For some reason my neck's all hot. "Thanks."

Ezra grins and takes a step back. "I need to head out. Are you going to the VCBA meeting?"

Tomorrow is our monthly Volana County Beekeepers Association meeting. Led by none other than *my mom*. Ezra and his family shouldn't show up; it spells bad news. So why do I still want to see him again? I can't do this. Bad. It's all bad.

But I don't say any of those things. Instead I give in and smile. "Yeah. See you there."

Chapter Five

ON THURSDAY, MOM and I attend the Volana County Beekeepers Association monthly meeting, held at Plié, the dance studio in downtown Volana. Our meetings are fairly low-key and casual, and my participation usually includes setting up all of Mom's PowerPoint presentations the night before. But every once in a while, Mom drags my socially awkward ass to the front of the room to help her with a presentation. While I'm my most confident talking about bee-keeping, I still turn into a nauseous mess up there.

Luckily, today my duties are purely technological. I'm already nervous enough as is.

I haven't seen Ezra since yesterday. Which is a good thing. A very good thing. I have to face the facts: Ezra's a Blumstein.

This summer needs to be about my future. *Not* the annoyingly attractive boy who is off-limits. My dream of working at Hazeldine Honey—and one day running it—isn't worth ruining for some boy.

The Volana County Beekeepers Association is painfully small. Other nearby counties, like Sonoma or Napa, have a huge number of members. For whatever reason, our minuscule slice of Northern California doesn't want to save the honeybee all that badly. But I like our tight-knit group. The downside of being small, though, is a lack of funding. We can't even afford to rent out a decent hall or auditorium space, instead setting up at Plié.

The dance studio is basic. One open room, mirrors on the side with barres, molded water stains on the ceiling tiles. It smells vaguely of feet. The overhead lighting is dim, but the skylight helps, even if it's seven at night.

I unfold ten chairs—wishful thinking on my part—while Mom sets out a side table of drinks and one of those huge platters of cookies from the supermarket. The supersoft, crumbly kind with pink frosting and sprinkles. To go with it, a liter of Sprite and a bottle of wine.

We're classy.

To stave off anxiety while we wait for the other families, I rearrange the cookies on the platter. Other than the Blumsteins, there are the Millers, a family on the edge of Volana County who have a small but thriving apiary. Bev always shows up, and the other members are hobbyist or uncommitted beekeepers who lose interest after realizing they can't harvest honey until they successfully winter for one year.

"Stop touching the cookies," Mom says, tugging her laptop from her tote bag. I hold up my hands in surrender, and she nods to her bag. "Mind grabbing the binder?"

I dig through Mom's tote and find the binder full of different topics we cover throughout the year. Last night I made an elaborate PowerPoint on swarm prevention—the topic of today's meeting—with key points on robbing prevention as the summer dearth ramps up.

The Millers filter in and take seats in the front row. They're a large family, and tonight Joyce Miller, who's in her seventies, is here with her adult granddaughter. They smile at me, and I wave from my seat beside Mom, crossing and uncrossing my legs. Bouncing my foot up and down. Scoping out the crowd for the Blumsteins with sweaty palms.

Maybe they won't show.

Due to the unfortunate news of Ezra being a Blumstein, I forgot to tell Mom that Penelope came looking for her yesterday. But, true to her word, Penelope showed up this morning to see Mom at Waxing Poetic. As a result, Mom was in a *mood* when she got off work earlier, and I didn't bother pushing for details.

"Josie," Mom says, sensing my restlessness, "can you pull down the projector?" She squats in front of her laptop, opening PowerPoint, which is the extent of her technical knowledge.

"Sure thing." I hop up, happy to have something to busy

myself with. I reach onto my tiptoes, feeling for the metal ring, but it evades my grasp. I loathe being short.

"Let me." A hand reaches from behind and pulls down the projector screen with the ease of someone who must be at least six feet tall. I pivot on my heel—and smack right into Ezra Blumstein-Abramo's chest.

"Oh!" Stepping back, I glance across the small, slowly filling room to where Mom fiddles with her laptop. "Thank you. I'm . . . vertically challenged." And socially challenged, but I'm sure he's figuring that out if he didn't at LaLa's.

But Ezra smiles. A little bit lopsided. A whole lot of charm. He tucks his hands into the pockets of his corduroy blazer; his light brown waves are neatly brushed back. "What would you have done if I hadn't shown up?"

"Stand on a chair," I deadpan, and he tips his head back to laugh. It's not the worst sound in the world. Fighting the grin on my lips, I wipe my sweaty palms off on my skirt and shift my weight onto my heels. "I should go. Got a meeting to co-run." And by "co-run", I mean clicking the next slide button on Mom's laptop.

Ezra's thick, expressive eyebrows lower conspiratorially. "Of course." He steps aside and does an *after you* motion with his hands. And not a moment too soon because Mom is working her way toward us.

"Who's this?" She's wearing her patented friendly smile, but her eyes are narrowed just so. Maybe she *can* sniff out the Blumstein DNA.

"Mom, this is—"

"Ezra," he says, and I press my eyes shut in disappointment as he adds, "Blumstein-Abramo."

Mom's about to shake his hand but pulls away, the smile tightening into a grimace. "Ah, you must be Penelope's son."

"Hope you don't mind us crashing the meeting," Ezra says, his expression amused, as if he finds this whole situation funny. Meanwhile it's giving me hives.

Did Mom hear us talking? Is that why she came over here? Also, why is she so rude? Ezra isn't to blame, and my face flushes with embarrassment—my cheeks a clear indicator how poorly I'm reacting to this situation.

"We usually don't let nonmembers into meetings," Mom lies convincingly.

I shake my head at how quickly Mom loses her moral compass when it comes to the Blumsteins. Nonmembers are always allowed. Besides, the other Blumsteins are members, much to my mom's chagrin.

"We can leave," he offers, glancing at me ever so briefly.

Mom sighs, and I'm relieved she remembered her conscience. "No, it's fine. I guess. Enjoy the meeting." She hooks her arm through mine and drags me over to our corner. "Josie, why were you talking to the Blumsteins' grandson?"

"He helped with the projector." This isn't a lie, technically. "But we barely talked." Tonight. We barely talked tonight. If I convince myself I'm telling the truth, the lie isn't as poisonous.

Mom purses her lips, the bright berry of her lipstick popping against her skin. "Well, stay away from that boy. That entire family is more trouble than they're worth," she says, swiping her water canteen from the lectern and taking a long sip. While she drinks, her attention shifts to Penelope as Ezra joins her in the back row; her eyes narrow. But then she caps the water bottle and says, "Let's get this meeting going; we're already five minutes behind schedule."

I sit to the side with the laptop and PowerPoint as Mom stands behind the lectern. Every few minutes, my gaze flickers over to the Blumsteins in the back row. It's ridiculous, but I can't help it. Knowing Ezra's in the room makes the dance studio feel ten times smaller. And it wasn't even that big to begin with.

What exactly does it say about me, about this situation, that my eyes keep finding Ezra's?

Or that there's an uptick in my heart rate and sweat on my palms?

I have no idea, but James Funderburk never made me feel *any* of these things.

I shift in my seat until Ezra's no longer in my line of sight. I flick to the next slide when Mom prompts me to, and pretend like this is another ordinary VCBA meeting.

"In conclusion, swarming should slow down during the warmer months, but improper hive management can lead to unhealthy swarming later in the year. If you do see any swarms, please report them! We have extra flyers you can hang up around town." Mom motions to the table by the door before closing her binder, balancing her forearms on the lectern. "Now, I'm headed out of town next week, but Josie will help run things in my absence."

A slight murmur ripples through the crowd. Everyone is as shocked by Mom's decision to leave town as I was. But she doesn't elaborate, which isn't surprising. When Gran moved, she didn't tell anyone about the Parkinson's. She announced she was retiring, upended her life, and moved to Florida. Running from disease and time.

Mom begins packing her binder and laptop. "As a reminder, next month's meeting will be skipped in favor of our annual Fourth of July potluck. This year the Andersons are kind enough to host. I'll send out an e-mail at the end of the month with a reminder."

Since no one has questions, Mom adjourns the meeting. The legs of metal chairs squeak against the polished hardwood as everyone abandons their seats in favor of the dessert table.

I nod to Mom's tote bag with the laptop and notes binder. "Want me to drop that off in the car?" I ask, because I'm hyperaware that Ezra's on the other side of the very small room with his mom. I need to get out of here.

Mom squeezes my arm. "That'd be great, Bug. Thank you!"

I heft the bag onto my shoulder and scrounge up the car keys from Mom's jacket, folded over the nearest chair. "No problem!"

I weave my way out of Plié but see Bev Nakamura, my mom's best friend, standing by the door. I *adore* Bev. She and her wife, Antonia, make all of our bee products in the guest bedroom of their house. Beeswax candles, solid soaps, lip balms—all by hand. Bev harvests the beeswax, prepares it, and dyes it, while Antonia does the dipping and carving.

"Hey, Bev," I say as I pass her.

"Hey, hon." Bev wraps one arm around my shoulders, halting me in place. She lowers her voice and adds, "Your mom told me about Gran. How're you holding up?"

"I'm okay." I smile, but my gaze catches on Ezra and his mom slowly making their way toward us.

"I'm around if you need any help while Emma's gone, you hear?" Bev squeezes my shoulders. In her free hand is a mug of wine—we have a bring-your-own-cup policy at meetings to cut down on waste—and the vinegary sweetness burns my nostrils. "Where you headed off?"

"Putting my mom's supplies away." I motion to the bag and binder, subtly trying to wiggle from her grasp.

"If I could've guaranteed I'd have a good kid like you, I wouldn't have gotten my tubes tied." Bev snorts. The apples of her round cheeks are flushed, probably thanks to the wine.

Too much information, I think, but I smile. "Thank you?"

Loosening her grip on me, she heads toward Joyce Miller, who's loudly broadcasting how she visited the home of L. L. Langstroth, the father of American beekeeping. I hurry away and out the open doors. The air outside is cool, even though it was in the mideighties today. No matter the season, Volana's temperature always dips at night, thanks to the cool fog from the nearby coast. Northern California and Mother Nature are a fickle combination.

Dressed in a skirt, long-sleeved top, and cardigan, I wish I'd opted for jeans or a jacket. Or both.

Mom's parked the Honda at a metered spot across the street and I cross easily, as downtown Volana is dead asleep after eight p.m. The silence is nice after the anxious buzz inside the studio. I manually unlock the door and lug the bag into the back seat.

I lean against the car for a moment and shut my eyes, imagining a future where I'm the one running the VCBA meetings. I've never yearned to be a part of something as badly as I've yearned to be officially a part of Hazeldine Honey.

When I open my eyes, I'm surprised to find Ezra standing on the other side of the street.

He lifts his hand up in a short wave. "Hey."

I cross the street, meeting him in the middle. I'd be lying if I said I hadn't hoped to run into Ezra again, even if this is possibly the worst place for us to have a conversation. We barely had time to talk inside with my mom hovering. At least we're alone now.

"Hi." I twist my sleeves down over my cold fingers. "What're you doing out here?"

"I saw you come outside, and . . ." Ezra shrugs. "Thought I'd say hey."

I should be annoyed, right? Why am I not annoyed?

"Hold on." I lead Ezra around the side of building so we're no longer in the line of sight of Plié's doors or windows. "We can't . . ." I trail off. "My mom's in there and it's too weird."

Ezra's eyebrows arch. "So we can't talk? In public?" He ducks down to my level. "Is that why we're conversing in the shadows outside? Dare I say *lurking*?" He has way too much fun giving me a hard time. A tawny wave has worked its way loose, curling against his forehead, and it takes all of my self-control not to reach out and push it back.

I have to look away. Because my internal chorus of *He's a Blumstein!* doesn't sound so convincing anymore. "I, um—I need to get back inside."

"Josie," Ezra says, his teasing tone gone. He reaches out for my hand, and his thumb accidentally slips beneath my sleeve, brushing the inside of my wrist. "Wait."

The touch is deceivingly innocent. But the warmth of it spreads through my limbs, pooling in my belly. "What?" I pull my hand free and tuck my sleeved hands underneath my armpits, glancing at him. He's backlit by a streetlamp, once again reminding me of how handsome he is.

"Do you care about the feud? I know your mom does, but do *you*?" Ezra's eyes are wide, imploring. "Because if you do, tell me and I swear I'll leave you alone. I just thought . . . maybe you liked talking to me as much as I like talking to you." He tucks his hands into his pockets.

My breath catches in my throat. Because I really, really don't want him to leave me alone. I should want that. I should have zero feelings about Ezra. There should be a void, a black hole. But there's not. Not even close.

I run my fingers nervously through my curls. "I don't know." Because Ezra raises a good question. Do I care— beyond the fact that my mom cares?

"Remember, I'm technically only half-Blumstein."

I laugh even though I'm frustrated. "That's true. I guess I don't care. But I care what my mom thinks." As I say this out loud, I realize how true it is. I care about Hazeldine Honey, but I have little stock in the feud.

"Okay . . ." Ezra nods thoughtfully, his gaze meeting mine, and I don't turn away. "I can work with that."

I can't help but grin. Farewell, the last shreds of my self-control. "Oh, can you?"

He smiles, but it's not the usual, dimpled smile. No, it's slow and does something weird to my chest muscles. "Yeah," he says. "I can. But it might be easier if I had your number."

My cheeks warm. "Probably, yeah."

Ezra slides his phone from his pocket and unlocks the screen before handing it over. I tap in my information, hit save, and hold the phone out. His fingers brush mine as he takes the phone back, and there it is again: warmth, addictive warmth, at his touch. "Here. I'll text you so you have my number," he says, and taps at the phone's screen quickly.

My phone buzzes in my cardigan pocket. He lifts his brows expectantly, so I slide it out.

> **805-555-1425: I don't care what your mom thinks. And hear me out—maybe you should do the same?**

My already anxious and energetic heart trips over itself. Because he is quite convincing. "You think you're pretty charming, don't you?"

His brown eyes are taunting. "Not usually, no, but the fact you're smiling makes me think I might be onto something."

The thud of my heart mimics anxiety, but it's something far less sinister. It's excitement. But I'm afraid to speak, afraid of what to say to Ezra, whose confidence and kindness overwhelm me in the best way possible.

So we smile at each other, shy and wordless. A flirtatious stalemate.

"Josie? You out here?" A voice interrupts from the other side of the building.

"Shit, that's Bev. I have to go," I say, taking a step away from Ezra. Then louder: "Coming!"

Ezra tucks his hands into his pockets. "G'night, Josie."

"Bye, Ezra." I start walking toward the building and glance over my shoulder. "Mind waiting, like, thirty seconds before coming back inside?"

Ezra laughs softly and nods. "Sure."

I hurry back to the dance studio but pause beside the planted hydrangeas by the front door. Bev's not waiting for me, which eases my nerves, but I still take a moment to wipe the silly grin off my face before stepping inside.

Chapter Six

ON SATURDAY NIGHT, I turn down plans with Nan—
who I haven't seen since the day after graduation—to spend
the evening with my mom. She leaves tomorrow, and I'm
terrified. Excited for the opportunity to have full control
over Hazeldine Honey for a week, and dreading it at the
same time. Worrying I might mess everything up. Worrying
about Gran. Worrying I'm the Worst Daughter Ever because
I flirted with Ezra Blumstein-Abramo. I should have never
flirted with him in the first place. Not like it led anywhere—
he hasn't texted me once.

Luckily for me, I don't have to think about any of those
things tonight.

Mom's home from her shift at Waxing Poetic and comes

bearing gifts—burgers from LaLa's and a slice of black-berry cobbler. I worked in the apiary all day, outrunning my neuroses, and I just finished showering, where I may or may not have cried over the fact that my mom leaves in twelve short hours.

"Get the movie ready," Mom calls from downstairs, "and meet me in the kitchen!"

In order to do so, I have to navigate the piles of clothes and magazines that have turned our eclectically messy house into a complete state of disarray as a result of Mom's haphazard packing practices. She's not the most organized person.

After getting the movie cued, I join her in the kitchen, which took an odd brunt of the mess. In a sweet attempt to plan out my meals, Mom turned the contents of our kitchen upside down. In the end, there's a fat envelope on the kitchen table with enough pizza money to last me the ten days. Probably because all she discovered were boxes of Pop-Tarts, cans of frosting, and SpaghettiOs.

Mom and I don't cook. We survive on a questionable diet of takeout food and frozen meals. We rarely eat the vegetables in our garden, instead selling them at the farmers' market and pocketing the profit.

Mom plates our meals and sets them at the kitchen table. "You're going to be okay here by yourself?"

"It's only ten days," I say, dragging a French fry through a pool of ketchup.

"You didn't answer the question." She settles beside me at

the table, nudges her elbow against mine. "It's okay if you'll miss me. I'm pretty awesome."

"It'll be great." I hope my voice is all confidence, none of the wavering self-doubt I've spent the past few days failing to banish. On one level, I know I'm a good, competent beekeeper. But on another, I'm so deeply afraid I'll be in over my head. "And I'll totally miss your awesomeness when you're gone."

Mom grins, not picking up on my wobbly self-confidence.

"Bev's covering most of my Waxing Poetic shifts, but I told her to call you if she needs help or if her schedule changes," Mom says, ripping into her burger. "I also forwarded my work number to your cell phone for any swarm calls. Questions?"

I shake my head, distracted as I try to clean a ketchup stain off my top. "Nope."

Mom winks. "You've got this."

"I've got this," I repeat, conflicted.

Mom's always believed in me and my skills as a beekeeper, which is why she trusts me now and why it was so confusing when she pushed me toward college. As if it didn't matter how I memorized the development cycle of brood by the third grade or the fact I can spot a healthy queen faster than her. Now's the time to give Mom irrevocable proof that I'm meant to work at Hazeldine Honey.

"I'm going to miss you." She nudges my knee. "We've never been apart for this long."

The second she says it, my stomach turns. Because she's

right. I'm turning eighteen in two weeks and I've never been away from my mom for more than three or four days.

"You don't need to be nervous," I say around a deep, calming breath. "I'm practically a legal adult, after all."

"How could I ever forget," Mom murmurs, smiling faintly. A little sadly. Then, recovering, she jokes, "You make me feel old."

I stick my tongue out at her, and she laughs.

"Oh, remember to grab your prescriptions from the pharmacy. They're ready for pickup."

Medications aren't a blanket cure—or a cure at all—but they've helped. I still have anxiety, of course. But between the meds and cognitive behavioral therapy, my anxieties rarely interfere with my daily life. During the school year I have therapy, but Margie, my therapist, takes summer off to vacation with her family. Between my coping skills and medications, I do okay.

After we're done with our food, Mom grabs the to-go container of cobbler and hooks her arm through mine, dragging me into the living room. Tonight's movie selection is *Napoleon Dynamite*—a selection of the it's-so-bad-it's-good variety.

We settle on the couch, and I tuck myself against Mom. Her body is warm from running around the house packing. I breathe in the natural scent of her shampoo, the weird crystal deodorant she always uses, the eucalyptus oil dabbed behind her ears. The perfume of comfort, love.

Pressing my eyes closed, I don't watch the movie; I've seen it at least half a dozen times before. Instead I lean my head against Mom's and she snuggles me tight, fingernails ever so slightly digging into my arm, like she's just as afraid to let go as I am.

◇ ◇ ◇

Mom's gone the next morning, long before I wake up.

At seven thirty I roll out of bed and take in my room—faded posters, burned-out ceiling light, cherry-printed curtains. Since we live in a remote area, it's eerily quiet outside. Even more so in the mornings. The quietness weighs like a heavy blanket. Or maybe that's fatigue. I stayed up way too late last night reading the latest *Gest* release.

Gest now has the annoying habit of reminding me of a certain someone. Since the VCBA meeting, I've worked hard convincing myself of one thing: I don't like Ezra. More important, I *can't* like Ezra. Sure, he's cute and charming. But he's also a novelty. New guy in a small town. That will wear off. Eventually. He's not worth it.

The whole me-giving-him-my-number thing? A mistake. And I've decided it's good he never texted. Because right now—more than ever—I need to focus.

During Mom's absence, I'll have to perform hive inspections and keep an ear out for any swarm calls, but also drop off online orders from Waxing Poetic's webstore at UPS and watch Ford. The next ten days will be busy, so I put my social media upkeep on the back burner. Not like our three hundred Instagram followers—most of whom live in Volana—will miss my photos of queen spotting or video inspections. Later in the week I'll be working a few shifts at the store. But the main bulk of my days will be dedicated to hive inspections and logging inspection notes.

Sure, it'll be a lot of work, but the thought gives me a silent thrill.

Tossing on my robe, I head downstairs.

Before leaving, Mom made an attempt to right the chaos she left in her wake, but the house is still messier than usual. It'd be nice to clean up before she gets home. But for now, I step around the messes and pour myself a bowl of sugary cereal, ignoring the piles of clothes and magazines.

After drinking my body weight in coffee, I revel in the novelty of all my responsibilities. Today I should knock out a good ten hive inspections and log their notes into our Google spreadsheet. For an entire day, it's going to be a lot of hard physical labor. Ten hive inspections can be finished in five hours, but only if I make each one no longer than thirty minutes.

But it's good work, the type of work that fuels my soul, makes my heart pump stronger, happier, faster.

Outside, in our small supply office between the house and apiary, I unearth my two-piece bee suit and tug it on, tightening the ankle straps around my muck boots. Even if I'm comfortable doing hive inspections without much gear, when you're inspecting so many hives, it's easier when you're protected. As we move into the warmer months and closer to the honey harvest, even the sweetest of bees turn their defenses up as their honey storages grow. I don't blame them. We're the ones intruding on their homes, stealing their food and hard work.

Fully suited, I drop my cell phone into one of the large pockets on my pants and walk down to the apiary. After removing the telescoping cover of the first hive, I use my metal hive tool to loosen the inner cover of the standard Langstroth. I puff some smoke into the ventilation hole to calm the bees before doing a deep dive. I set the inner cover aside and I inhale, leaning over the top honey super. It's at least a third filled. The sweet aroma of honey and nectar and warm beeswax tickles my nostrils.

I fix my hive tool between the honey super and the second box, jiggling it to loosen the propolis—the sticky gluelike substance bees create to seal up any cracks. Then I lift the honey super off, grunting. It's at least forty pounds, and I'm careful setting it on top of the telescoping lid at an angle so as to lessen the chance of squishing any bees.

Brood is my favorite part of inspections. Honey is beautiful, sure, but brood? It's the coolest. The eggs, larvae, and capped brood are fascinating, and the bees covering the frame are nurse bees. All honeybees have roles inside a hive, but they're the youngest in a colony, and take care of the larvae, feeding them bee bread—a mixture of royal jelly and pollen—and regulating the brood temperatures.

Since I see everything pointing to a healthy colony—the eggs, mainly, as they're a sign it has an actively laying queen—I work faster through the other ten frames in the top brood box. Once I'm positive there aren't any swarm cells, I put the hive back together. Slowly and carefully, like Gran and Mom taught me.

Swarming isn't bad—it's the natural procreation of a hive as they expand and one half departs with the old queen, leaving a swarm cell or a newly hatched queen behind. But in backyard beekeeping, a swarm means hive instability and lower honey production. A way to prevent this is to split the hive in half before they swarm, so we check for the warning signs during inspections.

I fit the lid back on and unzip my hood, stepping back underneath the arbor and sipping from my water bottle. My heart pounds with this golden happiness. Working with the honeybees is magical.

The average person sees a honeybee as a simple insect. They can't differentiate them from a wasp to save their life. Or they don't know honeybees don't bite—they sting. And when they sting, they die. In this moment, I'm so absurdly thankful for my upbringing. For knowing about the bees like they're a secret.

As I walk back toward the office for a break, my phone buzzes in my pocket. Mom already texted me after she landed, so I doubt it's her. I tug off one nitrile glove and check the screen. An unknown number.

"Hello?" I ask, cradling the phone between my shoulder and ear.

"Hi, Emma? This is Rick from Parks and Rec."

"Hey, Rick, this is Josie. I'm taking over for my mom while she's out of town." With my foot, I nudge open the office and step inside.

"Oh! Hi, Josie. A hiker reported a swarm up in Eagle Ridge Park, off the lake loop trail, marker three. Do you have someone who can take care of it?" Rick asks, his voice mildly panicked, which makes me smile. Swarms are literally the most docile bees can ever be.

"Sure thing." Adrenaline and excitement make my hands shake as I find a pen and ask Rick a few questions, writing down the information on a scrap of notebook paper.

After I hang up, any confidence I felt during the phone call fades, and anxiety crawls up my body. I have to do a swarm pickup *on my own*. Which, for the record, I've never done before.

With my mom? Dozens upon dozens of times.

But never, ever by myself.

Why didn't I think of this sooner? Mom told me last night that she forwarded her work number to my cell for this exact reason. Did I think no one would call in a swarm while she's gone? I should've told Mom that I'd need Bev's help or someone else's from the VCBA. But . . . asking for help would've made me look unprepared and inexperienced. Like I'm not ready for this responsibility.

Taking a shaky breath, I try to quell my rapid heart, but it pounds away. Suddenly the office is too small, too stuffy. I lean over the workbench and crack open one of the windows. I yank off the bee jacket and pants, collapsing into the nearby orange velvet chair for a second.

There's no question: I *need* to be okay with this. If I'm going to be a full-time beekeeper like my mom, I might be doing several swarm removals a week during the spring and summer. My damned nerves can't get the best of me. And oh boy, are they trying. There's a mutiny happening inside me. My amygdala is on fire.

As I lift my hair off my neck, the tepid breeze cools me off.

And I get an idea.

Perhaps it's the anxiety, the fear of going it alone, or some excuse to see Ezra Blumstein-Abramo again, but I pull up his contact information on my phone. I shouldn't have, but I saved his number after the VCBA meeting. Ezra *did* say to let him know if we ever needed help with swarm removals. Hazeldine Honey comes first, but if I mess up the swarm removal? Well, it won't bode well.

I need Ezra's help. That's it.

Chewing on the inside of my cheek, I type out a text. Then delete it. Retype it. Read it over four times. And hit send.

ME: Up for a live bee removal?

Chapter Seven

IN THE HAZELDINE family, we have many rules. But there's an unspoken and cardinal rule dipped in gold: We don't ask for help. We're self-sufficient women. We especially don't ask for help from the Blumsteins, or any Blumstein-adjacent family members. And I betrayed that rule.

In the moment, it felt like a good idea.

Now? As I wait for his response? Not so much.

I push up from the armchair and wander around the office, collecting my swarm retrieval supplies. Tossing the various items—a spare bee brush, pruning shears, a bottle of Swarm Commander—into a milk crate as I go. I fold my protective gear and lay it on top. The sign we use for swarm retrievals, warning passersby about all the loose bees, is already in the car. I dump everything into my mom's Honda Element and hop inside.

As I adjust her seat settings, my phone vibrates in the cup holder.

> **EZRA: Right now? Count me in.**
> **Give me five min?**

A smile tugs at my lips, warmth surfacing to my cheeks.

> **ME: Meet you at the street**
> **corner by highway 10?**

> **EZRA: Perfect.**

> **EZRA:** 🐝🐝 ☺

I finish adjusting Mom's rearview mirror while telling myself not to be *too* excited. But the weighty anxiety of doing a solo swarm retrieval has lifted. Instead a different brand of anxiety heats my chest. As I reverse out of the garage, I catch sight of my reflection in the rearview mirror.

The girl in the mirror is weightless. Happy. Near unrecognizable. *Uh-oh.*

Blumstein Farms isn't far, but when I arrive at the street corner, Ezra isn't there yet.

I take the moment to fuss with my bangs. Wonder

anxiously if I put on deodorant this morning. Covertly, I sniff my armpits. Is it bad that I can't tell?

After a few minutes I catch sight of Ezra walking down the street. He's dressed in tan pants and a light-blue button-down, a backpack hanging off one shoulder. My chest tightens with a familiar anxiety because I *shouldn't* be here. I *shouldn't* be doing this. Everything about this situation is wrong. But all the logic in the world can't negate the excitement I feel as Ezra approaches the car.

I unlock the doors and he pops the passenger's side open.

"Hey." Ezra sets his backpack down before climbing into the seat beside me.

I rake my fingers through my hair. "Hi. Thanks for tagging along."

He clicks his seat belt into place. "Are you kidding? Thanks for inviting me. I never pass up an opportunity to get some free bees." He pauses. "Get it? *Freebies?*"

I bite my lip to keep from laughing. "So, you're the worst." But he's not. Not at all.

Beside me, Ezra smiles easily and pushes up the sleeves of his shirt to his elbows, revealing a tattoo. On his left arm is a half sleeve: lush watercolor honeybees larger than life, twisted vines of wisteria, a melting sun.

"Wow," I say before I can stop myself. "That's beautiful."

Ezra rubs his cheek. "Thanks. Got it last month on my eighteenth birthday."

I tilt my head. Huh. I'd never peg him for a tattoo guy—

not like I *know* Ezra—but it looks good on him. "The artist did a great job."

"Yeah." He hesitates a moment before adding, "I actually designed it. Not to brag . . . or anything."

"No, it's great." I eye the expansive tattoo, impressed. "Brag away."

Ezra draws his hand self-consciously over the tattoo. "Thank you."

"We should go," I say, taking three tries to turn the engine back on. Because apparently boys with tattoos are my ultimate kryptonite. Good to know.

The radio plays, buzzing static interlaced with a local classic rock station.

The seat belt digs awkwardly into my boobs, and the car's shocks are shot. We bounce like a sack of potatoes over every damn pothole. Volana County is made up of more than thirty towns and cities, but the epicenter is Volana itself. And because of this, the town is *old*, founded in the early nineteenth century and containing one of the last missions built after Mexico gained independence from the Spanish Empire. In other words? It's ancient and our roads are more pothole than asphalt.

"Where're we headed?" Ezra asks.

"Eagle Ridge Park." When he doesn't reply, I add, "It's only twenty minutes from here, across town. Technically it's in the unincorporated area outside of Volana. . . ." I trail off, because I sincerely doubt he's interested in Volana's zoning ordinances. The upside, however, is that Eagle Ridge Park is on the far outskirts of Volana; no one will run into us there.

"Oh nice! I've barely been anywhere in town yet," he says, stretching out his legs into the footwell.

"Swarms are always popping up there. My mom usually handles them, but—"

"She's out of town," he fills in. "That's why you invited me today, isn't it?"

My already red cheeks are no doubt deepening into crimson. "Perhaps."

"Hey, I have zero complaints," he says, and rolls down the window, hanging his arm out. "I was hoping I'd hear from you after she left."

We slow at a stop sign, and I glance sideways at him. A mistake to be sure, as the breeze mussed his hair and the joyful look on his face is so adorably boyish. Swallowing hard, I face the road. "Oh?"

"When I didn't hear from you, I don't know, I was hoping it was because of your mom and the ridiculous feud." His normally airy laugh is tainted with nerves. "Not because of me."

I bite my lip to tame my smile. "Not because of you."

"Good," Ezra says, and my smile widens.

We lapse into silence, and I'm left overly aware of how small the car is. The narrow space between our two bodies. The way he said "Good" like my answer was exactly what he wanted to hear.

After a few minutes of silence, Ezra asks, "Why do our families hate each other, anyway? Other than the fact my grandparents *aren't* the nicest people."

"You don't know the story?"

"Nope."

"I'm sure there are several versions of *why* the feud started, but what I've always been told is this: My great-grandmother Millicent married your mom's great-great-uncle or something?"

"Rewind for a moment," Ezra interjects. "We're *related*?"

I can't help but laugh. "Keep listening. So they got married and your family gave them three acres of land as a wedding gift. Then your great-great-uncle or whatever was drafted in World War II and died. My great-grandmother was devastated, but she moved on and married my great-grandfather. The land stayed in my family."

"I don't get it. I mean, it's sad, but clearly I'm missing something."

"We still live on the land *your* great-great-grandparents gave my great-grandmother. Where we keep our award-winning hives," I say, shifting my focus back to the road. "My great-grandmother learned all her beekeeping skills from your family, and—"

"When your family began winning the honey show, my family got angry?" he guesses.

"Bingo. From then on, it's been tense, but there's always something new they're fighting about." I tighten my hands on the steering wheel. This conversation is a painful reminder of why I can't like Ezra. "Honestly, it's tradition now more than anything else."

"Huh," Ezra says contemplatively. Beyond him and out the window, farmland and vineyards roll by, the sky smooth blue. "I imagined something *bigger*, considering how worked up my grandparents get. A land feud is fairly anticlimactic."

"What were you imagining?"

Ezra lifts one shoulder. "Your ancestor murdered my ancestor. Or something."

"Seriously?" I laugh. *"Murder?"*

Ezra laughs, running his fingers through his hair. "I don't know! Everyone acts like it's this huge deal. I let my imagination get the better of me."

"Well, for Volana a land feud is a pretty big deal," I say, glancing beside me as I talk. "Most land around here has been in a family for generations. The land isn't just their home—it's their livelihood."

"I hadn't thought of it that way." After a moment, he adds, "When I agreed to stay here with my mom, I wasn't prepared for so much small-town drama."

"Small towns are *all* about the drama. I thought that was fairly common knowledge. We're terrible gossips." We're out on the back roads, surrounded by farmland, and the street is flanked by yawning eucalyptus trees. A traffic sign reads BEWARE FALLING TREES, which is equally as alarming as it is funny. "Why did you and your mom come up here, anyway?"

"Oh." Ezra goes quiet for a moment. "My parents got divorced in April."

"I'm so sorry, I didn't mean to pry," I rush to say, wincing.

"Don't worry about it," Ezra says, and he smiles as if to show me it's okay. "My dad's kind of an asshole? That's why I came to Volana with my mom. Sticking around for the summer with him didn't sound like a good time. Besides, I'm going to Berkeley in the fall; I was going to migrate north eventually."

"Wow, Berkeley?"

"Yeah, it's . . . great," he says, but his voice lacks something. Like he's not the least bit excited to attend one of California's top universities.

We pull into the Eagle Ridge parking lot, but I steer onto an access road that loops around the back of the park. "I got the okay from the ranger to use the access road. This way, we won't have to walk as far with the swarm."

"Perfect." Ezra peers out the window as we struggle along the dirt road, drumming his hands against his thighs.

"What're you going to study?" I ask, slowing to a stop beneath a large oak tree.

"Environmental science."

"That's amazing." I turn the car off and shift toward him, pointing to my top. The same one I wore during graduation: *Destroy the Patriarchy, Not the Planet.* The words are stretched across my boobs. Something I should've considered *before* showing off my shirt.

Ezra's gaze slowly lifts from my chest to my eyes. "Nice shirt." He winks before climbing out of the passenger's side.

I fumble with my seat belt and hop out of the car, flushed. I almost made it the entire car ride without embarrassing myself.

Ezra stands beside me, apparently unaffected by what happened in the car. "Wow," he says, "this is gorgeous."

"I love it here," I say, and forcibly put what happened in the car into the back of my brain. Gorgeous is an understatement. Eagle Ridge Park is hilly, with two lakes and three trailheads, and lush with greenery. "The ranger said the swarm is off trail marker three. From here, it shouldn't be a far walk." We gather our supplies and pick our way through the underbrush onto the trail.

"Can I ask you something?" Ezra says as we walk.

As long as it isn't about me making a fool out of myself, I think. "Sure."

"Why don't you want me telling anyone that you turned down college?" he asks, ducking beneath a low-hanging branch.

"I didn't tell you everything at LaLa's." My mouth goes dry. "My mom doesn't know that I turned down my college acceptance. So. That's why."

Ezra does the least expected thing: He laughs.

I stop walking and glower at him. "Hey, don't laugh. It's a stressful situation and—"

"Sorry, sorry," he says. "It's just—you're fearless."

Now it's my turn to laugh. Because me? Josie Hazeldine,

Queen of All Things Anxious? I'm the complete opposite of fearless. I deflect and say, "Hazeldine Honey is a family business, and I want to take over as soon as possible. My mom wanted college and I didn't. So I found a solution."

I expect more laughter. Or judgment. Instead Ezra says, "You really love bees, don't you?"

I look down, embarrassed I wear my heart so obviously on my sleeve. "Yeah, I do. This summer . . . I want to make my mom proud." I glance up, but Ezra's stopped walking and he's smiling at me. "What? Why're you smiling like that?"

And by "like that," I mean in this gooey, melt-my-heart kind of way. Maybe I can enjoy the novelty of Ezra Blumstein-Abramo while it lasts? I mean, that's harmless, right?

"Because that's awesome. You know exactly what you want from life—and you're going after it. That's so rare."

I laugh, mostly because his comment fills me like carbonation in water. "Mmm, right. Tell that to my mom."

"Why is she so stuck on college?" he asks, picking back up and walking the trail. "My mom would be elated if I wanted to save her money and stick around."

"Financially, college wasn't in the cards for my mom," I explain. "She never went. I mean, I get it. She wants the best for me. But I wish what I want and what she wants were one and the same."

The words tumble out easily, and I'm surprised how not stressed I am right now. I glance at Ezra, who walks with the nuc box pressed to his chest, staring at the dirt puffing up around the edges of his boots. Despite being dressed in a button-down shirt *and* slacks, he's sporting Timberland work boots.

Ezra turns and catches me watching him, his lips quirking. "Well, for what it's worth, I think what you're doing is pretty admirable."

I shrug off the compliment, but it warms my chest. "Thanks."

The trail curves and the swarm comes into view. Our small talk quiets as we set our stuff in the dirt and prep for the removal. Since Ezra didn't bring any protective gear, I decide to brave the removal sans suit too. Besides, that's what my mom would do.

While it's visually frightening—an amassed glob of honeybees—they're harmless, homeless, flying slow with bellies full of honey, their queen protected in the center. People see one swarm of bees and freak out, often killing them.

The thought hurts my heart.

Ezra lifts the nuc box, balancing it on his hip. "Lead the way."

The swarm drips from a low-hanging branch right off the trail. They hum and buzz, gentle as a kitten's purr.

"Ripe for the picking," Ezra jokes, and I'm in awe of his ease. He's all levity. "Now, do you wanna hold the nuc box or shake 'em?"

I eye the branch, ignoring the hot beat of the sun against my arms and the fact that I forgot sunscreen. It's low, but I'm short. Too short. Ezra has the advantage and we need to do things slowly. "Box."

Ezra sizes up the swarm. You never want to approach a swarm unless it's safe. If you mess up—shake them too violently and somehow injure the queen—it's game over.

"Hey, ladies," I say, hoisting the empty nuc box up, positioning it right beneath the swarm. "Ready for your new home?"

Ezra gives me a funny look, his nose scrunched up. "You talk to the bees?"

I lift my chin. "I'd be concerned if you didn't."

Ezra grins, and I can't help but smile. He makes my heart beat faster. "Okay, Hazeldine, let's do this. You ready?"

"Whenever you are."

Ezra takes hold of the branch the swarm clings to, and gives it one steady, downward shake. It's amazing, unreal, how easily the honeybees fall into the box held to my chest. Like a drop of water from a faucet. A few stragglers remain, and Ezra lightly jostles the branch.

"Think we got the queen?" I ask, and he helps me lower the box carefully to the ground.

"We'll know soon enough." Ezra crouches beside me, so close the heat of his body radiates against mine. Close enough I can smell his deodorant and the coconut of his sunscreen. Close enough that we keep bumping into each other as we layer in the frames of beeswax foundation. But neither of us moves.

If the queen is indeed in the nuc box, the stragglers will fly inside, following the scent of her strong pheromone. If not, the bees will fly back out. It's a waiting game now. They'll follow the queen in twenty to thirty minutes.

We leave the nuc box with the sandwich board—CAUTION: LIVE BEE REMOVAL—and rest on the nearby trail bench with our water canteens.

"That was awesome." Ezra's face is flushed and his hair mussed. He nudges my arm. "You did great."

"Thanks," I say with a grin of my own. "I've never, um, done a swarm removal without my mom. I was so nervous."

"Really?" He takes a sip of water. "I couldn't tell."

"Well, I was. Thanks for your help," I say, slightly guilty.

All Ezra's done is help me since the moment I met him, and I've been stubbornly writing him off. The ridiculous thing is, I know why. Despite all my convincing and attempts not to, I'm starting to like Ezra.

"Anytime." He reaches out and plucks something from my hair, fingers grazing my cheek. "You had a leaf," he says, and holds the leaf up as proof before tossing it onto the ground. "If you get any more swarm calls while your mom is gone, let me know. I've had a lot of fun today."

"Me too," I say, which is terribly inconvenient. Why is he so freaking *likable*?

After a moment, Ezra asks, "Did you only invite me because you needed help? With this being your first swarm and all?"

I hesitate before answering. Because even though I told myself that earlier, I was just fooling myself. "No," I admit, but I can't bring myself to look directly at him.

Ezra fiddles with the carabiner attached to his canteen before setting it in the dirt. "Josie?"

"Yeah?" I glance beside me, thoroughly distracted by my heart's hyperactive pounding. Maybe it's the adrenaline, or maybe it's because he shifted slightly and now we're sitting close enough for our legs to touch. There's this yearning warming my stomach, and it's making me dizzy.

Ezra's hand grazes mine where it rests on the bench, and all this accidental—or not, I can't tell—touching is sending my nerves haywire. "I really, really want to kiss you," he says, studying my face. "Would that be okay?"

Never has a guy *asked* before kissing me, and the request throws me. Concern flits through Ezra's warm brown eyes until I say, "Very okay." My fingers curl around the collar of his button-down. Pulling him closer.

Ezra ducks his head and presses his mouth to mine, his hand cupping the back of my neck. The kiss is brief, a brush of his lips. After a moment, I tease his lips open with my tongue, and the kiss deepens. His breath catches in his throat—making this *noise*—and his mouth softens against mine. *Oh my God, I'm kissing a Blumstein*—and it's good! Better than good. Freaking glorious. It's alarming how good Ezra is at kissing.

I savor every second because this is the best kiss I've ever had.

Silently, we part and take a breath. The world—Eagle Ridge Park—falls back into place around us. Inside my chest, my heart is running elated laps. Because I'm actually doing this! I kissed Ezra, the one person I have every reason not to kiss. But instead of being wrong, it feels like what I've been missing. Ezra feels right.

Now that we're no longer glued to each other, I can see he's flushed. That kind of red that nearly makes all his freckles disappear. A red that lights something inside me on fire. I want to run my fingers across those cheeks to check if the heat reaches the surface. For now, I pull Ezra's mouth back onto mine before I can ask myself if this is a terrible idea.

Chapter Eight

ANY STRAGGLING HONEYBEES have migrated into the nuc box, and all signs point to a successful swarm removal. I shouldn't be disappointed, but I am. Like I'm desperate for an excuse to stay here, hidden away with Ezra. But we can't stay out here forever.

We work in tandem to close up the nuc box and seal it shut, readying the girls for transportation back to my house. I'm guessing Mom will want me to keep this new hive rather than sell it. Swarms are free, but we sell them as nucs. A nucleus colony is essentially a bee starter kit; people pay upward of two hundred dollars for them.

Ezra hoists the sealed nuc box onto his hip. "Ready?"

I gather our supplies. "Yeah."

We retrace our steps back to the car, silence stretching between us. Not an uncomfortable silence—more contemplative than anything else. After Ezra kissed me, he didn't say much. Neither of us did, actually. We kind of just smiled goofily at each other. But the silence is nice. For someone who overthinks literally everything, I'm finding it easy to avoid thinking about how my mom would burst a blood vessel if she knew who I've been kissing. My solution? I don't think of any of those things. Those are problems for Future Josie.

I mean, it doesn't have to be a thing. Right? Ezra's only here for the summer, a few short months. With my mom gone, we can have fun. Yes, he's a Blumstein, but if we're careful, no one has to know. It doesn't have to be complicated.

We reach Mom's Element, the orange color garish around all this nature.

Ezra places the nuc box in the back seat, and I belt it in, double-checking the straps to make sure the lid won't pop off during transport. I've driven many times with hives or nuc boxes in the car, and I'm always afraid something might happen and—*bam*—my car is full of bees. I love bees, but I'm already a nervous driver, so no, thank you.

"Hey," Ezra says when I shut the passenger's-side door, and I turn around. His cheeks are red from the heat, his hair mussed from when I ran my fingers through it earlier. No longer do I find his attractiveness unfair. It's . . . pretty nice.

Ezra slides both his arms around my waist and hugs me against him. I'm surprised, but recover, and tuck my face into the space between his shoulder and neck. An up-close-and-personal encounter with that smooth, intimate slope of his skin, which smells of sweat, boyish; my brain is full of over-eager hormones. His head rests against mine. The softness of this moment is confusing and comforting. Different than the kiss, but somehow just as good.

"So." Ezra loosens his hold on me and leans against the passenger's-side door beside me. "We live pretty close to each other, right? We can't see each other during the day, but what about at night? We could walk around town? Hang out?" He shrugs, and the gesture is endearingly sheepish.

Because of the aforementioned hormones and the fact I'd very much like to keep seeing Ezra, I agree. "Okay," I say slowly, my overactive mind kicking back into gear. "But no one can find out about this. We need to be really, really careful."

Ezra's gaze lifts to meet mine. "Okay," he says simply.

I hesitate, waiting for him to change his mind. But all he does is smile a dimpled smile and open the passenger's-side door, climbing inside. I drive us home, Ezra fiddling with the radio before settling on the static-ridden indie rock station that's broadcast out of San Francisco. As we reach our neighborhood, Ezra unbuckles his seat belt and turns to me.

"You can drop me here," he says, and I slow to a stop alongside the curb. "Thanks again for inviting me along. And everything."

That *everything* is loaded, and my face warms. "Thanks for keeping me company."

Ezra pops open his door. "See you later?"

"Yeah." For some reason, my hands are sweaty on the driver's wheel. "Bye, Ezra."

"Until next time, Josie." He jumps out of the car and quickly walks along the sidewalk, hands in his pockets. *Whistling.* As if whistling isn't the most conspicuous thing ever.

Laughing, I shake my head and pull away from the curb. As I drive off, I survey the quiet street. The only person out and about is the mail lady. No Blumsteins, no Bev. The coast is clear.

The adrenaline from earlier is beginning to wear off as I head home, a chorus of *Holy shit, that just happened* sounding in the back of my brain. But instead of feeling anxiety or regret, I'm . . . happy. Ridiculously happy.

I turn down the lane, squinting at the car in our circular dirt parking circle. When I'm closer, I roll down my window.

"Hey," Nan calls, glancing up from her phone. She's leaning with her back against her Mini Cooper and uses her free hand to shade her eyes.

I rack my brain. Did I forget about plans with Nan? What is she doing here?

"Hey! One sec." I steer the Element into the garage, unload the nuc box, and set it in the shade of the parking bay.

Nan wanders over, frowning at the nuc box. Then her attention flicks toward me as she declares, "We're having a sleepover."

I blink. "Okay?"

"You bailed on me last night, so I'm here to collect." She grins, but there's something barbed to her smile, like it hurts. I should've guessed she'd be pissed. Being best friends with Nan Johansen is a fine balancing act. One I perfected over time. One I enjoyed, like she was a puzzle only I could crack. Too bad I'm a clumsy, clueless mess now.

"I have to install this nuc really quick, then we can hang out?" I gesture to the box by my feet. A box vibrating from the hum of the honeybees inside.

Nan sighs. "Fine, fine. I'll wait inside."

I toss her my house keys and hoist the nuc box up, then carry it through the garage and out into our backyard. Installing a hive doesn't take long, but by the time I'm done setting the swarm up in their new home, sweat trails down my back and I'm in desperate need of a shower.

Before heading into the house and my impromptu sleepover, I check my phone. The new message alert causes my heart rate to pick up, a steady drum inside my chest. I lean against the garage shelf of half-empty paint cans, and read.

> **EZRA: This is dorky, but today was the best day I've had in a while. Are you free tomorrow?**

I'm almost embarrassed how happy this text message makes me. Happy in a way I don't want to look at too closely. No, I want to live it—live this weightlessness, this excitement.

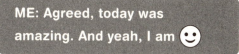

ME: Agreed, today was amazing. And yeah, I am 😃

EZRA: Meet you where you dropped me off tomorrow night? Around 10?

ME: See you there!

EZRA: Can't wait 😊

I lock my phone and press my eyes shut. Not even bothering to try calming my pounding heart; it's a lost cause.

◇ ◇ ◇

Nan and I stuff ourselves full of pizza from the one restaurant willing to deliver to the outskirts of Volana, eating on the floor of my living room while Ford snores on an epic pile of blankets in the corner. We're still spread out on the floor, our legs kicked up against the couch. Nan's blond hair fans out across the carpet, and *Arrested Development* plays on the television, a show we've watched together so often we can quote the first two seasons by memory.

Even if we're having a good time, I'd rather be with Ezra right now. Which makes me feel like an even shittier friend than I already am. I've kept too many secrets from Nan. Golden State and my fictional college plans, not to mention

Ezra. Nan might not be the *best* friend in the world, but she's still mine.

"So," I say, drumming my fingers on my pizza-bloated stomach. "I have something to tell you."

"Oh?" Her voice is curious, gossipy.

I swallow hard. "I kind of met someone."

Nan's mouth drops open. *"What?"* She sits up, using one hand to wind her hair into an artfully messy bun. "What's his name? Tell me everything."

"Ezra." I hesitate, sitting upright with my back to the couch. "He's the Blumsteins' grandson."

Nan's blue eyes widen. *"Ooh.* Intrigue."

I groan. "It sounds even worse out loud: I kissed a Blumstein."

"He kissed you? Jos, this is a big deal!" Nan grins. "Tell me about him."

I braid and unbraid my curls, tugging at the split ends. "We met on graduation night."

Nan hits continue when Netflix asks us if we're still watching. The next episode plays. "That was, like, a week ago! Why didn't you tell me sooner?"

"I guess I didn't want to jinx it?" I say, but that's a lie. Why *didn't* I? Ezra's been firmly at the forefront of my mind for a week now. Is it because I've grown so used to keeping secrets from Nan it's become second nature? Or because I wanted to keep Ezra wholly to myself? But we *kissed* today, and I'm bursting to talk about it. "Sorry I didn't tell you sooner."

My best friend sighs dramatically. "You're forgiven." She makes a rolling motion with her hand for me to continue. "What else?"

"I didn't know he was a Blumstein, though, when we first met."

"Which only makes it hotter."

I can't help but laugh. "No, it makes it more complicated."

She lifts a brow. "Admit it. The sneaking around has to be the tiniest bit fun."

My cheeks redden and Nan falls into me, laughing. "Shut up."

After a moment, she rights herself. "Hey, I'm glad you met someone decent. I was worried the Unfortunate Event known as James Funderburk made you go all chastity belt on me until college."

I frown, because that's *not* what I said when I declared being done with dating last summer. James was pretty unfortunate, though. I mean, the first time we kissed, we were on his parents' couch. He felt up a pillow, confusing it for my boob. I should've jumped ship right then and there.

"I never said chastity belt," I say. "But this thing with Ezra, it's not serious. He's only here for the summer."

"We're only here for the summer too."

I silently curse myself; I need to be more careful around Nan. I'll tell her about GSU, I swear I will, but not tonight. Tonight, I want to hold on to the magic I felt with Ezra back in Eagle Ridge Park. Tonight, I want to have fun with my best friend and forget all the heavy things weighing me down.

Nan's not paying attention to my blunder, though. "Ooh, maybe we can double? I'm *this close* to landing the White Whale. He's coming to town later this month."

The White Whale is Emery's cousin Nick, and Nan's summer conquest. The *Moby-Dick* reference is due to his initial disinterest in Nan when he was in town over spring break, which only fueled her desire to win him over. Everything's a competition to Nan Johansen. White Whale or not, the idea of double-dating with Nan sounds like a nightmare.

"Maybe," I say, then add, "What the fuck is a chastity belt, anyway?"

Nan's expression is downright gleeful as she grabs her phone from her purse, spends a quick second on Google, and turns the screen toward me.

"Nope!" I push the phone away, laughing. "Forget I ever asked."

Laughing with me, Nan flicks through the different pictures. "I don't know, Jos, this one would suit your skin tone."

I shriek, and we fall into a fit of laughter.

It's almost like old times.

I miss the old give-and-take of our friendship. Our prime was middle school, when we first met, back when life wasn't as complicated. In middle school, making friends wasn't easy with an anxiety disorder. And Nan never made me feel awkward. She's always put up with me and all my neuroses, her abrasiveness a shield for me to hide behind.

With Nan, I didn't have to make any decisions or branch out socially. We were two oddballs coming together. Nan, with her note cards, intensity, and graphing calculator. Me, with my anxiety medication, collection of honeybee paraphernalia, and weighted blanket.

Every once in a while, there's a glimpse. Like when we both quote a Tobias Fünke line at the same time or she buys me my favorite lipstick without me asking when she's at the fancy mall in Corte Madera. But with high school and hormones and college, all our small differences grew larger.

Nan likes to drink and party; I like my bees and staying in on Friday nights.

Nan can't even play mini-golf without turning it into a do-or-die competition, whereas I couldn't care less about who wins when she and I are having fun.

And the biggie: Nan's moving to LA, and I'm staying in Volana.

When I tell her about GSU, I hope she'll eventually be happy for me.

Later, when Nan's snuck a big glass of my mom's dessert wine and she's starting to slur her words, I officially call it a night and drag her into the upstairs bathroom. Over the sink, we both wash up and brush our teeth.

"What happened to your hand?" she asks, staring at my reflection in the mirror.

"Just a sting." I finish washing my hands and dry them off.

"I don't *get it*," she mutters, her words sloppy.

I flick off the bathroom light and she follows me into my bedroom. "Get what?"

"Why you bother with beekeeping." Nan flops onto the air mattress I dug out of my closet, her feet hanging off the end. Hot-pink toes wiggling as she talks. "Like, it's your mom's job, I get that. But it's not *yours*, Jojo."

I loathe being called Jojo—she only does it when she's drunk. It's a battle I don't even bother with anymore because fighting with a drunken Nan is the Worst. I crawl into my bed, heart oddly heavy. Nan's never understood why I love beekeeping. She knows I love it, but it doesn't compute inside her head. Like the fact that manual labor, outdoors and in the sun, is fun for me.

"You'll see," she says, curling up onto her side. "In LA, things'll be different. Better."

"Yeah." I lean over to my bedside table, switch off the lamp. Stare at the shadowed ceiling above my bed and sigh. "Things will be different, all right."

Chapter Nine

MOM CALLED EARLY this morning to check in and update me on Gran. While I sipped coffee and Nan slept, Mom filled me in on her first twenty-four hours in Florida. We've both witnessed how Gran goes through periods of lucidity and senility, but Mom was still surprised to see how, well, *normal* Gran was acting yesterday. As if the half-inch scratch on Rosa's cheek wasn't Gran's fault. Gran's appointment is on Wednesday, and Mom promised to update me more after they spoke with the doctors. When she asked how my first day went, I didn't lie. I didn't need to because yesterday went very, very well.

I haven't spoken with Ezra yet, and I'm caught somewhere between excitement and debilitating anxiety over meeting up later tonight. Good thing I spent the entire day working through hive inspections, a methodical and calming salve on my nerves.

After eating dinner, I kill time with binging a new anime and then I head upstairs to shower. Nan didn't stick around, not when I explained how much work was waiting for me in the apiary, and the house has returned to its odd emptiness. This much freedom feels wrong, but I'm going to milk it for all it's worth.

I pair my phone to my Bluetooth speaker and blast Jenny Lewis, singing along to the lyrics and psyching myself up. All this energy churns my stomach. Sometimes, excitement and anxiety are so painfully similar, I have to stop and ask myself what I'm really feeling.

Excitement, I decide as I dig through my closet after showering. My low-level and constant anxiety is still there, but for some reason Ezra doesn't contribute to it. Weird. I step back from the mirror and do one final once-over. My outfit is casual yet sophisticated—for Volana, that is. Thick leggings beneath a long swishy skirt, a T-shirt, cardigan, and boots. I gave up on my hair, and the curly mess is tangled back into a bun. My minimal makeup isn't a statement; I can't apply it without resembling a clown. All in all, this is probably as good as it's going to get, so I head downstairs to feed Ford.

A bit before ten—my stomach fluttering with excited nerves and *not* anxiety—I hook Ford to his leash, turn off all the lights, and slip outside. It's chilly, the fog from the coast rolling in, and I button up my cardigan as we walk down the lane. Ford trots slowly behind me, and I'm envious of his canine obliviousness right now. Are dogs ever nervous about, well, anything? Lucky bastards.

I turn right onto Highway 10, which is less of a highway and more like a quiet two-lane road, and scan the approaching street. The moment I spot Ezra, my lips pull upward automatically. He doesn't notice me right away, his gaze downcast to his shoes as he leans against the streetlamp with his hands tucked deep into his pockets. So *casual*. Infuriatingly casual. Infuriatingly cute.

My heart rate kicks up a notch when he notices me.

Ezra's smile lights up his face. Like he's just as happy to see me as I am to see him.

"Hi." When I reach the street corner, Ford waddles over to Ezra, emitting this low and pathetic whine as he begs for pets.

"Hey." Ezra quickly pats the top of Ford's scrubby little head, then steps toward me. His hands find my waist as he pulls me closer for a hug. I savor the contact—the heat of his hands on my lower back.

"Where to?" I ask when we let go, and tuck my free hand into my cardigan pocket because my palms are already sweaty with the best kind of nerves. Nervous-excitement nerves.

"I was thinking the Vale?" Ezra says, nodding his head toward the darkened highway.

The Vale is a small park not far from our houses. "Sure," I say with a smile, and we start walking. There aren't any sidewalks along Highway 10, just dirt shoulders and over-grown weeds with ill-placed streetlamps, most of which are burned out, but the moon above makes up for any lost light. Ford trots slowly in our wake.

"How was your first full day working solo?" Ezra asks, his voice low like a whisper even though we're all alone out here. But something about the time of night, all this darkness, calls for hushed tones.

"Good, actually." We turn left off the highway, and Volana Vale Park spreads out before us. "Busy but . . . good."

Compared to Eagle Ridge, the Vale is more of a community park with its picnic tables, BBQ pits, and jungle gym. But the trees and pin drop–still quietness make up for its otherwise bland scenery. In the distance, crickets chirp, toads croak, and my permanently anxious soul is instantly calmer. Nature has that effect on me.

"I can help out," Ezra offers as we walk the cobblestone path weaving through the park.

"No, you don't have to—"

"I want to," he says, his voice soft.

"Oh." My stomach warms. "If I need help, you'll be the first person I call." As much as I want to jump on his offer—and company—inviting Ezra to help work in the Hazeldine apiary isn't my smartest move.

Unless my goal during Mom's absence is discovering all the different ways I can betray her trust. I'm actually not sure what Mom would hate more: that I've kissed Ezra or that I turned down GSU. Probably college. Either way, smart moves haven't really been on the agenda lately.

"Let me know." Ezra swings his backpack off his shoulder and unzips the top. "Here good?" He motions to the spread of grass situated between two small knolls.

"Perfect."

Ezra reaches into his backpack and tugs out a wadded-up blanket. He flaps out the checkered fabric across the grass and sits down.

I lower myself onto the picnic blanket and tie Ford's leash to the backpack straps. Ezra removes a few more things from his bag, including a battery-operated camping lantern, several comics, and a stargazing guidebook. "Wow, what else do you have in there?" I joke.

"I'm an Eagle Scout," Ezra says, turning on the lamp. "I'm *always* prepared."

"Seriously? An Eagle Scout?" I laugh, because that doesn't track with my image of Ezra. He's all button-down shirts and comic books. Obviously he enjoys the great outdoors, but this surprises me. Goes to show I don't know him all that well.

My stomach does this funny little flip because I realize I *want* to know him that well.

I want to know everything.

"Yup." He stretches onto his back, pillowing his arms behind his head. My eyes stray to the slice of skin exposed between the hem of his shirt and the waistband of his pants. "If you think small towns are dramatic and gossip-filled, try listening to a conversation between Scout moms." He shudders comically.

Laughing, I lie down beside him, one hand resting on my stomach, the other open-palmed between us. Not a moment passes before Ezra shifts, reaching one hand down to hold mine. Like the other day, I don't bother trying to calm my heart. I can't. Not when he's touching me.

"This is nice," I say, hushed. Because it's nice—and confusing. I readjust on the blanket so my head rests against Ezra's shoulder. Down by my feet, Ford curls up with a contented snort. Lying here, with the air so clean and crisp it makes my lungs ache, I stare up at the stars. They're so bright out here in the country.

"Not too boring?" Ezra asks.

"Nope." Part of me wonders if being around Ezra could ever be boring.

Our hands are growing sweaty, but neither of us pulls away. "Good," he says with a low laugh. "I was nervous."

The fact that Ezra was nervous calms me, like we're on an even playing field. "I was nervous too." I don't tell him about my anxiety disorder, though. There's nothing romantic about mental illness. It rarely brings people closer to you. If anything, it drives them in the opposite direction.

"Really?" He turns his head, cheek against the blanket, and I do the same. So close our noses brush. "You don't seem nervous."

I can't help but laugh. "You still have a lot to learn about me, then; I'm always nervous. A constant, low-level nervousness."

"Can't wait." He grins, those dimples deepening. "I'm all ears."

"For what?"

"Tell me more about yourself. About Josie Hazeldine."

I snort-laugh, rolling onto my side and propping myself up with my elbow. "Okay. Fine," I say, like I'm not all floaty over the fact he wants to know more about me. "For starters, my full name is Josephine Delilah Hazeldine."

"Oh, that's, uh—"

"Awful?"

"Mmm, I dunno," he says, shaking his head. He mirrors my pose, lying on his side, propped up. "Josephine Delilah Hazeldine has quite the ring to it."

"Funny." After a moment, I add, "I think my mom did it because my gran did it to her—Emmaline Hazeldine, but she goes by Emma. Family curse or hazing ritual? I'm not quite sure."

"Well, for what it's worth, the name fits you."

I study Ezra's face in the faint light. The pull of his lips, like a faint yet permanent smile. "Thanks?"

"Why don't you believe me?" he teases, nudging my foot with his. "I like your name.

"Uh-huh." I fight my grin and ask, "What about you?"

"What about me?"

I hold up my hand. "I know roughly five things about you." I tick my fingers as I talk. "Your name, the fact you're apparently an Eagle Scout, you're an excellent artist, you have amazing taste in comics, and you're going to Berkeley to study environmental science."

Ezra flashes me a grin. "That pretty much covers it."

I lift an eyebrow expectantly. "You know my biggest secret. We're seriously unbalanced."

"Fine." He huffs, but his tone is light. "Berkeley is a really good school and all, but I wanted to go to RISD, the Rhode Island School of Design. My dad found out, and we had this huge fight about my future. According to him, studying to become a comic book artist wasn't a good use of my time."

Something inside me quiets, deflates. I was teasing, but Ezra told me something real. A dim, faraway part of my brain warns me that this is bad. That knowing more about Ezra— the real and hurt and delicate parts—won't end well. But that part of my brain? It's easy to ignore.

Ezra smooths his hands across the blanket, eyes cast downward. "Maybe that's why I find you so, I don't know, admirable? Unlike me, who gave up at the first sign of struggle, you went after what you wanted, full tilt. Even if your mom wants something different for you."

Those words fill me up—softening all the doubt I've felt about my life lately, my decisions. Naturally, I want to deflect. Convince him I'm not admirable. That I'm an anxious weirdo. I don't, though—but I also don't focus on his kind words. Instead, I ask, "Why do you have to give it up? Just because you're not going to RISD doesn't mean you can't still pursue art. Right?"

As Ezra releases a heavy sigh, he meets my gaze. "Yeah, you're right. I did just start drawing again. Berkeley's where I'll be next year, so I should probably get more excited. . . ." The lantern illuminates a sad smile quirking the side of his mouth. "I don't know. I'll figure it out. I always do."

Even if Ezra admires me, I admire his calmness, his ability to believe everything will work out fine. But it's more than that. On some level, it's like Ezra gets me. And being understood is a vastly underrated emotion.

I offer up a small smile. "We're even now."

"Oh, good." He laughs softly. "I was worried."

"You enjoy making fun of me, don't you?"

"Yup. Ten out of ten, would recommend." Ezra shifts closer, wrapping one of my curls around his fingers. "But there are . . . other things I enjoy just as much."

My face warms, and I lean closer. "Yeah? Like what?"

Ezra drops my curl, his fingers trailing my cheek and wrapping around the back of my neck. Then his lips brush mine. A simple, innocent kiss that leaves me aching for more. So I pull his mouth back onto mine. And as I kiss Ezra, something inside me surrenders—yes, I like kissing him. I already knew that. But now that I know more about him, I like *him* even more.

This might be a problem.

Chapter Ten

BY WEDNESDAY, I take Ezra up on his offer to help me in the apiary, and try not to think of what a betrayal it is to Mom. I shower before work, a rare occurrence as I usually wait until I'm all sweaty and done for the day. But then again, I'm normally not beekeeping with a supercute boy, and yes, I'm that self-conscious.

I like Ezra, even though he's a Blumstein. Even though the more time I spend with him—and the more I like him—the harder it'll be to end whatever this is when Mom comes home. Dimly, I'm aware of all these things, but they don't slow me down. Not in the least.

As I fiddle with my hair—my mind drifting to how it felt with Ezra's hands in it—my phone buzzes on the bathroom counter: *MOM CALLING*. After scooping my curls into a ponytail, I answer.

"Hey!" I say, probably way too energetic for only ten in the morning.

"Hey, Bug." Mom's voice is warm but worn. "How're things?"

I tuck the phone between my shoulder and ear as I walk downstairs. Ezra's due over any minute, and I try shoving any guilt into the far recesses of my mind. "Good. Yeah, it's a lot of work, but I have it under control."

"Glad to hear it," she says, and pauses. "Your gran and I finished up with the doctor."

Oh. My stomach clenches. I forgot today was Gran's appointment. The guilt I semisuccessfully shuttered resurfaces, and I lower myself onto the bottom step of the staircase. "How'd it go?"

"Honestly, the appointment was a bust. They don't have a reason—a *medical* reason—as to what caused the rapid progression of Gran's Parkinson's since her fall. Or if there is a cause."

"Then you need to find another doctor," I say. "Their answer can't be that they don't know. That's bullshit."

Mom laughs, but it's fractured, tired. "Trust me, I feel the same way."

"Okay, then what's the next step?"

"They need to run tests to figure out what's going on." She hesitates, her voice cracking. "I don't know what to do.

Other than convincing Gran to come home, I don't know what I *can* do."

Then, thousands of miles away, Mom begins to cry.

Mom and I are emotional creatures. Our house was very touchy-feely when I was growing up. But she's always put on a brave face for me, rarely lets me see her weaker moments. Crying during *Little Women* is one thing. Crying over Gran is another; it tells me something is really wrong.

In response, my eyes dampen. "I'm sorry."

Mom sniffles and half laughs. "Oh, Bug, I don't want you to worry. I'm sorry, it's just—it's stressful. So damn stressful."

"What can I do?" I ask as someone knocks on the front door. Mom doesn't notice it on her end, or if she does, she doesn't mention it.

"You're already doing plenty. With the business handled, I can focus completely on what's happening here. And Gran needs my full attention."

Across the foyer, Ezra's face pops into view through the sidelights alongside our front door. He waves, motioning for me to let him inside. I hold up my finger, conflicted by all the emotions running through me at once.

"Let me know if there's anything else I can do. And tell Gran I say hi."

"Of course. She's having more testing done tomorrow, and we should have the results back early next week. Or that's what the doctor said. I'll keep you posted."

We exchange our goodbyes and I hang up, running my

thumb beneath my wet lashes. I sniff back my sadness and stand up to unlock the front door.

"Hi," I say, and motion for Ezra to come inside. Like this is normal, me inviting a Blumstein into our house.

"Bad time?" he asks, studying my face.

"My mom called." Ezra's face remains inquisitive, curious, since I've never explained Gran's situation to him. But it isn't my secret to share, so I parcel out the truth and say, "My grandma isn't doing too well; she moved out to Florida a few years ago. My mom's visiting her."

"I'm sorry. You wanna talk about it?" Ezra's hand rests on my forearm, and the space between his brows scrunches up in concern.

"I'm fine." To show him how much, I work a smile onto my lips. "Thanks for the offer, though."

"I'm here if you change your mind."

Something about that almost breaks me, and I lean into Ezra, hug him. Feel the solid weight of his body, the steady drum of his heart, the heat of his skin. Other than Nan and my mom, I've never really had people to confide in before. Even with James, there was this invisible line we never crossed when it came to how much we shared with each other. Sure, we got close physically, but emotionally, we were pretty distant.

Ezra's hand wraps around my waist, and he rests his chin on the top of my head. I take slow, deep breaths until the threat of tears subsides. I step back, my hand finding his, as I admire him. His slim-cut jeans and striped button-down, rolled and cuffed to his elbows, the colorful splash of his tattoo.

"You ready to start?" I lead him through the living room, into the kitchen. As I do so, I try to take in our house like a stranger would. It's not fancy, but it's nice. Cute. Certainly lived in. Messier than usual, thanks to Mom.

Ezra pauses in the kitchen, where Ford has roused from his nap. As Ezra kneels down to pet the dog, his shirt rides up, showing the groove of his lower back.

Averting my gaze, I return to the living room and turn down any framed baby photos. In one of them I'm 100 percent butt naked, and inexplicably posing with a bouquet of wildflowers. *Thanks, Mom.*

There shouldn't be anything else especially embarrassing downstairs. Upstairs there are even more framed baby photos and I likely left a few bras on my bedroom floor, but it's not like Ezra's going upstairs or anything.

My already-red face heats.

Turning from the staircase, I join Ezra in the kitchen.

He's full of this adorable energy, smiling wide. "So. I take it you like honeybees."

I lean against the kitchen counter and laugh. Mom went a little heavy-handed with her decorating. There's enough bee-related paraphernalia in this house to prove we're beeks, in case there was any doubt. Bee-embroidered pillows, jars of honey in the kitchen, a tapestry chronicling the life cycle of a honeybee. An entire kitchen wall to our left is decorated with gold-painted hexagons. It's *a lot*.

"Too subtle?"

Ezra holds up his hand, narrowing the space between his thumb and forefinger. "Just a tad."

We smile at each other for a second before I clear my throat and nod toward the sliding glass door. "Apiary's out there. Let me get Ford settled." I fetch a dog biscuit for Ford and check his food bowl before leading Ezra outside.

"The main part of the apiary is farther back," I say, gesturing out to the yard. "But we keep bees all around, wherever we find the space."

Ezra tucks his hands into his jean pockets, soaking it all in: the sunshine and oak trees and rosebushes. "It's beautiful."

"Isn't it?" I skip across the grass to the office. "This is where we keep all our supplies." The door is unlocked and I push it open, flicking on the overhead bulb. "Lemme grab my gear. One sec." For a while, I tried leaving my suit out on a hook under the arbor, but the raccoons living in the arbor (it's a problem) tore it apart.

"Nice little place you got here," he says from behind me.

I glance over my shoulder; he's peering in curiously. "My mom converted it a few years ago." Stepping deeper into the office, I make room so Ezra can check it out.

Ezra roams around, and I try not to be embarrassed by our little office as I lift my two-piece bee suit from its hook by the door. Like I did in the house, I self-consciously wonder how Ezra views the space.

The stuffed shelves, the ratty velvet armchair that is most definitely older than I am. The stacks and stacks of old notebooks with years of handwritten hive notes. Our Northern California Honey Show ribbons decorating the walls. The ancient freezer stuffed full of old honeycomb and drone brood. The wonky space heater Mom is convinced will burn the office down if we ever use it, but we're too lazy to move it. It's nothing fancy in here, but it's another little slice of myself, exposed for Ezra.

Ezra glances past me, up at our award-adorned wall. "When you say twenty-four ribbons," he says, "it doesn't sound like very many. But in person?" He lets out a joking whistle.

"Impressive, right?" I move to stand beside him.

The corner of his mouth turns and his dimple appears. "Twenty-four is a nice, even number, don't you think?"

"Oh, like you care who wins next month."

Ezra holds both hands up in surrender. "I don't care. But it'd be a shame to get another ribbon and mess with all that symmetry," he teases, and gestures to Mom's perfectly displayed ribbons. They *are* symmetrical, but we have a space for the twenty-fifth.

I laugh and nudge his ribs with my elbow. "You and your family are all talk. I mean, you haven't won in *years*. Maybe you should put your money where your mouth is."

Ezra raises his eyebrows. "Oh? And how would I go about doing that?" As he shifts toward the door, his hand trails my hip. I focus on his mouth, and let's set the record straight: Ezra has one very nice-looking mouth. Full lips, pouty, with a freckle on his bottom lip I'm now just noticing.

Surely my face is bright red, but I lean against the doorway and lift my chin. Ezra ducks down to kiss me, and the kiss is warm and soft. A slow-burning tease that I have to cut off now because if I don't, I'll spend the rest of today kissing Ezra in this work shed. Not a bad way to spend time, but not exactly a good idea, either.

"C'mon." I press my hand to his chest and break the connection. "We have work to do."

"I suppose you're right." Ezra sighs, but he's smiling in a way that nearly makes me trip over my own feet. Together we leave the little office and head down to the apiary.

The path from the office leads down the wooden steps embedded in the hill, linking the apiary with the rest of the yard. On either side of the apiary are wild berry bushes, their blooms already clustered with honeybees. Ezra follows me as I step down the stairs.

"Whoa," is all he says.

"Welcome to the Hazeldine apiary," I say, and spread my arms in a grand gesture. "Not all the hives are harvestable this season, but we do pretty well for ourselves."

"This place is amazing," Ezra says, edging on awe.

"Thanks. It's one of my favorite places in the world."

I lead him down the path into the thicket of the apiary. Since the morning sun is starting to shine hot in the sky, the girls are out collecting pollen, the rainbow of colors laden on their back legs as they touch down on the landing strips outside of their respective hives.

Beneath the arbor, Ezra unbuttons his shirt and hangs it on the back of the nearby Adirondack chair, revealing a white tee beneath. I don't get to admire him much before he pulls on his suit. I do the same. They're an unfortunate side effect of the warming weather. Since we're entering the dearth, the girls are more hostile than usual.

The dearth is when the nectar flow dries up. Less nectar means less honey. Which means angrier bees. Well, I shouldn't say angry—they're protective. They buzz with purpose, and when the heightened hum gets louder, you know they're losing their patience with you poking around in their home.

Side by side, we inspect in silence. Mom would implode if she saw Ezra handling her hives, but with the both of us working, the time goes by faster. We break for lunch, eating sunflower-seed butter and blackberry jam sandwiches on the patio, then we're back at it.

Everything about this situation is wrong, but I'm glad I invited Ezra. I knew he liked beekeeping, but it's different to experience his knowledge and care firsthand. To stand beside him and enjoy the same strange hobby. It's refreshing and wonderful; I'm more comfortably and authentically *myself* than I have been in a long time.

All because of Ezra.

Ezra, the boy I am most definitely falling for. Not just

because of the way he looks or how he kisses—I really like who he is as a person. It's a terrifying and confusing realization. Because I am 100 percent unable to stop myself.

In the past, I've only been attracted to the guys I've dated—if that. I didn't actually like them as people, which is probably bad in hindsight. Liking the way Ezra looks and how he acts is overwhelming. And weird. And nice.

Clearly I'm conflicted. The person I finally, actually like is probably the only one in Volana who is strictly off-limits. And it might just kill me.

"Thank you," I say as we wrap up the last hive of the day. My arms ache and my lower back is sore, but I wouldn't trade this work for anything in the world. We each carefully carry a few frames of honey we pulled from the more industrious hives.

"Thank *you*. I had a blast." Ezra's smile is an infectious thing.

I study the frames of honey in my hands. They're sticky sweet on my gloves, and the scent tickles my nostrils. Brood might be my favorite part of a hive inspection, but capped honey is gorgeous, especially when the light hits the wax in the right way. It glows golden, the capped wax over each cell delicate and opaque.

"About what I said, in the office." Ezra slows as we walk up the wooden steps to the top of the yard.

"What'd you say?" I ask, my mind now fully on that kiss.

"You know I don't care who wins that thing, right?"

"*You* don't." I head for the office and nudge the door open with my foot. "But your grandparents and mom care."

Ezra loosens a sigh. "Yeah. They do." He hands me the frames of honey, and I stack them in the mini fridge beneath the desk. "Do you care?"

I consider his question as I finish storing the honey. "Yeah, I do. I love Hazeldine Honey. Maybe more than anything. And the win would mean a lot to my mom."

"Okay," he says thoughtfully, and begins to remove his bee suit. I try to ignore how his white T-shirt clings to his chest. "That's fair. But I'm neutral, okay? Call me Switzerland."

I laugh, fumbling as I remove the honey-and-propolis-stained bee suit. *So* attractive. Not like my sweat-stained tank top beneath is any better. We both ditch our suits; I leave mine behind in the office, hung up by the door, but Ezra carries his out with him.

"Thanks again for all your help," I say, locking up the office behind me.

"Not completely selfless." His face is flushed, hair matted to his forehead, and all I want to do is kiss him. "I wanted to see you today—preferably in the daytime. And I figured the sooner you were done, the sooner we could hang out?"

When I smile, I feel it throughout my entire body. "Yeah, okay." My gaze slides past Ezra, up the hill to the house. "Where does your family think you are, anyway?"

"With a friend. Which isn't technically a lie. I'm covered for a few more hours. I can make you dinner?"

My heart warms. "While I love the sound of that, there's no food in this house," I say, and we head into the air-conditioned kitchen.

"Challenge accepted," Ezra says, and begins rifling through the pantry.

Bemused, I perch on the kitchen table. "You're not going to find anything edible."

"Why are there six cans of half-used cake frosting in here?" He pokes his head out of the pantry. "What the hell do you and your mom eat?"

"Cake?" I shrug. "Or just the frosting. It's an excellent nighttime snack."

Ezra just stares at me in horror. "Are you kidding?"

"Nope." I laugh at his unease. *"What?"*

"I can't be the first person to tell you that's unhealthy, right?"

"I have a perfectly good clean bill of health. My mom, too."

"Pretty much everyone in my family has heart disease or diabetes, so I try to eat healthy." Ezra shakes his head, but he's smiling. "Your mom sounds like a trip. Too bad she hates me."

"She hates your family, not you," I point out, even though I really don't want to think about my mom right now. "You're very . . . unhateable."

Ezra grins in response, ducking back into the pantry. A moment later, he reappears with a box of noodles I've never seen in my life. He rattles the box. "They're not expired. How does pasta sound?"

"Sounds perfect," I say, and try to abandon any concerns over what my mom thinks.

Ezra then proceeds to cook me an actual meal. I direct him to our garden and he returns with a few heirloom tomatoes, which he chops up and mixes with olive oil. When he puts on one of our frilly aprons—courtesy of Gran—I laugh so hard my sides hurt. Today might be one of the best days I've had in a long time.

"This is so good," I say once we're seated on the couch with our bowls of pasta. "Amazing."

He laughs, balancing his bowl on the arm of the couch. "It's pasta. It took me ten minutes."

I point at him with my fork. "Exactly. I'm very easy to impress. I'm surprised our stove even worked."

Ezra shakes his head affectionately, returning to his pasta.

We watch *Fullmetal Alchemist: Brotherhood*, which Ezra's never seen before—a criminal offense. It's nice. As someone with social anxiety, I find it's rare to come across a person who doesn't judge my awkward moments or put me on edge. Being around Ezra is easy, effortless. Borderline addictive.

After we're done eating, Ezra hits play for another episode, and we lie down on the couch. Ezra is behind me, his arm casually draped over my waist. I try to focus on the show, but all I can think about is Ezra's arm. How his hand shifts, rests on my thigh. How the length of his body is pressed against mine.

Impulsively I shift onto my back and hook my fingers

through the collar of his shirt, pulling his mouth down on mine. Just for a moment. A long, glorious moment.

Until he pulls away and says, "Josie?" He's propped over me, and his chest rises and falls rapidly. Part of me is proud—I did this to him. I made Ezra breathless.

"Yeah?"

"I don't know what we're doing, but . . ." He breaks off, rubs his cheeks with one hand. "I like you."

"I like you too," I whisper, afraid of the admission. Because it's true. I like Ezra—probably too much. It's almost funny. Despite the fact my anxiety constantly has me on guard, I didn't see this one coming.

I didn't count on liking him this much.

Chapter Eleven

FOR THE FIRST time in a while, I'm excited to sleep over at Nan's house—I need someone to talk to about Ezra. And since my mom is never, ever finding out, that leaves Nan. She texted last night and invited me over, and even though spending the evening with Ezra is more appealing, I said yes. At first it was out of guilt, but now I'm actually eager to hang out with my best friend.

Bev's coming by at three to take over my Thursday-afternoon shift at Waxing Poetic, as well as Ford for the night. The last hour of work drags by at a glacial pace. The store is busy, but it's in bursts. Currently I'm in a lull. I practically *feel* every minute tick by. Sure, it may be more stressful dealing with customers, but at least the time passes quickly.

In the lulls, my mind wanders to Ezra. I saw him again last night—he came over and we stayed on the couch and kissed until my lips turned numb—but the second I lost sight of him walking down the lane, I began missing him. Which is ridiculous. Right?

Or is this normal?

I scroll on my phone, debating about whether or not I should text Ezra and see if he can sneak away before I go to Nan's. But I stop myself. Bad idea, right? Or is it a *great* idea? Before I make up my mind, the bell above the door jangles. I stuff my phone into the cubby and look up.

A smile breaks across my face because Ezra lopes across the store, weaving his way between the wine barrels. "Hey!" Did I conjure him into existence or something?

"Hey," Ezra says, his grin mirroring my own as he reaches the counter. "And before you panic about me being in the store"—he grabs a jar of honey at random from the nearest shelf, and plunks it down in front of the register—"I'm a customer with a perfectly valid reason to be here."

Full of laughter and something effervescent I can't quite name, I slide the jar of honey closer and punch the item code into the register. "What're you up to today?"

"Other than missing you? Not much." He leans his forearms onto the counter and studies me through fringed eyelashes. My stomach somersaults. "Are you *sure* you're too busy tonight to hang out?"

"Fifteen seventy-five," I say, and Ezra gets out his wallet.

"And yeah, I'm sorry. Nan asked me over and I'm already a shitty friend. I felt bad."

"When are you going to tell her about GSU?"

I groan, reaching below the counter for a gift bag and dropping the jar of honey inside. "Ugh, I don't know. Soon." I shove an artful tuft of tissue paper inside and hold the bag out for Ezra. "Here you are."

Ezra takes the bag. "Don't be so hard on yourself."

"I'll try. Sorry about tonight." A dangerous thought flits into my head, and I check the time. Bev's not due for nearly an hour. "Come here."

Giving me a quizzical look, Ezra rounds the counter. I hop off the stool and open the back office door, pulling him inside by his shirtsleeve. The inside of Mom's office is dark and cramped, without any air-conditioning.

"What're you doing?" Ezra asks as I partially close the door, leaving it open enough to hear the bell.

I reach up to kiss him, which shuts him up. Fast. Ezra's hands thread through my hair, and he backs me up against the wall. I melt against him, all the anxious noise inside my head turning to soft static. The kiss is almost too much. Maybe it's the circumstances, or maybe it's because things are shifting between us, but I'm overwhelmed. Or maybe it's because Ezra's a very good kisser. Whatever the reason, I'm left with my heart pounding and warmth spreading throughout my body.

The bell rings in the storefront.

"Shit," I murmur against his lips, and slide out from beneath him. Ezra leans against the wall, breathing heavy, which makes me smile.

Through the crack in the door, I peer into the store—and all the bubbly warmth inside me fades. Because Bev's early. I whip around and hold my forefinger to my lips. "Be quiet. Bev's here."

Ezra sobers, nodding in understanding before shifting farther into my mom's tiny office.

I run a shaky hand through my hair and slip outside. "Hey, Bev!" My voice sounds loud and weird.

Bev sidles up to the counter cheerfully, but her eyes are narrowed in confusion—or concern, I can't quite tell. "Hey, hon. How're things?"

"Good! The store's good!" Internally, I cringe. What is *wrong* with me? Bev frowns, and I swear her gaze wanders to the partially open office door. I shift on my feet to block her view. "You're early."

"By ten minutes." She looks away from the office and focuses on my face.

Wait. How long were Ezra and I inside the office? *Oh boy.*

Face steadily turning red again, I scramble for a reason to get Bev out of the store. There's no exit in my mom's office. Not even a window for Ezra to shimmy out of. I turn to Ford—bingo. "Do you mind walking Ford over to the square? He needs to use the bathroom, and I'll wrap up here."

Bev hesitates. But her expression softens into something

normal; I've passed the test. "Sure thing." She slides Ford's leash off the counter, clips it to his collar, and heads out. The second the bell rings, I turn on my heel and open the office door, finding Ezra perched on the edge of my mom's desk.

"You need to leave," I say, motioning for him to get up.

As he passes me, his fingers trail my arm. "I shouldn't have come by—"

"Don't worry about it. Bev's taking Ford to the square. When you leave, turn left, loop behind the pharmacy, and from there you can walk Highway Ten back to your house. She shouldn't see you."

Ezra backs out from behind the counter and grabs his honey. "You have no idea how badly I want to kiss you goodbye."

"I might have an idea," I say with a smile.

My heart tugs the farther away he becomes, until he's out of the store. I collapse my head onto the counter. That was a close one. Bev almost outed us.

And it was totally worth it.

⬡ ⬡ ⬡

Nan howls with laughter, sloshing vodka-spiked lemonade on her shirt. "At Waxing Poetic? You didn't!"

"Oh, I did." My drink is strong, the sourness of the lemon making my eyes water, the heat of the vodka burning my throat. I take a big gulp and finish telling Nan about today's misadventures. Filling her in on everything she's missed. Over the last hour, I've caught Nan up on my relationship with

Ezra, pandering to her out of the guilt I've developed over all my secret-keeping.

After letting Bev take over, I drove Mom's Element into the Volana foothills, the swanky neighborhood where Nan lives. When Nan and I first became friends, going over to her house used to scare the shit out of me, although I would've never said that because I was eleven. It's a modern, palatial one-story house with cement walls, marble floors, and slightly pornographic art. It is the direct opposite of my house, which is soft, homey, and full of quilts. Years later, I still struggle to feel comfortable here—like I'm a misplaced country bumpkin or something.

"Told you the sneaking around would be hot." Nan tips her glass back and gulps. "I'm almost jealous."

I blush, laughing. "It's not *that*. It's . . . Ezra."

"You think your mom would care if she found out?" She leans over the edge of the couch to pet King, their giant Doberman, who rolls onto his back on the area rug and exposes his tummy.

At the VCBA meeting—was that only one week ago?—Mom dragged me away from Ezra, telling me to stay away from "that boy." Nan idolizes my mom—and I get it, she's awesome—but there are some lines you don't cross in the Hazeldine family. Kissing Ezra definitely crosses said line.

"Yup." I slowly draw out the word. "She'll care. Trust me."

"Still," Nan says, tripping over the rug as she stands, "I think it's great."

I set the drink on the coffee table and drag my fingers through my unruly hair. "Really?"

Nan heads to the living room's wet bar to refill her glass. "Ezra's the perfect summer fling."

Something about the way Nan says this curdles my stomach. Not like I didn't consider his temporariness before this moment. But still.

My brain is floaty from the vodka, and I push up to see her over the back of the sofa. "Right," I say hollowly. "He is."

"Tell me more, tell me more," Nan sings in a *Grease*-inspired cringey falsetto, wobbling her way back to the heavy leather couches.

I turn around, letting my head fall back into the cushions. "You know it all," I say, which is true. I didn't quite get into the details of how much I like Ezra, how he occupies my brain constantly. How I wish I were with him right now, not her. There are parts of Ezra I'd rather hold close to my chest, not turn into gossip.

Nan boos my lack of participation but launches into her own summer fling: Nick. Emery's cousin is coming to town next week, and my best friend loves nothing more than a challenge. As she talks, she tips back her second—or is it third?—drink. I press my palm to my stomach, vowing to lay off the vodka if I'm going to be the sober one to Nan's drunken ass tonight. One of us should stay with it, and it's clearly not going to be Nan.

I don't like to drink, but when I arrived, Nan's parents and brother were out at the movies, and she made a beeline for the wet bar. Poured us two drinks like we were sophisticated, talking about our love lives over cocktails. No doubt re-creating some daydream in her head from our fictional future in Los Angeles. And I played along.

After Nan's done funneling vodka into her body, we hide out in her room and watch a movie so her parents don't find out we got drunk off their vodka when they get home. They have the opposite stance on drinking than my mom: zero tolerance.

I've always been jealous of Nan's bedroom, with its connecting bathroom—shower and a separate soaking bathtub—and a small walk-in closet. Nan's parents are a bona fide power couple and own half of Volana County's commercial real estate.

While Nan turns on the TV mounted on her bedroom wall, I grab my phone from my duffel bag and my heart warms at the notification on the screen.

> **EZRA:** So I fell into a blackberry bush behind Waxing Poetic, but I successfully made it home without Bev seeing me. Currently covered in like dozens of thorn scratch marks, but it was worth it.

I grin, holding my hand over my mouth. I perch on the

edge of Nan's bed and type out a response.

> **ME: Oh no! 😫 Glad you made it relatively safe.**

> **EZRA: How's Nan's?**

> **ME: Not bad?**

I hesitate, then send a follow-up.

> **ME: Wish I was with you, though.**

"Josie?" Nan stands in front of me, waving her hand. "Hello?"

Quickly, I lock my phone. "What? Sorry."

She rolls her eyes. "We have *Pretty in Pink*, *Sixteen Candles*, *Say Anything*," she says, rattling off movie titles she's preselected for the night. "Take your pick."

I sit on the bed with my back to the headboard, palming my phone. Resisting the urge to check the screen when it vibrates because Nan will only get more annoyed with me. This is supposed to be *our* night.

"Whatever's fine," I say, yawning because vodka makes me tired.

"*Say Anything* it is." Nan grabs the remote for the Apple

TV and hits play. Alcohol has the opposite effect on her. She's extra energetic, trying to pull me from my sleepiness. "I could totally go for a dose of young John Cusack." She smiles wide, her teeth perfectly straight and white. Like a toothpaste commercial come to life.

The movie plays and she rests against the headboard, enraptured by a film we've both seen an innumerable amount of times. I shift, stretching out on my stomach with my cheek pressed to a throw pillow. Resisting the urge to check my phone. Forcing myself to be a good friend. Because as cutting as Nan can be, she's still my best friend. I never made friends easily. Either from the social anxiety itself or the barriers it created, I'm unsure.

Nan and I aren't the perfect friendship fit anymore. We're drifting apart, but that doesn't mean I want to lose her. I've seen the rare and softer parts of Nan's personality. Even if those softer parts have hardened as we've gotten older, they still exist.

When I tell Nan about staying in Volana, I hope she'll support me. That she'll look back on seven years of friendship warmly—like I do—and be happy for me. Because beneath it all, the girl who ate lunch with me on my first day of sixth grade—when I was perpetually friendless and she'd just transferred schools—still exists. She has to.

Chapter Twelve

"HOW HAVE I lived in Volana County for three weeks and never seen the river?" Ezra marvels as we unpack our swarm gear.

"Because you're always hanging out with me and I *hate* the river," I say, lugging the wooden nuc box over to the patch of grass.

It's Sunday, and the mid-June heat is nearly unbearable at noon. Earlier this morning, I got a swarm call and invited Ezra along. For his help, but also for his company. For a day where we can find some stolen moments together.

The swarm's on residential property backing up onto the Russian River, in an unincorporated part of Volana County. The house is higher up on a grassy knoll with a slope down to the rocky-sand beach. The swarm hangs out from underneath their fence. I approach it curiously; the bees have been there for some time, creating a makeshift home and drawing out comb.

I groan—this isn't a swarm retrieval, but a *hive* retrieval.

When we arrived, I talked briefly to the owner—a gruff, uninterested man holding a Lagunitas beer—telling him I was here in place of my mom and would remove the bees, but it could take several hours depending on the complexity of the situation. The man barely spoke to me the entire time; his only priority was to get the bees off his property before his kid's birthday party tomorrow afternoon.

"Why do you hate the river?" Ezra asks as he helps unpack our supplies.

Even if I'm infinitely calmer around Ezra than anyone else I've ever met, I'm also more . . . let's go with easily distractible around him. He messes with my ability to wholeheartedly focus on any task at hand. Today is no different. Maybe it's because he looks really, really good today, and I have a functioning pair of eyes. I mean, he's wearing shorts! I've never seen his bare legs before. And while they're entirely unremarkable, my stomach flutters.

"I don't know. It's always seemed gross. Mucky."

Glancing between the river and me, he lifts a brow. "Looks perfectly clear and refreshing to me."

With a playful sigh, I toss his bee suit at him. "C'mon, let's get this show on the road. The hive isn't going to remove itself."

"Aye, aye, Captain," he jokes.

Like the first swarm retrieval, we set up a nuc box, but that's where the similarities end. The bees have drawn comb, and I do something I've seen my mom do in similar cases.

"Can you grab some rubber bands out of the car?" I ask Ezra, zipping up my suit. "Back seat in a coffee tin."

While I wait, I snap on some nitrile gloves. I didn't bring any regular leather gloves, which I'm regretting. My hands are already sweating. Nitrile is thinner, and bees are less likely to sting it because it's an unnatural texture. Leather gloves are familiar to them from an evolutionary standpoint; they know they can sting leather. Unfortunately, nitrile make your hands sweat like no other.

"Here," Ezra says, dropping a handful of rubber bands onto the grass.

"Thanks." I kneel down and use my elbow to pop out the beeswax-coated plastic foundations from the frames Mom keeps in the swarm kit, leaving the empty wooden frames behind. I leave a few regular ones in the sides of the box and lay the emptied ones out on the grass.

"What're you doing?" He crouches beside me.

"This isn't a swarm," I point out. "They have an established hive. It's underneath the overhang on the fence, in the shade, so they're protected. They've drawn comb, which looks like it has honey and brood on it. I'm going to transfer them over."

While my words are pumped full of confidence, I half

expect Ezra to second-guess my approach. To ask me if I know what I'm doing. But all he does is move out of my way and say, "Let me know if I can help."

I glance sideways at him, appreciative. "Thanks."

Using my hive tool, I break off the gorgeous lobes of comb, and use a rubber band to secure them to the frame. Then I lower the frame into the nuc box. I do this for three frames, until all the large pieces of comb are removed, moving slowly and methodically.

By the time we're done, it's taken me two hours to re-home the hive. Since this is an actual hive and not a swarm, we have two options: waiting until sundown, or setting up an extra box where the hive used to be and collecting it early tomorrow morning. We do this because there could be foragers out in the area, and if we move the hive before they return, they'll become homeless and die.

We're on private property, but I still set up the sandwich board sign—CAUTION: LIVE BEE REMOVAL—and step away from the hive, unzipping my suit as I go.

Ezra lets out a low whistle. "That was impressive."

I laugh, heat in my face. "Nah."

"Take the compliment. You deserve it," he says, grinning wide. Those dimples, I swear.

"Thank you." Flushed from the heat of the sun *and* the heat of his gaze, I free myself of my bee suit, then plunk down on the grass so I can rest and have a drink of water. "It's so hot."

Ezra settles beside me and leans his weight back on his

hands. "You know, there is a perfectly good, refreshing body of water mere yards away."

I roll my eyes, my body still buzzing from the high of the bee removal. "Ezra, we can't go swimming."

"And why not?"

I tilt my head to one side. "Because we're working. We're *professionals*."

"You're working. I'm the moral support," he says. "And besides, we're done!"

While I hate to admit Ezra might be onto something, it's awfully hot. I'm sweaty to the point where my deodorant has waved a white flag, and even the gross Russian River is appealing. "I don't have a swimsuit."

"Wade in," he says. "You're wearing shorts."

I narrow my eyes at Ezra, and he grins wildly. "Fine," I say, and he pops up to his feet, reaching down to haul me upright.

I place my hand in his and let him pull me to my feet. "What about the owner?"

"He drove off a half hour ago."

I nod. And it's not like the river is his. "Let's go. But only for a minute, okay?"

He's already running toward the water.

I take off my shoes and ball my socks together, following him to the rocky shore.

With zero regard for his clothes, Ezra chucks off his shoes and runs into the Russian River.

Laughing at his lightness, at his pure ability to be calm and enjoy himself, I tentatively follow. He's the kind of person who's never, ever anxious or put out by anything. I'm equally as fascinated as I am jealous. Honestly, it makes me like him even more.

The first step into the river is heavenly. Icy-cool water laps around my ankles.

Ezra drifts on his back, shirt clinging to his skin, hair floating around his head like a halo. "See? Isn't this an excellent idea?"

"The best you've ever had," I say dryly, inching into the river so it reaches my calves. I lean down and cup my hands, then splash water onto the back of my neck. I go as far as my thighs but stop before getting my shorts wet.

Ezra floats by, kicking slightly, sprinkling me with water. "That's it?"

"I don't want to get my clothes wet."

"They'll dry. Seriously, it's worth it." He swims closer, and his legs brush mine beneath the water as he stands in the muddy embankment. Before I can react, Ezra's wrapping his arms around my waist and pulling me into deeper water.

"Ezra," I say, trying to sound stern but I'm laughing, my clothes already damp from being held against his body. I can't see his face but know he's grinning that charming grin of his.

"See?" When we're in the middle of the river, he loosens his hold on me. "The water is great!"

I splash him in the face. He sputters, then splashes me

back. We're both laughing and having way too much fun. But I deserve this, don't I? I've been working—so hard—and it's incredibly nice to screw around for once.

The laughter and the water and the warmth of the sun fill me up in a way I could've never expected.

I study Ezra as he treads water across from me in the river. The crinkle between his brows. The Roman arch of his sun-freckled nose. The slight part in his lips. The droplets of water glisten against his skin. How his wet T-shirt clings to his body, like he isn't even wearing one. The anxious thrill I get when I realize I *want* to see him without a shirt on. The accompanying swoop of my stomach because that might happen this summer.

I swim closer, our treading legs knocking into each other beneath the surface, and wrap my arms around his neck. Ezra's mouth finds mine. For some reason, I expected intensity, passion. Instead, the kiss is slow, lingering, sweet. Intoxicating all the same.

"You know," Ezra murmurs, resting his forehead to mine, "I wasn't looking forward to staying in Volana for the summer. But meeting you . . ." He trails off.

My fingers knot in his hair in response. I'm so in over my head, aren't I? But this doesn't usher in anxiety. No, I'm safe here, treading water in the Russian River, holding on to Ezra.

"I'm glad you didn't stay in Santa Barbara."

He leans back, a shy grin on his face. "I'm glad I met you."

"I'm glad I met you too," I say, my voice thick.

Ezra's shy grin morphs into something more confident, and his hand finds mine. "C'mon. Let's go dry off."

$$\Diamond\Diamond\Diamond$$

I made the decision to leave another nuc box behind at the swarm retrieval site. Staying until sundown would've meant hanging around that guy's property for four more hours. So I set up the nuc box, closed up the main hive and put it in my car, and left the owner of the house a voice mail telling him I'd be back in the morning.

Ezra and I stretch out in my backyard under the hot-hot June sun, and let the sun dry our still-damp clothes. My head rests in the crook of Ezra's shoulder, and one of his arms is propped up beneath his head. Our fingers are interlaced, palms sweaty, but neither of us cares.

"Do you—have you heard when your mom might be coming back?" Ezra asks.

My eyes are closed, the heat leaching any remaining energy from my body. Mom touched base with me on Thursday after Gran finished her PET scan. We're waiting for the results, which are supposed to come in on Monday.

"She's planning on flying back Wednesday morning." Wednesday used to sound so far away, but in reality, that's three days from now. And since today is halfway over, we only have two full days.

"Oh. That's—"

"Soon?" I peel open my eyes and blink at the sun.

Ezra adjusts his position in the grass. "Yeah. All this sneaking around. It's hard enough seeing each other now when she isn't even in town."

"I know."

"So, uh, when she's back, are we still . . ." He breaks off, tracing the ridges of my knuckles with his thumb. "What does that mean for us?"

Something heavy and conflicted tugs at my chest. Ezra's right—our time together is limited already. Mom coming home will be another limitation. The logical part of my brain tells me to shut this down now. Except the thought of no longer seeing Ezra hurts. The kind of hurt I want to outrun for as long as possible.

"I don't even know what we are," I murmur, embarrassed, even if it's true. We've never talked about it. Labels are fairly irrelevant in a secret relationship. But if I'm going to keep on lying to my mom—and lie to her *face*—then I need the confidence of knowing Ezra and I are on the same page.

Ezra mirrors my position and lies down on his side. From a bird's-eye view, we probably look like two parentheses curved into each other. "Josie." When I meet his gaze, his brown eyes are soft, vulnerable. "I *really* like you. If I could, I'd take you out on dates and post dozens of ridiculous selfies of us together because I'm in this with you."

My mouth goes dry, and I'm like an old-timey cartoon—my heart thumping outside my chest. Not trusting my words, I press my lips to Ezra's. But after a moment, he gently shifts away. Raises his eyebrows. Damn. I actually have to communicate. I shouldn't be nervous, but I'm afraid I'll say the wrong thing and he'll take his speech back. Rewind his feelings.

"My mom coming home will complicate things," I say carefully, "but I don't want us to be over. We'd need this to stay between us."

Ezra kisses me before pulling back and saying, "So. Will you be my secret girlfriend?"

I laugh at the ridiculous term, but nod. "Depends. Will you be my secret boyfriend?"

"Yep." His eyes glint happily. "But for the record, *I* don't want to keep *you* a secret. But I will because there's so much on the line for you this summer." Ezra tucks a wayward strand of hair behind my ear. "Know that, okay?"

"Okay." I rest my forehead against his, our legs tangled together in the grass. As happy as I am, I wish this situation were different. I wish my mom weren't so petty. I wish Ezra had a different last name. I wish I didn't have to hide him—this openhearted, courageous boy—in the literal shadows.

But Ezra's right. There's a lot on the line for me this summer.

Mom and Hazeldine Honey are so important.

And yet, as I stare into Ezra's eyes, they don't feel as important as they once did.

Chapter Thirteen

THE SCREEN FLICKERS as Mom adjusts, ducking her head awkwardly to get into view. "Can you see me now?"

I tilt the laptop screen back and flash my mom a thumbs-up. "Yep!"

The cheerfulness is forced, though, because my stomach is knotted preemptively. Waiting for the bad news Mom is no doubt about drop. I was able to ignore Gran's situation and Mom's impending return during the weekend, especially since I spent most of it with Ezra. But late on Monday afternoon, Mom wanted to FaceTime. On the day Gran got her scan and blood tests back.

"Oh," she says, bringing her hands to her mouth, "it's so good to see your face, Josie!"

"You've barely been gone a week. And you'll be home Wednesday, right?"

She drags her fingers through her dark hair, which has fallen prey to Florida's humidity. Ever watch the episode of *Friends* where the gang goes to Barbados and Monica's hair expands like a Chia Pet? Yeah, that's what my mom's hair looks like right now.

"About that . . ." Her focus falls beyond the screen. "Wait, I'm getting ahead of myself. I've missed you so much."

"I've missed you too," I say, and a stab of guilt—*Hello, my old friend*—hits my stomach. While my mom has missed me and being home, I've barely spared a minute to miss her. I've been too busy with Ezra.

"How's Gran?" I ask to redirect the conversation. As if Mom might read the guilt on my face.

Mom worries her bottom lip between her teeth. "The good news is I'm bringing Gran home with me."

My eyes go big, round. "Wait. What? You convinced her to come home?"

Mom and I hated it when Gran moved over three thousand miles away. But at the time she was of sound mind. We couldn't have kept her here even if she'd *wanted* to stay. She packed up the essentials, leaving Ford in our care, along with the house and her bees, and took off. Gran's health must be worse than I thought if Mom convinced her to come home.

"The doctor called us in this morning. Her Parkinson's is getting worse," Mom says, fiddling with her leather bracelet.

"When the doctor said he wasn't comfortable with her living out here alone, she listened." Mom breaks off with an uneasy laugh. "That's when I knew she understood how bad it was."

Gran is stubborn. She never listens to anyone—not her children or grandchildren, not the weather forecaster, and especially not doctors.

"When I asked if she'd be willing to move home, she didn't fight me," Mom continues, squinting like she's holding back tears. "But I can't get her packed up and out of here by Wednesday. We have a follow-up with her neurologist on Thursday to go over a treatment plan and get a referral for some local doctors."

"When are you coming home?"

"I canceled my ticket, but I haven't booked a new flight home yet. There's . . . so much to take care of here. I'm thinking the end of next week?"

"You're going to miss—"

"Your birthday," she interrupts with a sad smile. "I'm so sorry, Bug, I know I said I'd make it home in time."

I shake my head, blinking fast. It's silly to get upset over my birthday when Gran's sick. Birthdays are nothing; they're just days. "Mom, it's fine. I'm sorry Gran isn't doing better. Um, hold on." I bend down, out of view, and swipe at the tears lining my lids. Pause for a second, ducked beneath the kitchen table, breathing.

Exhaling slowly, I sit back up and face my laptop. "Sorry!

Dropped my phone." If Mom suspects I'm lying, it doesn't show. "What can I do to help?"

"The doctor suggested a few care homes in the area," she says. "But I want her living with us. Care home costs in California are astronomical. I already asked Rosa if she'd be willing to move to California, but it was a no-go. Once I'm home, I'll have to hire someone else for part-time help, but until then, if you can clean out the study, that'd be perfect."

"Of course." I press my palm to my roiling stomach. "Is there anything else?"

"Nope. I've seen your hive notes on the Google sheet and everything looks like it's going well. Keep on doing what you're doing." Mom rests her chin in her upturned palm. "This is a lot, but I'm so proud of you."

Mom's praise washes over me like warm water. She's proud of me—and not for getting into college. No, she's proud of what I've done here, how hard I've worked. Because while I've been having fun with Ezra, I've been working hard.

Never have I spent so much time with the bees. My back aches constantly, and I have a funky sunburn on my neck and shoulders from the sunlight burning through my bee suit. But I've never doubted that this is what I want to do. If that isn't an indicator of passion, I don't know what else is.

"It's no problem," I say, my voice small. Like I'm afraid to acknowledge her praise out loud.

"What else? Tell me everything! How're things at home?"

"Good—great." At least I don't have to lie because this is

the truth. "Everything's the same, only it sucks because you're not here." My mind flits to thoughts of Ezra, of his dimpled smile, his laughter and quiet understanding. I've never kept a secret like this from Mom before—well, unless you count me bailing on college.

On the screen, Mom's expression is so sad and sweet and I miss her fiercely. "If we can come home sooner, we will. But for now, it'll probably be the end of the month. You sure you can handle everything?"

Without a thought, I say, "Of course. Keep me posted, okay?"

"I will." Mom drags her fingers through her frizzy hair again. "Thanks for being strong. All this Gran stuff isn't easy."

"No, but I'm happy to help."

"You're the best." Mom smiles and I'd give anything to hug her right now. "I miss you. And I'll be home soon."

"I miss you too."

"Okay, I need to go wake Gran. She's been napping a lot lately. I love you, Josie."

"Love you, Mom."

We say goodbye and I close my laptop before dropping my face into my hands.

The house is strangely quiet. Just the *tick-tick-tick* of the Betty Boop clock. The anemic wheeze of our air-conditioning unit. I start crying. It sounds wrong, too loud. But the tears I kept back during the video chat are finally free. They pool in my palms, splash the kitchen table, burn my chapped lips. *I want my mom.* I hate that that's right where my mind goes, but it's what I crave. I want someone to tell me everything's going to be okay. That Gran will be okay.

Even if it's all a lie.

◇◇◇

Once my tears dry, I begin cleaning out Mom's study.

Putting files into boxes. Dragging an office chair with one wonky wheel into the garage. Scrubbing down the attached guest bathroom. When Gran still lived with us, she stayed in the study since there are only two bedrooms upstairs. After she moved to Florida, Mom converted it into her work space for the paperwork end of our business. Invoices and order forms and bank statements. It hasn't been too difficult to clean out, but I'll probably need an entire extra day to finish.

I slide onto the study's hardwood floor and rest my back against the vintage armoire. Exhausted, I begin arranging folio folders into banker's boxes. Somehow I've been cleaning and organizing for hours, and the quantifiable progress— the boxes packed, the study clearing out—has made the Gran-induced anxiety bearable. But as I sit and look around the room, sadness and anger fill me back up.

I hate how life works. How easily the parent becomes the child. The reversal of roles.

In a hive, there's a misconception that the queen—their mother—leads. They dote on her, feed her predigested food, groom her, remove her feces from the hive, but she's not in control. Her pheromones control hive behavior, but the moment the queen begins to falter, no one cares about the queen. They only care about the health of the hive. At the first injury or drop in pheromone, they replace her, turning a viable egg or young larva into a queen cell. The new queen will emerge and kill the old queen. Regicide.

Long live the queen? Yeah, not so much. More like *off with her head*.

With people it's different. With people, we care. And we do everything within our power to keep them here, on earth, with us. To ease their pain. The honeybees are right about a lot of things—but that's not one of them.

As much as I wanted Gran to move back to Volana, I'm struggling to find the positives in this situation. Sure, Mom will be gone longer, which means more time with Ezra. But that's hardly a fair trade.

Maybe later, when I'm not so upset, I can revel in this. Ezra and I went from having one more day together to over a week. And when Gran's actually here, I'm sure it'll hit me. After all, life hasn't been the same since she moved to Florida. What makes Hazeldine Honey special is it's *generational*. A line of women, starting with my great-grandma Millicent.

Yet this darkened part of my heart knows it'll never be the same. When Gran left, the Parkinson's wasn't too bad. She was still cognizant and barely had a tremor. She could still put on her lip liner without straying too far. But it's all been downhill since. Worse since her fall, like it somehow accelerated the disease.

People with Parkinson's often die from starvation. I made the mistake of Googling the disease a few years ago. It isn't considered a terminal illness, but it will kill you. As the muscles begin to deteriorate and the patient loses control, they might choke on their own spit, or be unable to swallow food at all. It's a gruesome end, and I hate it.

I hate watching strong women bend to time and disease.

I'm still working as the sun drops in the sky, barely visible through the small picture window in the study. My stomach's rumbling and I'm debating whether or not I have the energy to make dinner when our novelty doorbell, set to the tune of ABBA's "Dancing Queen," rings.

With a grunt, I push the banker's box to the side and stand up. I'm bone-tired from cleaning—and crying. I reach the front door and peer through the sidelights. Taking a deep breath, I unlock and open the door. "Hey," I say, trying to sound normal. "What're you doing here?"

Ezra steps inside the house, but his bright face turns quizzical. "You weren't texting me back. We were supposed to get dinner . . ." He pauses and glances around the living room. The normally closed study doors are flung open; the boxes I have yet to move into the garage spill out. "Is everything okay?"

"Y-yeah," I say shakily, and retreat farther into the

house. I can't believe I forgot. Ezra has the car for the night, and we thought we could drive a few towns over for dinner. If I weren't so emotionally exhausted right now, I'd be mad at myself. I lean down and stack some boxes. "Sorry about the mess."

Ezra wraps his hand around my arm and tugs me upright. "Josie. What's going on?"

My throat tightens, and I stare at his chest, the soft-looking sweater he's wearing. A hot, clawing feeling tightens around my esophagus, and my eyes burn. I motion wildly to the boxes and the study. "My mom asked me to help, um . . . my gran . . ." But I barely get any words out. They crack, and I begin to cry.

Ezra pulls me against him. I'm so fucking tired of crying. It's like all the tears I've held back for Gran, for missing Mom, for being scared about the future, have unleashed a torrent. I fist my hands against Ezra's sweater and hold on to him. Because he's here and he's real and he's mine, for now. All of this doesn't hurt as much when I'm leaning on Ezra.

Eventually the torrent lightens up. Ezra leads me into the kitchen and sits me down on a barstool alongside the counter. He disappears for a second before returning with a box of tissues.

"Here," he says, and offers up the box with a tentative smile.

I wipe at my eyes before blowing my nose. "Thanks." I ball the issue up in my palm and stare at the floor. Embarrassed. Vulnerable.

Ezra lowers himself into the stool beside me. "Do you want to talk about it?"

"Not yet. If that's okay."

"Of course it's okay," he says. "How about I make you some dinner?"

My neglected stomach rumbles. "That'd be—yeah, thank you."

Ezra squeezes my hand before standing up and ransacking the kitchen. I lean my elbow onto the counter and rest my head in my palm. So exhausted. But a warmth spreads throughout my limbs as Ezra grumbles over the only dinner options: SpaghettiOs or a frozen dinner meal with freezer burn. He mutters something about how unhealthy both the options are before finding a can opener for the SpaghettiOs.

I'm lucky. I'm uncomfortable and scared, but I'm lucky.

After Ezra and I eat our SpaghettiOs, it's barely nine thirty. But my eyelids are drooping.

"You should go," I tell him. "I'm sure I'll feel better in the morning."

Ezra dumps both bowls in the sink and lifts his brows. "Are you sure? There's nothing else I can do?"

As if on cue, Ford waddles into the kitchen. He stands between the two of us and wags his nonexistent tail excitedly. "Actually, mind letting him out?"

"Sure thing." Ezra heads to the patio door and Ford follows. They both disappear outside.

I drag my feet into the living room and plunk down on

the couch. Curl up on my side and pull one of Gran's quilts over my body. *Until Ezra's back with Ford*, I tell myself as my eyes close. But I wake up to a gentle jostling, someone's hand on my shoulder.

When I open my eyes, Ezra looks sheepishly down at me. "I'm sorry," he whispers. "I was going to carry you upstairs. It sounded very chivalrous inside my head."

"Sorry. Light sleeper." I sit upright but lean into Ezra. Let the weight of my body rest against his chest. I'm half-awake, but I don't want him to leave. "Can you stay? Until I fall asleep?"

Ezra nods, and I lead him upstairs. He's never been in my bedroom before. Should I be embarrassed by the baby pictures? The box of tampons on my desk? The Costco-size bottle of zit cream on my vanity? Fortunately, I'm too tired to worry about it and flop onto my bed. I pat the spot beside me, and he only hesitates for a moment before climbing into bed.

Ezra's body curls around mine, and he holds me against his chest. I press my face into the space between his neck and shoulder, my cheek resting against bare skin. Reflexively, his arms tighten. And I let myself be held and comforted until sleep pulls me under.

$$\Diamond \Diamond \Diamond$$

Bright sunlight wakes me.

I squint open my eyes and sigh. I forgot to close the blinds before bed. My bedroom's eastern exposure is a real pain in the ass sometimes.

One by one, yesterday's events come back to me. Mom's FaceTime. Gran's declining health. Nothing the doctors can do . . .

Too lazy to get up and close the blinds, I roll over—and find myself face-to-face with Ezra. He must've fallen asleep waiting for *me* to fall asleep, and he's still out. Sleeping with one arm tucked under his head. Fringed lashes curl against his freckled cheeks, and the morning sun brightens strands of gold in his hair. Steadily and evenly, his chest rises and falls.

Last night, Ezra helped more than he'll ever know. Just by being there, he made the unsteady solid again.

Before I can turn away, Ezra blinks open his eyes.

And sees me staring at him like I was watching him sleep.

I try to ready myself with an excuse, but he smiles. "Good morning."

Embarrassment fading, I smile in return. "Morning."

"What time is it?" he asks, yawning as he gets out of bed. *My* bed.

I glance at the clock on my bedside table. "A little after eight."

"Wanna make breakfast?" He smiles wider and his dimples make an early-morning appearance.

"I'd love to."

After I brush my teeth and change, I find Ezra downstairs in the kitchen.

"You actually have pancake mix," he says, holding up a box. "Nonexpired too."

I crack a smile and lean my elbows onto the counter. "It's a miracle."

Ezra gathers a bowl and all the ingredients, shooing me off when I offer to help. As he cooks, neither of us brings up last night. Like spending the night together wasn't incredibly intimate. I mean, the only person I've spent the night with outside of my family is *Nan*. And that definitely doesn't count. I didn't even spend the night with James! Maybe it wasn't special for Ezra, but I don't think I'm ever going to forget what it felt like to wake up with him beside me.

Ezra divvies up the pancakes and we eat outside on the back patio steps, balancing our plates on our laps. The bee yard is barely visible down the hill, and the morning fog is beginning to burn off. The air is fresh and clean, and I feel a million times better than I did last night. The initial pain has passed, and I'm left slightly numbed by reality. Gran's worse. She's coming home. There's nothing we can do.

"I'm sorry," I say, around bites of pancake, "about last night. Crying all over you. I'm pretty sure I used you as a tissue."

Beside me, Ezra sips his orange juice. "S'okay. How're you doing now?"

"Better." I fiddle with my fork. "Um. I FaceTimed with my mom yesterday. She's staying in Florida until the end of next week."

"Oh!" Happiness flits across his face, but it fades. "*Oh. Is your grandma okay?*"

Exhaling carefully, I begin to tell him all about my gran. About her moxie and spunk and perfectly lined lips. Her love of beekeeping and how she instilled a reverence in me from a young age. About her disease and the doctors without answers.

The entire time, Ezra just listens.

When I'm done, he sets his plate aside and wraps an arm around me. "I'm sorry."

I lean into his embrace. "Me too. Last night, having you here . . . it helped."

"Good, I'm glad. If you ever want to talk more, I'm here."

"Thanks." I return to my pancakes, but Ezra hesitates.

"I want to apologize if I crossed a line," he says, tapping his foot against the bottom step. Almost like he's nervous. "Sleeping over—falling asleep—was an accident. I shouldn't have, especially without clearing it with you first."

"Ezra—"

"I'm just saying, nothing will ever happen between us without your full consent, okay?"

"Okay. I really appreciate that," I tell him, "but no worries. Last night was great."

He glances sideways at me, his brows raised.

"What? I like your company," I say simply, and return to my pancakes.

Ezra laughs softly and nudges his leg with mine. "I like your company too."

My chest tightens with a confusing warmth.

In the bright morning light, it's easier for me to view this Gran situation with a clear head. Her coming home is for the best—we can take care of her here. And as a result, I'm getting another week with Ezra.

The extra time is a good thing—for many reasons. I need to figure a few things out.

Figure out what exactly is happening inside my heart.

Chapter Fourteen

ON WEDNESDAY, THE day Mom was supposed to fly home, Ezra and I go out for ice cream.

"Might be faster going inside," I say, peering out the car window as we roll up alongside the building. Get Creamed is nothing special on the outside, but from the size of the crowd, you know it's good. The drive-through line is heinously long. Like In-N-Out on a Friday night long. "That okay?"

Ezra flashes me a grin from the passenger's seat. "Up to you. You said Bev's working at Waxing Poetic, right?" He taps his fingers on the car door in time with the radio.

As luck would have it, everyone's accounted for today. The elderly Blumsteins are in San Francisco for an appointment, and his mom is helping at the vet clinic in Rosedale, the city neighboring Volana. Bev's covering the store and should be squirreled away at Waxing Poetic until closing.

"Yup." I even called her before picking up Ezra to confirm her whereabouts. Like I'm living in a spy movie or something. But she answered the store's landline phone. "We're good."

I pull into Get Creamed's tiny parking lot, managing to fit the Element in one of the remaining spots. "Ready to have your taste palate blown?"

Ezra's brows raise as he unbuckles the seat belt. "Is that a challenge?"

"Always."

Get Creamed is a Volana institution. It's tiny, with limited seating and chalkboard menus with their rotating ice cream of the month. The air is sweet, warm. Their entire decor is funky and exaggerated—large chairs, neon signs, and local artwork. A smaller line than the one outside snakes from the register through the parlor.

Ezra and I get in line. The tile beneath my boots is checkered, green and white. The walls are papered in pin-striped metallic. It's heinous and loud but perfect.

"What're your recommendations?" he asks, his shoulder pressing comfortably into mine.

"You can't go wrong with any of the flavors." I lean into him.

"What about the honey lavender?"

"It's their flavor of the month," I say as we shuffle forward in line. "They make it every summer. It's delicious but super-sweet. Like cavity sweet."

"Okay, that's definitely in the running." Ezra stares down at me. A slow and appreciative smile lights up his face. This is so easy, so normal. What would it be like to just . . . date Ezra? Not in secret? Go out in public every day? The space between our bodies narrows, and I find myself reaching for his hand, intertwining my fingers with his.

Ezra squeezes my hand, then clears his throat and begins rattling items off the menu, adding commentary. "Sweet corn? That's a flavor?"

I laugh. "It's not awful; a little weird, though. My favorite is cayenne chocolate."

He scrunches his nose, making his freckles merge into one large super freckle. "No offense, but that sounds gross."

"It's chocolate! How is chocolate gross?" I shake my head at him in disbelief. "Everyone likes chocolate."

Ezra leans closer and stage-whispers, "I don't like chocolate." His lips brush my ear, and my face warms.

"Blasphemy," I stage-whisper back, unable to fight the huge, dorky grin on my face. Because something simple, like bantering over ice cream flavors, makes me so happy.

We reach the register, and I smile in surprise. "Olivia! When did you get a job here?"

Olivia tucks her hair—now dyed Creamsicle orange—behind her ears. "This is my first week," she says, leaning across the counter. "The tips alone, plus free ice cream? Dream job."

"Awesome!" I haven't seen Olivia or Moira since our run-in at LaLa's on graduation night. A burst of social anxiety unravels in my chest, making me feel extra awkward. For no reason—also known as anxiety's modus operandi. "Can I get one cayenne chocolate cone and . . ." I turn to Ezra. "What do you want?"

"A double-scoop cone of honey lavender, please."

"Sure thing!" Olivia punches something into the touchscreen register, gaze flitting between Ezra and me.

"Olivia, this is Ezra." I hesitate, then add quietly, "My boyfriend."

Olivia's mouth pops open comically, but she recovers with an energetic wave. "Nice to meet you."

Ezra nods his head, grinning wide. "Likewise."

As he busies himself looking for his wallet, Olivia winks at me. Then she taps her cell phone on the counter. Clearly she wants the dirt on this situation. And I get it. I made a *huge fuss* last summer after I ended things with James. But Ezra is no James Funderburk.

Olivia scoops our dessert, and I slide my Get Creamed loyalty card onto the counter. She hands us each our cones, then picks up the card to punch it. "Hey, your birthday is Monday, right? If you show your ID, you get a free sundae and the entire staff has to sing."

"I might just do that," I say. While being sung to in public is one of my top three worst nightmares, it's hard to pass up free ice cream. "See you!"

"Your birthday is next week?" Ezra asks as we head outside with our cones. I might be imagining it, but he sounds . . . almost panicked.

I nod slowly as we wander toward my mom's car. "Yeah. But it's not a big deal. I don't even have anything planned."

"You aren't having a party?"

"Me? Voluntarily throwing myself a party?" I internally shudder. But Ezra doesn't know the scope of my anxiety or the fact I take medication. "I have pretty bad social anxiety, so a huge party is the opposite of a good time."

We perch on the bumper of Mom's car, and I sneak a glance beside me. Gauging his reaction, searching out his features for judgment. Of course there's nothing there but quiet understanding.

"No parties. I'll remember that."

A smile tugs at my lips. But my surprising desire for him to *understand* me has me adding, "Like, small things trigger my anxiety too. I hope that, um, won't be an issue."

"Why would it be?" He knocks his knee with mine.

I shift my body toward his. "Thanks for understanding." Anxiety has always felt like a big deal to me. Maybe because other people—from teachers to classmates and even James Funderburk—made it into an inconvenience, a weakness. Like my anxiety needs to be fixed, rather than just being another aspect of who I am.

"Thanks for being honest." He takes a bite of ice cream, winces from the cold. "Hey, um, I have to tell you something."

My anxious heart trips over those ominous words. "What?"

"Every summer, my dad and I go on a camping trip. I didn't even consider he'd still want to go this year. But my mom told me yesterday that he'd like me to join him next week." Ezra takes a bite from his ice cream and stares off in the direction of the town square.

"Where? Santa Barbara?"

"Yeah. We go to this campground on the coast." He glances back at me. "I'm sorry. Trust me, I tried getting out of it, but it was a no-go. I had no idea it was your birthday on Monday until three minutes ago. I feel awful."

"Oh." Disappointment flushes and prickles through my body. "For how long?"

Ezra presses his lips together. "I talked with him on the phone today. He actually sounded like he wants to spend some time together. I'm driving down Saturday, so probably until Thursday?"

"My mom's flying in early Thursday morning," I tell him. She e-mailed me her and Gran's ticket information this morning. I was so ecstatic. A whole other week to spend with Ezra. A week that just disappeared before my eyes.

"Seriously?" Ezra laughs, but it's flat. "Fuck. I'm so sorry, Josie."

On an emotional level, being with Ezra is effortless. There aren't any games, and I'm just as comfortable with him as I am alone. But the external obstacles are frustrating. The crushing disappointment of Ezra leaving town makes me want to curl up into a ball. I wanted one more week with him. One week, that's it.

Tears burn my eyes.

Ezra's the only person in my life right now who I'm not lying to. The only one who sees me for me. He's validated me and my choices. Made me feel brave for turning down Golden State. Around him, I'm my true and authentic self. And I don't want him to leave.

Not on Saturday.

Not when the summer's over.

"I'll make it up to you," Ezra promises, then presses his ice cream–cold lips to mine.

As I kiss him back, I try to reframe this situation inside my head. I can't change our circumstances, but I'll take advantage of what I have. For once, I'll try living in the present instead of always, always in the future.

◇◇◇

For the next forty-eight hours, I spend all my free time with Ezra. Plus some time when I probably should've been working. But I'll have many Ezra-less days to catch up on my apiary work when he's gone. Or that's how I reason with myself.

On Friday, Ezra and I try making an early dinner together. This quickly turns into *him* making *me* dinner, because apparently I inherited my mom's complete inability to cook. But today arrived much too quickly; Ezra leaves tomorrow morning for Santa Barbara. I only have him for a few more hours, since his mom and grandparents want him home by eight for a late family dinner. Luckily, Ezra has a huge appetite, and two dinners in one night isn't a problem for him.

I perch on the kitchen counter as Ezra puts the finishing touches on the skillet-seared chicken. In another pan are sizzling potatoes and red peppers. He's wearing one of Gran's old frilly aprons again, and it's entirely possible my heart can't take it.

"Okay," Ezra says, plating the chicken and sliding the roasted potatoes and peppers alongside it. "Dinner is served."

I hop off the counter and we sit outside on the patio. Balancing our plates of food on our knees as we sit beside each other on the swinging love seat. "Who's going to feed me when you're gone?" I joke, savoring a piece of chicken. Ezra really can cook—it's amazing.

Ezra laughs. "Glad to know I'll be missed."

I nudge my shoulder against his. "You know I'll miss you—you *and* your cooking skills." Joking somehow makes this hurt the tiniest bit less. Because if I tell him how much I'll miss him, I'll probably start crying and ruin this moment.

"I'll miss you," he says, "but I won't miss your cooking skills. Or lack thereof. You ever think you'll get the burned chicken smell out of the kitchen?"

"Ha-ha," I say, because I totally torched our first attempt at dinner and the charred carcass is stinking up the kitchen. We eat in silence for a moment, just the sound of our forks and knives clacking against the plates. Then I ask, "You all packed for tomorrow?"

Ezra bobs his head, setting his now-empty plate on the side table. "Yeah, not looking forward to it, though."

I frown, wishing he could stay right here with me. "Why don't you two get along?"

"Mostly it's because I'm not the son he wanted or envisioned." Ezra stares at his hands. "I'm not into sports; I like to read comic books and draw. I take after my mom—I'm pretty emotional and okay with that. But to my dad"—he shrugs—"it was weakness. I got a lot of 'crying is for girls' and 'don't be a pussy' talks as a kid."

I set my plate on the ground and turn to him. "Holy toxic masculinity, he sounds like a dick." My face reddens. "Um. No offense."

Ezra laughs, but it's flat. "Yeah. He is. But he's also my dad, and I love him. It's complicated. Honestly, he hasn't made much of an effort since the divorce. That's the only reason I'm going. It's, like, the first time he's actually wanted to see me in months."

I reach for his hand and say, "I've never really met my dad."

My dad is living in Oregon or Washington. Wherever he is, it's definitely the Pacific Northwest. I get postcards around my birthday, but that's about it. He left when I was a baby and is basically a glorified sperm donor. Mom always made sure I felt loved by her and her alone.

Ezra shifts toward me on the bench. "Really? When did your parents split?"

"They never married. My mom met him at one of his gigs. He was a local musician. One drunken night later and"—I gesture to myself—"but from everything my mom told me, he's a good guy. When she told him about the pregnancy, he was supportive, stuck around. But after I was born, he got an opportunity to teach music up in Oregon or Washington, and my mom told him to go."

"You miss him?"

I shift on the wooden bench, folding myself against Ezra, and he wraps an arm around me. "No. How can I miss something I never had? He used to visit when I was really young, but I don't remember him. Besides," I add, "my mom's all I need—all I ever needed. When I was growing up, she made sure I never felt like I was missing something, you know? Between her and Gran, I was whole."

Ezra presses his lips to the top of my head, and I shut my eyes. Relax into the moment. Talking with Ezra—*sharing* with Ezra—is surprisingly easy. I find myself wanting to share more about myself, and to know more about him in return. Because the more I know, the more I like.

Across the stretch of yard and apiary, the sun turns the sky into shades of pink and orange. Down the hill, all the foraging honeybees will be returning to their respective hives for the night. Ezra gently pushes his foot into the patio so the bench sways, and my heart is too big for my chest.

"Are you sure you have to leave tomorrow?" I ask selfishly,

imprinting every moment so I can recall it when I'll miss Ezra so much it'll hurt.

"Yeah. Unfortunately." He rests his head against mine. Then he says, "Fuck, I'm gonna miss this."

I don't have to ask what he means. By the time he returns, Mom and Gran will be back from Florida. Everything will be different. And even if we're going to try navigating those changing waters, it doesn't mean we're not upset. Not clinging to this.

We aren't losing each other, but we're losing something we'll never get back.

I twist around to face Ezra and kiss him. My eyelashes are damp. "I'm going to miss you too," I murmur against his lips, then tighten my arms around his neck. Hold him as tight as possible. Ezra hugs me against him, and we sit there. Wrapped up in each other.

Eventually we let go, and Ezra smooths my curls back from my face. "I've never felt this way about someone before. I like you so much, Josie."

A combination of anxiety and relief hits me. Anxiety over the intensity of my feelings, over the mess I'm making out of my uncomplicated summer romance. Relief that Ezra feels the same. Like we're in this mess of our own making together.

"I've never felt this way either." As I say this, I realize the truth in my words. I *haven't* felt this way before. James Funderburk was the disappointment that kept on disappointing. This is decidedly *not* disappointing. Confusing, yes, but never disappointing.

We sit on the love-seat swing—kissing and talking and kissing some more—until the alarm Ezra set on his phone for family dinner buzzes. *Time's up.* We go back inside.

"Sorry I can't stay longer," Ezra says when we're standing by my front door. "My mom made family dinner mandatory tonight."

"How about I walk you home?" I offer, because I want to eke out as much time as humanly possible. "To the street corner, at least?"

Ezra smiles. "Yeah, okay."

I grab Ford's leash, and the old-man dog waddles behind us as we make our way down the long driveway and onto Highway 10. The days might be longer, but the temperature is already dropping. I itch to hold Ezra's hand, to lean closer, but resist. With Ford, I have plausible deniability if someone sees me out here with Ezra. I was walking the dog and ran into him.

"I know this trip is a bummer and the timing's the worst," I say as we approach the street corner between our two houses, "but I hope you have a good time with your dad."

Ezra glances down fondly. "Thanks. I hope so too."

We slow to a stop at the corner, and Ford waddles off into the grass. I bite my bottom lip and force a smile.

"See you when you get back?" *When everything's different,* my brain finishes.

"Of course. And I'll text you while I'm gone, okay? And take pictures! You'd love the—"

I cut him off by tossing my arms around his neck and hugging him. Ezra laughs, his hands tight on my waist. Ford's leash tangles around us. "Bye, Josie," he murmurs, his mouth warm against my ear.

"Bye, Ezra." But I don't let go. Not yet.

A car honks. I stumble back and turn around. An Oldsmobile idles along the one-way street up to Blumstein Farms. And behind the wheel is Penelope Blumstein-Abramo.

"Hey, Ez, you're going to be late for dinner," she says, sticking her head out the rolled-down window. Then she adds, "Nice to see you again, Josie."

"I was just walking Ford," I blurt out.

Penelope looks from me, to Ford, and finally back to her son. A small smile pulls at her lips. "You know I don't care if you two hang out, right?"

Ezra and I stare at each other.

"Really?" I ask. All this time it never occurred to me that Penelope isn't like my mom, like her parents. "You won't— you're not going to tell my mom?"

Penelope shifts the car back into drive. "Why would I? In my opinion, this feud is ancient and ridiculous. Unlike other people in this town, I don't waste my energy on hatred."

"Oh." Penelope has rendered me near speechless. "Okay."

"Have a nice night," Penelope says to me. Then to her son: "See you at the house."

"I'll be right there," Ezra tells her.

The Oldsmobile putters up the hill and we're alone once again.

We're both quiet for a moment before he says, "Huh. That was—"

"Surprising?"

"That's one word for it." He laughs, breathless. "But this is good. Right?"

"Yeah, definitely."

Is it possible my mom will have a similar reaction? No—I've witnessed her animosity, her anger. Penelope's lived outside of Volana for almost two decades; she isn't entrenched in this like the rest of us.

Ezra doesn't deserve to be treated like some shameful secret. But luckily, that's a worry for the future.

I almost feel bad for Future Josie.

Chapter Fifteen

I CRADLE MY cell phone between my shoulder and ear, eyeing the closet. Despite my occasional snoopiness, I don't like going through my mom's things—her level of disorganization gives me hives—but she's insistent I unwrap my birthday gift today on my actual birthday.

"Where in the closet?" I nudge the door open.

"Behind some shoeboxes," Mom says on the other end. "It's already wrapped."

"Okay, hold on, I'm putting you on speaker." I switch her over to speakerphone and set the phone on the carpet.

Mom's room is a disaster. Piles of clothes. A cluttered vanity. Stacks of books on business management or guides on beekeeping. I rarely come in here; this is an excellent reminder why. The closet isn't much better. Half her clothes aren't even on hangers, rather layering the floor. Boxes of all varieties sit on top of the clothes, and I shift them aside, and—aha!—a wrapped gift. I lug the large square wrapped in floral paper out from the closet.

"Found it," I say, shutting the disaster-zone closet behind me. I pick up the phone and carry everything to my room. "Mom, this is too much."

"You don't even know what it is yet," she teases.

Keeping her on speakerphone, I smile and peel back the tape. If I had to guess—and let my imagination run wild—an Ultra Breeze bee suit awaits me. They're top of the line and ventilated so you don't die of heat exhaustion during long summer inspections. The size and weight are about right.

I pull back the paper and flip the plastic-wrapped package over. "Oh!" I am so glad FaceTime didn't work and we're having an old-fashioned phone call. Because I don't want Mom seeing the disappointment on my face.

"Like it?"

"Yeah!" I throw every ounce of enthusiasm into that one word. Because in my hands is a college dorm bedding set. The pattern is cute—the comforter vintage chevron in blues and greens, with solid sheets and pillow covers. But utterly useless. The size is a twin XL for the weirdly long mattresses in dorm rooms. Add that to the shower caddy and shoes she got me, and I'm amassing quite the collection of college freshman essentials. "Thank you so much."

"Oh good," Mom says, and I can practically hear her smiling. "We can exchange it if you don't like the pattern?"

"No, it's perfect," I say, setting the bedding aside. Hopefully that means she kept her receipt. "Hey, I gotta go."

"Right! Nan's taking you out?"

I nod, even though Mom can't see me. "We're going to watch that new Marvel movie." Nan has a thing for Chris Evans.

"Happy birthday, Bug," Mom says. "I love and miss you. See you Thursday!"

"I love and miss you too."

Fuck. A wave of guilty nausea overcomes me as we hang up. I hide the bedding in my closet. It's salt in the wound, reminding me—in case I forgot—that I'm lying to my mom about more than Ezra. I slide my closet closed. Out of sight, out of mind.

Besides, Nan honks twice and I hurry downstairs to meet her.

I begged Nan not to throw me a party, and she actually listened. After the movies, we're coming back here for a sleepover. It's perfectly low-key, and if I can't spend my eighteenth birthday with Ezra, this is second best. He's been gone for maybe fifty-two hours—who's counting—and a heaviness fills my gut; I miss him.

After checking on Ford, I lock up and head to the idling Mini Cooper in the driveway. The first day of summer is appropriately hot, and sweat already pools beneath my armpits. I duck into the car, grateful for the AC.

"Happy birthday, Jos!" Nan lifts a tubular item above our heads and—*pop*—confetti rains down on us. "How does it feel to be legal?"

Laughing, I shake the confetti from my hair. "Fairly similar to being illegal." I shift to hug Nan, looping my arms around her neck, and she gives me a good squeeze.

Nan hands over playlist control as we drive to the small movie theater in downtown Volana. The movie theater is right beside our favorite haunt, Pigs' Feet Café, which is a county chain, and we pop inside for coffees.

Pigs' Feet is big on minimalism—dusky white walls, wooden tables, local art—and expensive beans. But Nan offers to buy since it's my birthday, so I order a large iced mocha latte. We wait for our drinks beneath the ironwork winged pig hanging from the rafters. A local artist made it a few years back. It's Pigs' Feet's unofficial mascot.

"How're things with lover boy?" Nan leans her hip against the counter, using one free hand to fluff her flawless blowout.

I wrinkle my nose and say, "Never call Ezra *lover boy* again. Super creepy." The barista shouts my order and I grab my drink. "But we're good. Sucks he isn't in town for my birthday."

"Medium double-shot, low-fat cappuccino," the barista announces, and Nan takes her drink.

As we head next door to the theater, she hip checks me. "You're going to have a great birthday! Stop moping."

"I'm not moping," I say, completely aware of how defensive and mopey that statement is.

Nan sighs dramatically and hooks her arm through mine, dragging me into the theater.

◇◇◇

The movie lets out after six, and my stomach is rumbling as I climb into Nan's car. Since it's the longest day of the year, the sun is still high in the sky, and the temperature hasn't begun dropping yet. As much as I wish I were with Ezra, spending my birthday with Nan's been good.

For the first time in a while, things are fairly effortless between us. Nan hasn't brought up LA all day—a miracle. It instills hope that she finally understands me. Like it might all be okay when I tell her my choice to stay in Volana.

"Why don't we pick up some food?" I suggest.

Nan drives down Main Street in the direction of my house. "Nah," she says, "let's get delivery."

My stomach grumbles. "But LaLa's is right there." I nod my head toward the car window as we pass the restaurant. Jokingly, I press my palm to the pane in longing.

"Let's stick to the plan, okay?" Nan says in this oddly rigid voice. It's *my* birthday—I should be able to call the shots. But then she smiles and adds, "I didn't want to ruin the surprise, but you know Marcus? He's including one of those huge cookie 'pies' for your birthday."

"Oh." My tight shoulders relax. Marcus works at Croccante, the fancy pizzeria in Volana, and he's friends with Nan's brother, Charles. "Okay, that's awesome. I'd never turn down free dessert knowingly."

Nan *tsks*. "Trust me, Jos. This birthday will be one for the history books."

We drive the rest of the way home in music-heavy silence, and I'm relieved by the empty driveway. Not like I thought Nan was going to throw a party on *my* birthday, but the thought haunted the back of my brain during the movie.

"Did you already put in the order for the pizza?" I ask, fishing my house key out of my purse.

Nan glances up from her phone. Behind her, the sea-glass wind chime clatters in the light summer breeze. "Hmm? Oh, not yet."

"Can you?" I unlock the front door, take a half step into the shadowy living room. "I'm starv—"

"SURPRISE!"

The overhead lights flick on and a good two or three dozen people pop out from behind the couch, in the kitchen, and even behind some potted plants. I shriek and clutch my chest, unable to move past the threshold into my house. Because of course Nan didn't throw me a party. She threw me a *surprise* party. Which is, like, the worst thing you can do to a socially anxious person.

I grit my teeth and accept my anger because it's much easier to manage than my anxiety.

"Happy birthday," Nan sings, giving me a little shove past the threshold.

Someone cues up a playlist on the TV's speakers, and a bunch of people come over to wish me happy birthday. I grin, nod, and try not to bitch them out because it's not their fault. It's Nan's. Nan, who is my best friend and who should know the last thing I'd want is three of my friends and another two dozen strangers getting drunk in my house.

I spot Olivia and Moira in the kitchen and extricate myself from Nan's grasp. The kitchen is slightly more tolerable. It's crowded—someone brought a keg—but I'm happy to see two people I actually like.

"Happy birthday," Olivia says when I reach them. She takes a sip from her beer and offers me a limp smile. Like even she knows this is my living nightmare.

"Thanks." I cross my arms, upset that my eyes are hot.

Sometimes, when I'm anxious, I cry. Like all the pressure—my chest, my head, my skin—becomes too much. Every sound, every touch, barbs. It *sucks*. It makes me feel vulnerable and weak. Unable to cope with the simplest of situations. Normally, removing myself helps—but I don't have anywhere to go. This house has always been my safe space, but Nan's taken that away. My chest is tight, my lungs unable to fully fill with air.

Moira frowns, her dark purple painted lips creasing. "Not your jam, huh?"

I laugh bitterly. "Nope."

Olivia sighs, shifting her orange waves over her shoulder. "Nan said you'd love it. We weren't so sure, but . . ." She trails off with a *What can you do?* kind of shrug. High school was a lesson in learning how Nan was an unstoppable force. Olivia joked once that Nan is like a less likable, more materialistic Paris Geller from *Gilmore Girls*.

"Yeah, well, Nan was wrong."

Moira sets her cup on the counter and squeezes my arm. "Hey, maybe it'll be a blast? You never know!"

I smile a tiny bit. "Yeah. Maybe." If only I could be a little more like Moira.

"Where's Ezra?" Olivia asks, and waggles her brow suggestively. We texted after they met at Get Creamed last week, and she's all caught up on my unexpected summer romance.

"Out of town."

Olivia pouts. "Bummer." But then the song changes, and she says, "Oh, this is my *favorite* song," and grabs Moira's hand, leaving me alone in the kitchen.

Well, not alone. Being alone would be preferable right now. Instead I'm stuck with a bunch of people I've never spoken to partying inside my house. It's like Nan invited our entire senior class, plus some of the junior class— which includes her annoying little brother, Charles, his friends, and their friends from the country club. At least

James Funderburk isn't lurking around here too.

With a tight-chested sigh, I fill a red cup up with soda from the fridge and retreat back into the living room. I keep my eyes peeled for an escape route, somewhere to hide. I'd leave, but abandoning the house—and our apiary—unattended with a bunch of drunken teenagers is a sure way to piss off Mom.

On the far side of the living room, I lean against the bookshelf. Trying to fold into myself. Nan spots me, her face already flush, and runs over.

"Isn't this the best?" She's smiling so wide I'm afraid her face might cramp. She sips from her cup and burps. Then laughs.

"Oh yeah," I say dryly, "the best."

Nan either doesn't want to acknowledge my sarcasm or simply doesn't pick up on it, but she leans forward and envelops me in a sloppy hug.

"I'm so glad you're having fun." I don't bother hugging her back. The anxiety, the disappointment of it all, is too much. Nan smacks a kiss on my cheek, then surveys the crowd. "Have you seen Nick?"

"Why would I?" I ask, confused. Nan hasn't mentioned her White Whale lately.

Nan nudges me. "I invited him. Isn't the timing *perfect?*"

My stomach turns with understanding. This party isn't for me; it never was. Emery, Nick's cousin, is a big partier. From what I've heard, Nick's similar. And Nan's parents would never, ever allow her to throw an unsupervised party.

Especially not with boys. When Nan's mom found out she was on birth control, she grounded her for three months.

Before I can confront Nan, she says, "Oh! There he is!" and disappears into the crowd.

I blink back my frustrated and anxious tears, downing the rest of my soda. The funny thing is, I'm not even that *surprised*. Just hurt. And the tiniest bit angry. Like I should've seen this one coming. I hope Nick's worth it. After tossing my cup in the trash, I eye the staircase.

Whoever Nan got to set up the party when we were at the movies taped a sign saying upstairs was off-limits. And I hope everyone listened, because my bedroom is pretty much the best option for an escape.

The sea of people between me and the staircase is daunting. If I cared about parties at all, I'd have to give Nan props: It's packed. She definitely knows how to throw a rager. I push away from the bookshelf and stand on my tiptoes, searching for the best route through.

I'm about to take the plunge and run—or more accurately, elbow my way through the mess of people—when someone catches my eye. A tall someone, with brown hair, wearing a button-down. His back is to me, but I shake my head. It isn't Ezra. Ezra's in Santa Barbara.

But then the person turns around.

"Ezra!" I call, waving my arms like I'm landing a small aircraft or something. "EZRA!"

My flailing finally gets his attention, and we lock eyes.

Grinning, I point to the staircase. He nods, and I push my way through the crowd. People bump into me. Someone's beer sloshes onto my sandals. But I don't care because Ezra's here.

Ezra's waiting on the bottom step, and I yell, "What're you doing here?" when I reach him.

He points to his ear and shakes his head. The music's too loud, and it's not like I want to stay downstairs for another moment. I grab Ezra's hand and tug him upstairs. Luckily, the sign and closed doors have kept people away from the second story. I push into my bedroom and lock the door behind me. The music is still audible, but it's muffled.

I have no shame and launch myself at Ezra, wrapping my arms around his neck. "What're you doing here?" I hug him tighter. "More important, how?"

"Whoa, there, birthday girl." He laughs and swings me off my feet in a hug. His presence is the perfect birthday gift. "Hi."

"Hi," I say, and he kisses me. It's quick. A hello.

"I normally hate surprises, but this is a surprise I can get behind." We kick off our shoes and relocate to my bed with our backs to the headboard. "How're you here? You weren't supposed to get back until Thursday!"

"Kind of a long story? My dad and I actually got along," he explains. "I told him a little about you, and how I was missing your birthday. His advice was to get back in the car and not let you spend your birthday alone." The song changes downstairs and people start whooping in excitement. Ezra laughs. "You know what I mean. What the hell is going on down there, anyway?"

"Nan threw me a surprise party," I say flatly.

His face falls. "Oof. I'm sorry."

I shrug, no longer caring about the party or Nan. "Things are looking up." I lean against him, and he wraps his arm around me in response. "I'm so happy you're here. You have no idea."

"I have an idea." He kisses my hair. "I missed you."

"Missed you too." I shift even closer to him and sigh my relief. Perfectly at ease. "So the trip went okay?"

"My expectations were very, very low." Ezra hesitates. "But it was nice. Now that the divorce is finalized and he's on his own, my dad seems better. More mellow. Happier."

"Good!"

"We even went surfing. The campground's on a beach."

"You surf?"

"If by surfing you mean falling on my ass for two hours and giving up to make s'mores, then yes, I surf."

I laugh, relishing this—his company, the comfort I feel around him, the relief that my birthday isn't ruined. "I'm glad it went well."

"Yeah, me too." Ezra grows quiet for a moment. "We had some good talks, and he was obviously trying to make amends. It was nice, but weird. He even apologized for what he said about art school . . . but I also realized that I don't care as much about his opinion anymore."

"Yeah?" My heart aches at the sincerity in his voice. He's a *good* artist, and he deserves to have people believe in him. "You're talented, Ezra. I'm glad your dad's coming around, but even if he doesn't, you're still ridiculously talented."

He laughs nervously. "I don't know about that, but you were right. Just because I'm not going to an art school doesn't mean I can't study art. Right?"

I sit up to face him. "Right! Does this mean you're going to take art classes at Berkeley?"

"Maybe?" He grins, sheepish. "I haven't made up my mind."

I poke him in the chest. "Well, I think you should."

Ezra bites his bottom lip. "I have been drawing more lately."

"Yeah?"

He hesitates, then leans over the bed and grabs his backpack, pulls a tablet out of it. He turns it on and pulls open an application. "I started this after we moved here."

I peer at the screen, at the neatly sectioned breaks and scenes. "Is that a graphic novel?"

"Not yet." He flips through the digital panels, some colored in vibrantly—like his tattoo—others line work and empty text blocks. From this cursory glance, Ezra's talent is obvious. I can barely draw a stick figure, let alone an entire fictional world.

"Can I?" I hold out my hand.

Ezra nods and passes me the tablet. He nervously rubs the back of his neck as I start at the beginning. The title page has a bursting, colorful drawing of a honeybee—larger than life, similar to his tattoo—with a wisp of a girl standing beneath it.

"*Hive Mind*?" I ask.

"It's a working title." He toys with a thread on his button-down.

I nod and swipe to the next page. Only a few panels are fully fleshed out, but I can already tell it'll be beautiful. I flip through the application, studying the images. "What's it about?"

Ezra watches with a mildly panicked expression. "I'm focusing more on the art, but it's like *Pushing Daisies* meets *Chew*?" He pauses, gaze shifting off to the left. "How douchey of me was it to say that?"

I laugh, swiping back to the beginning. "Not douchey at all." In silence, I study the images, my heart full. What I saw of his tattoo was a mere highlight of Ezra's talents. You can sense the passion, the dedication, in his art. I set the tablet down and say, "While I commend you studying environmental science, this is what you should be doing, Ezra. This." I tap the screen for emphasis.

"I don't know." He scrubs his face, which makes his cheeks red. "You think so?"

I nod emphatically. "Yes, yes, I do."

Ezra grows quiet for a moment, dropping his hands to his lap. "I'm glad you like it," he says. "I mean, I kind of started drawing it because of you."

I raise both brows. "Me?"

"Yeah. I don't know, I guess you made me realize that if you love something, you should chase after it, even if everything's pointing you in the opposite direction. Like my dad."

"Or my mom," I say faintly, but my heart's gone feral inside my chest. Because we're talking about art and beekeeping, but it sounds like . . . well, it sounds like so much more.

Ezra studies me, sitting still with his back to the headboard. His expression is serious and strangely hopeful and I want to kiss him. So I do. In an instant, his body softens against mine. All my concerns, all my thoughts, about the party downstairs fade away. No one will miss me, and I'd much rather be here. With him.

Ezra's responsive to my touch, mouth on mine, fingers combing through my hair. We pause and reposition until I'm on my back and Ezra's propped over me. His hand runs the length of my body, from my neck down to my kneecaps.

The kisses alternate from quick and teasing to long and explorative. Ezra's hand hesitates before slipping beneath my shirt, his palm skirting across my bare stomach. Not wandering any farther up or down. Which is frustrating and confusing. Over the past few weeks, there has been *so much* kissing, and I'm not ashamed—I want him to touch me.

I'm wearing a T-shirt and a gauzy peasant skirt, both of which are cumbersome right now. In the way. I reach for Ezra's hand, which rests on my hip, and slide it lower.

"What're you doing?" His mouth is against my ear, breath hot.

A small flash of panic strikes me in the chest. What if Ezra doesn't want to take this further? I assumed, which is always a bad idea—

Ezra's palm slides along the inside of my thigh. "Josie, is this okay?" he asks, voice hazy and thick.

"Yes." I run my fingers down his back.

"If, at any point, you want to stop, we stop."

"Okay," I say, tilting my mouth to catch his. "The same goes for you."

He smiles against my lips. Kisses me hard.

The gauzy material of my peasant skirt bunches up, and I shift my hips. With Ezra's help, I pull the skirt off, the material pooling around my ankles. I pull at Ezra's shirt and he removes it. We alternate ditching our clothes until we're both in our underwear.

"*Oh.*" Ezra says this in an exhalation, the word escaping as he looks at me. My underwear is plain, black, nothing exciting. My bra matches at least, but it's worn black organic cotton. For the first time in my life, I wish I'd listened to Nan when she tried to convince me to buy actual lingerie.

But my worries over my drab underwear set are shoved to the back of my mind when Ezra shifts, and I feel him pressed against my thigh. I'm not embarrassed—thrilled, if I'm being honest—and I lean forward, grabbing a quilt from the end of the bed and pulling it over our bodies.

Beneath those button-downs and slacks, Ezra's body is all lean muscles, his skin hot against mine. As our bodies press together, I expect things to speed up, but they slow down.

Ezra's fingers slip beneath the waistband of my underwear and then he's touching me. He asks again if I'm okay. I kiss him in response. He asks if what he's doing with his hands feels good—and it does. It's *fantastic*. It's so fantastic I touch him in return.

We do a lot of things in that bed, but we don't have sex. He's gentle and attentive and actually cares about making me feel good—a far cry from James Funderburk. There's a give and take. There's respect in every touch.

The birthday party I abandoned is still raging beneath us downstairs when we're done, but I no longer care. I'm exhausted in the best way; I don't even know what time it is. Ezra rests beside me on the small twin-size bed, naked except for his boxers.

"Was that okay?" he asks, voice heavy.

"More than okay." I shift onto my other side so I'm facing him. "Pretty great, actually."

We kiss, and when he pulls away, he says, "You have a good birthday?"

"The best birthday," I answer truthfully, my heavy eyelids inching shut.

Weightless, I curl against Ezra. My birthday wasn't what I'd hoped—or even imagined. And yet, it turned out amazing. The tight panic and fear—the love of controlling every aspect of my life—lessens, second by second. All of it fades. Like a finger unfurling around a ledge. One by one, my grip lets go.

And I fall.

Chapter Sixteen

I STARE AT the gift bag on my dresser with a frown.

Nan must've forgotten to give me the birthday gift Monday night, because I found it on the living room's sideboard earlier. And I don't know if I should unwrap it or shove it into the back of my closet. Ezra's due soon to take me out to celebrate my birthday, and I don't want to be in a bad mood for our date.

As mad as I am at Nan, she didn't mean any harm. She wasn't being malicious. That's the thing about Nan. She isn't necessarily cruel, she's just selfish. Nick was coming to town and she needed a way to see him, unsupervised. Nan doesn't *think* sometimes. Which is, in itself, infuriating.

I pluck the gift bag from the dresser and unwrap it.

Inside are three items layered in tissue paper.

The first is a limited-edition tube of my favorite lipstick I never, ever buy because it's too expensive.

The second is a novelty Tobias Fünke T-shirt with an illustrated David Cross covered in blue paint and a speech bubble that reads: "I'm afraid I just blue myself."

The third is a snow globe, and Nan attached a sticky note to it.

> *J,*
> *For when you're homesick.*
> *Love,*
> *N*

I shake the snow globe, and glitter flakes to represent fog fall around a miniature downtown Volana. Local tourist shops and wineries sell them. Inexplicable tears prick my eyes as I tilt it upside down, then right side up. Maybe Nan isn't so oblivious as I once thought.

Wiping my eyes, I set the gifts aside and grab my phone.

> **ME: Thanks for the gifts** ❤
> **Have fun in Paris**

Nan leaves this weekend for her graduation trip to Europe, and I'm glad to have some space while she's gone. The gifts lessened my anger, but I'm still hurt. I need some time to calm down and finally think of the best way to break the news to her that I won't be going to LA.

Telling Nan will be easier than telling Mom, though. She and Gran return tomorrow morning. Funnily enough, my lie about GSU doesn't weigh on me as heavily as my lie of omission about Ezra. Maybe because my carefree summer fling is complicating—fast. I thought sneaking around with Ezra would be fun and exciting and, above all else, distracting. And it has been. But it's also . . . serious and confusing and amazing.

Ezra's due soon, so I toss on my outfit—a sundress with cap sleeves and tights—and coat my lips with the red lipstick Nan gave me. I run downstairs to take care of Ford, since Ezra warned me we'd be gone for most of the evening. Once Ford has peed and I've filled his food bowl, I lock up and wait outside.

Barely a minute passes before the Oldsmobile rumbles down the lane.

"Hey," I call out, waving as Ezra parks. I don't expect him to get out of the car, but he does. My chest warms, flutters, because he's wearing these dark green pants with his Timberland boots and a checkered button-down. My already nervous heart beats even faster.

"What?" he asks with a laugh, and shuts the car door. "Why're you looking at me like that?"

I bound down the steps. "Admiring the scenery."

"Uh-huh," Ezra says, and grins knowingly. "You're thinking about me naked, aren't you?"

Laughing, my face hot and red, I stop in front of him.

"Nope." Now I am, but I don't tell him that. This is as close as we've come to discussing what happened the other night. The memory flushes my body with warmth.

Ezra envelops me in a hug, then steps back and says, "You have my full permission to think of me naked."

"Psh," I joke. "Like I need permission."

Ezra tips his head back and laughs. "Fair enough. C'mon. We have places to be."

Settled in the passenger's seat of the Oldsmobile, I glance sideways at Ezra. "So. Are you going to tell me where we're going?"

"Nope." Ezra drives down the shadowed lane and onto Highway 10. "But, since I'm feeling generous, I'll give you clues."

Normally this tactic would annoy the shit out of me. I like plans. I like knowing where I'm going and what I'm doing. And, as evidenced by my birthday party, I hate surprises. But instead of upset, I'm charmed. I'm so fucking charmed.

"Clue number one: the first night we met." Ezra turns onto the Highway 101 South ramp, then merges with the stubborn commuter traffic.

"*That's* the clue?" I ask. "That's not even a complete sentence."

"It'll all make sense in due time," he says sagely.

I settle back into the passenger's seat. "Sure it will."

Ezra takes advantage of the carpool lane, and we speed down the 101, passing through Petaluma and the Novato

Narrows. Almost everything is south of Volana, so I don't have a solid idea of where we're going.

As we pass the Richmond–San Rafael Bridge, Ezra says, "Okay, clue number two: Volana has two of these."

"Your clues suck."

"Or are they the perfect amount of complicated?"

I toss Ezra a skeptical look—I'm not mad, a smile tugging my lips. "If Volana has two of these, why are we going elsewhere?"

Ezra mimes zipping his lips shut and turns up the stereo.

Okay. Volana has two of . . . *what?* I rack my brain, but I honestly have no idea.

Highway 101 eventually gives way to the Golden Gate Bridge, San Francisco sparkling in the distance. I roll down my window, inhaling the fresh, salty air. The fog is thick, clouding up the sunny sky. Hundreds of tourists walk the bridge, stopping to take pictures.

"Is it safe to assume we're going to the city?" I ask as we near the toll booth.

"Yep." Ezra fishes out a FasTrak from the glove compartment, and the small device beeps as we pass through the toll. "Want another clue?"

"Hit me." I roll up the window and readjust my dress over my legs.

Ezra moves into the right lane, taking the Nineteenth Avenue exit. "Your final clue: We're both fans."

I frown, trying to piece together the three clues, but

all I come back with is nonsense. "I give up."

Chuckling, Ezra says, "We'll be there soon."

Outside the window, Golden Gate Park and the Conservatory of Flowers pass by. A park *would* align with our interests. But being a fan of a park isn't a thing. Ezra keeps on driving, though. A few minutes later, he pulls into a pay-to-park lot. As Ezra pays, I scope out the darkening San Francisco street. Haight Street, to be exact. Thankful I brought a jacket, I slip it on before ducking out of the car.

Cool wind whips at my dress, and Ezra returns to the car. "Ready?" he asks, buttoning up his own jacket.

"Sure." I hook my arm through his, trusting him and his mysterious plans. As we exit the parking lot, I add, "If you lead me into a surprise party, you're dead to me."

"The punishment fits the crime," Ezra says, and we wait at a crosswalk, leaning into each other to keep warm. "Is San Francisco always this cold?"

I laugh quietly. "Usually. And it's *not* that cold. Your Southern Californian is showing."

Ezra shivers. "Agree to disagree. I've barely spent any time in San Francisco before," he says, and we cross the street when the light turns. "My grandparents would come visit us in Santa Barbara. My dad took me here when I was younger. We went to the Exploratorium, I think?"

"Oh yeah, the Exploratorium is great. Like, every elementary school in Volana County takes a field trip there at some point." I scope out the street Ezra leads me down.

Up ahead, a line snakes out of a bookstore. *Bingo.* Something Volana only has two of.

"The Booksmith?" I try working in the rest of his clues. "For . . . something to do with books?"

Ezra pulls me in front of the store. Before I even peer inside, my attention is grabbed by the huge poster in the window.

MEET THE BRAINS BEHIND *GEST*! WRITER KIRK J. NEILSON AND ILLUSTRATOR NEENA DAVIS IN CONVERSATION!

"No way!" I tackle-hug Ezra, who laughs, his arms encircling my waist. "That's tonight? We're going?"

Ezra beams down at me; the corners of his eyes crinkle nicely. "Yup! Let's get in line."

We join the end of the line, which moves quickly. The fact that Ezra thought to do this, well, it plucks all my heartstrings. Is this swooning? Am I swooning right now?

"It's been torture not telling you about this," Ezra says, bouncing up and down on his toes. "I had the idea last week."

"Understandably. Awful clues aside, this is awesome."

Ezra squeezes me. "I'm glad you like it. Just in case this is the only real date I'm able to take you on this summer, I wanted it to be perfect."

"Best date ever," I say, and reach up to kiss him on the cheek.

◇⬡◇

The tickets Ezra bought in advance guaranteed us seats and a spot in line for the book signing. The reading and conversation portions were fascinating and hilarious. Kirk and Neena know how to work a crowd, and it was beyond fun to learn about their creative process. Throughout the whole thing—as my butt went numb from the metal chairs—I held Ezra's hand, feeling incredibly lucky.

"Oh shoot," I say as we're clapping, the crowd either funneling out of the store or to the back, where the signing will be held. "I don't have anything for them to sign."

"I've got you covered," Ezra says, and motions to the backpack slung over his shoulder. "Eagle Scout, remember? In honor of being prepared, I swiped your collection."

I scoot out from the row of folding chairs. "You stole my comics? *When?*"

"On your birthday." Ezra grins as he pulls his backpack around and unzips it. "Here you are," he says, handing me my stack of *Gest* comics. "Take your pick."

"I should be mad at you right now." I clutch the comics to my chest. "But I'm not."

Ezra winks. "And therein lies my charm."

He's not wrong.

The signing line moves slowly, but I'm in no hurry. This night has been effortlessly good, and I don't want it to end. We're in line behind a girl in a vintage knee-length dress with intricate beading who's talking animatedly with Kirk and Neena. Off to the side, a boy with seriously enviable curls watches with a warm smile.

"Thanks so much," the girl says, and scoops up her comics.

Arm in arm, she and the curly-haired boy walk out of the Booksmith together.

When it's our turn for the signing, Ezra tenses beside me. Like he's nervous. Maybe because he's facing something he so desperately wants. Or because he's a mega nerd. Who knows? But I take his hand in mine and, for once, don't act socially awkward. It's actually nice to be on the other end of things.

"Hi," I say to Neena and Kirk. They're seated behind a folding table decorated with images from *Gest*. "I'm Josie and this is Ezra."

Neena smiles, holding out her hand. Vintage bangles slide down her dark, toned arms, and her nails are painted cherry red. "Nice to meet you!"

I shake Neena's hand, then Kirk's. They both seem genuinely happy to be here.

"Thanks so much for this," Ezra says after a long, silent moment. "Really. I'm such a big fan. . . ."

Kirk looks up from my copy of *Gest*, volume two, my favorite volume, that he's signing with a metallic purple Sharpie. "Thank *you* for coming. Meeting our fans is always a delight."

Ezra bobs his head nervously, pushing up the sleeves of his button-down. Neena takes the copy Kirk signed and spends a moment signing it.

"Here you are," Neena says, and turns to Ezra. "Would you like us to sign anything?"

"Oh! Right." Face reddening, Ezra pulls a fancy bound

edition of the first six volumes of the series from his backpack. "Thank you."

"No problem," Neena says, flipping open the book. "Awesome tattoo, by the way."

"Ezra drew it," I blurt out, because apparently, I'm *that* person now.

Kirk slides the bound edition in front of him, glancing up at Ezra. "For real?" he asks, pushing back his floppy red hair. Then to me: "Your boyfriend is talented."

Ezra mumbles his thanks, face redder than Neena's nails. We say goodbye to Neena and Kirk, peeling away from the crowd. I stow my autographed comics in Ezra's backpack and shrug my jacket on. Ezra does the same, the heat in his face steady.

"Kirk J. Nielson said you were talented," I say in a sing-song voice as we exit the store.

"He was just being nice." Ezra rubs his face with his palm.

I nudge him. "Why would he do that? He didn't have to say anything at all." The tiniest grin pulls at Ezra's lips. "C'mon, it was pretty awesome."

Ezra laughs gruffly. "Okay, yes it was. Even if I feel like a loser. I clammed up."

I take his hand in mine. "You're not a loser. Sure, you went quiet there for a moment, but you came back from it."

"I guess . . ." He trails off, studying the dark street. When he looks back at me, he's smiling. All nerves lost. "It was pretty awesome, wasn't it?"

"Super awesome," I say, and when I suggest we grab something quick to eat on the drive home, Ezra agrees.

As we drive in the direction of Volana, I'm silently freaking out—in a good way.

We might've only met three weeks ago, but Ezra gets me more than anyone else. More than Mom. Definitely more than Nan. Ezra understands me in a way that isn't logical and doesn't make any sense. But at the same time it's right and solid and real. I don't think I've ever felt as accepted by someone—for all my good and all my bad—as I do with Ezra Blumstein-Abramo. This might be the best feeling in the world and I'm desperate for it to last.

Ezra takes an exit outside of Rosedale, and we pull into Amy's Drive Thru.

"I thought you hated fast food," I say as we join the line of idling cars.

"Well, yes, but it's your birthday celebration and you love junk food," he says. "Also, Amy's is awesome. They have healthy frozen meals and stuff. So this is the best of both worlds."

"You're weird." I lean across the center console to kiss him.

We place our orders, and as we eat, I have to admit Ezra's right—the food is pretty good.

The drive back into Volana passes far too quickly. It's near eleven at night, and the entire town is cloaked in darkness.

"Tonight was . . . perfect. Seriously, Ezra, thank you," I

tell him as he pulls to a stop in front of my house. It's like I blinked and the night's come to an end.

Ezra turns the Oldsmobile off and glances over at me. It's dark, but my eyes adjust to see his dimpled smile. "Anytime." Something shifts in his expression, like he's remembering it can't be *anytime*. "Want me to walk you?"

"So gentlemanly," I joke, but I take him up on his offer. Hand in hand we walk up to the house. The weak porch light attracts a few moths, and the wind chime clacks in the breeze. After I unlock the front door, I turn to him and say, "Nothing changes because my mom's coming home, okay?"

I expect Ezra to say something, but he doesn't. Instead he leans down, takes my face in both hands, and presses his lips to mine. The kiss is fervent and intoxicating, and before I question myself, I open the front door and tug Ezra inside.

"What're you doing?" he asks with a laugh.

"Being opportunistic." I reach up and kiss him in the darkened living room. I kiss him on the stairs, and in the hallway outside my bedroom. Then I push him onto my bed and climb onto his lap.

"This okay?" I ask, my hair falling from one shoulder as I lean over him.

Ezra's response comes in the form of a kiss. Mouth on mine. No hesitations. *Urgency.* I thread my fingers through his hair, and he explores the expanse of my back, hands hot against the thin fabric of my dress. The kissing is phenomenal. Like lose-my-mind good. I'm shaking slightly, which is embarrassing.

When I reach for his belt, Ezra gently pushes me back. His gaze is locked onto mine. Intense. "We don't have to have sex." He swallows, Adam's apple bobbing. "Or do anything, for that matter. I can leave. No pressure."

"No! I want to. I want to." My heart pounds so fast, I swear Ezra can hear it. "If you want to?"

Ezra laughs deeply. "Yes. Want doesn't even begin to describe it. But if you change your mind, let me know, okay?"

"Okay." I'm nodding, kissing him.

It's not like I haven't had sex before. But I'm *enjoying* this. Enjoying the way he touches me. The sex I had in the past didn't come from a place of desire or want. I had sex because I thought it was something I *should* do. That night with James was a whole lot of awkward and never enjoyable.

But something tells me I might enjoy being with Ezra.

We regain our rhythm. The kissing. The touching. The kind-of-embarrassing noises we both make. I'm more cautious taking off my clothes, but Ezra tosses them off so fast—it's like I blink and he's naked. And he's beautiful. With his help, I unzip my dress and pull it over my head. We tug a quilt over our bodies, readjusting as Ezra leans over me, fumbling with the clasp on my bra.

I've seen naked guys before, but there's something about Ezra that's different. I didn't quite take the time to appreciate it the other night. Anxiety doesn't fill me—rather anticipation—

as he digs through his pile of clothes on my bedroom floor for his wallet and the condom he promises he has in there.

"Aha," he says, lifting up the small square wrapper. Then he joins me beneath the blanket. "God, you're beautiful." He kisses my lips, my neck, my collarbone. "Are you sure you want to do this?"

"Yes." I press my palm to his cheek, guiding his face so I can look him in the eye. "I'm sure."

Ezra takes his time, touching me like he did in my bedroom on my birthday. Then he grabs the condom, carefully opens the package, and rolls it on. I silently thank the goddess because I've actually never had to put on a condom before. Unless you count that banana in the ninth grade.

"Um," Ezra says, propping himself up on his elbows, "will this be okay? Or do you want to be on top? Or we can—"

Laughing, I pull him closer. And closer. Until there's no space left between our bodies. At first, it's awkward. Which is to be expected. But the awkwardness melts away. Ezra kisses me, asking again if I'm okay, and I assure him I am, indeed, very okay. More than okay. After that, something between us clicks. It's intense and sweaty and surprisingly good, even if it's over too soon.

Sex isn't like how they show it in movies; I already knew that. We're awkward elbows, knocking teeth, embarrassing noises. But we're also all emotion. Long kisses and making sure the other is enjoying themselves. And we do.

Afterward, I hold Ezra in place, wrapping my arms around

his neck and burying my face against the smooth slope of skin along his shoulder, perfectly at ease. Breathing him in. The way we lie, his heart beats against my chest, and it's so fast. I stroke his back and run my fingers through his hair, kissing all the freckles on his cheeks and nose.

Sometime later, Ezra murmurs, "My mom needs her car back for work early in the morning. I should . . . probably . . . bring it back. Right?"

I laugh quietly at his reluctance. "I mean. Yes? But I don't want you to go."

Ezra props himself up on his elbow. "How about this? I'll set my alarm for five. She doesn't work until seven. Win-win."

Pressing my lips to his shoulder, I nod. We quickly clean up and set our alarms. I help Ezra wrap the used condom in, like, twenty pieces of tissue, and I shove it into the bottom of the trash can in my bathroom. I vaguely remember Nan mentioning something about how you should pee after sex, so I do.

Back in bed, Ezra kisses me good night. Neither of us mentions that this'll probably be the last time we spend the night together. At least here. But we'll figure it out. We have to.

"Good night," I whisper, and nudge his foot with mine beneath the sheets.

Across from me, Ezra smiles sleepily. I almost want to say something as he shuts his eyes. Force this day to never, ever end. But barely a moment passes before his breath evens out with sleep.

I roll onto my back and stare at my bedroom ceiling.

I had sex. Good sex. With a guy I really, really like, who was kind and respectful and giving. After my failure with James, I thought this wouldn't happen for me. I thought I'd given up. But I didn't give up. Not really.

I was waiting for the person who didn't just accept all the parts of myself I've grown to dislike—my anxiety, my weirdness, my social awkwardness—but who liked all of me, idiosyncrasies and all.

Ezra's that person. *My* person.

And I don't want to let him go.

◯◯◯

Ezra's alarm goes off before sunrise.

Groggily, I sit up in bed even though my biggest desire is to burrow beneath the blankets. Blink a few times to try waking myself up. My brain clumsily turns back on—but barely.

"I should go," Ezra whispers from beside me in the dark, and I nod my heavy head. "Josie, I . . ." He hesitates as I let out a huge and endless yawn. He leans closer to rest his forehead against mine. My sleepy brain wonders what he was going to say, but I forget to care as he presses a light kiss to my lips. "See you tonight?"

"M'okay." I yawn again and hug him as tight as my half-awake body will allow.

Ezra holds me for a moment before sliding out of bed.

I lie back down as he gets dressed in the dark, smiling

sleepily. "Bye, Ezra," I whisper as he crosses to my bedroom door.

Ezra hesitates in the doorway before saying, "Bye, Josie." Faintly, I hear his footsteps. The front door shutting. Then he's gone.

Chapter Seventeen

MOM BOOKED HER and Gran's return flight into the Volana County Airport—a tiny, two-terminal building in nearby Rosedale. Since the airport isn't too far from home, I drive Mom's car over to pick them up. The tickets were more expensive, but she wanted to ease the trip as much as possible for Gran. No flights into Oakland or SFO and a two-hour Airporter bus ride.

As I drive past the street up to the Blumsteins', my stomach does a funny little flip. Ezra left so early this morning and I barely remember the hazy goodbye. But I remember last night. Every single detail. Graphic novels in San Francisco, healthy fast food, his warm lips on my collarbone. The perfect night.

Overall I'm feeling pretty great when I pull up to the airport. Besides the amazingness of Ezra, I did well with the bees during Mom's absence. Hopefully she'll see that—and my value—and agree I belong here in Volana. It won't matter that I turned down Golden State University or that I'm literally sleeping with the enemy.

I cling to these hopes because—for once—life is good. And I don't want the good to end.

The parking lot is busy, and I circle the pickup area three times before I spot Mom. If she weren't the one wheeling Gran, I'm not sure I'd recognize my grandmother. I steer the Element to the curb and unlock the doors, heart lodged in my throat. I'm not surprised, not after the FaceTime on graduation night and Mom's descriptions of Gran's condition, but it still steals my breath.

Gran's shrunken. Despite the heavy leopard-print sweater she's wearing, it's clear she's thin, all bones and papery, sagging skin. Her hair is shone short, silver gray. The only similarities are her clothes—flashy, colorful patterns, large earrings, shakily applied makeup.

I shift the car into park and hop out to help them with their luggage.

Mom's tamed her dark hair into a bun, and her skin is sunburned. She wheels Gran to a stop beside her car, a grin breaking wide across her face.

"Josie!" She tosses her arms around my neck, hugging me so tight I'm afraid she might crush my larynx. But I don't care.

My mom is *back*. She's here. When she was gone, it was easy to distract myself from how much I missed her, but now? I wrap my arms around her neck, hugging her back just as tight as I try not to cry.

When we part, Mom's bleary-eyed, and turns away, pretending to fuss with her suitcase.

"Hey, Gran," I say, my expression tentative. Unsure. Will she recognize me?

Gran trembles as she lifts her chin. Her arms are folded limply in her lap, and her neck strains with the effort. "Josephine?"

My insides exhale with relief.

I nod and don't let myself cry. Because I kind of want to cry. All the prior knowledge, all the prepping in the world, couldn't prepare me for actually seeing my gran reduced to a shadow of her former self. Where did my gran go? The one who was vivacious and snappy and venomous if you ever got on her bad side.

"Yep, the one and only." I lean down and carefully hug her. As if she might break under the pressure of my embrace.

"Missed you, Button," Gran whispers in my ear, and I can't stop the tears springing to my eyes.

"You too." I sniffle and step back.

I help Mom load up the Honda Element with their two suitcases and situate Gran in the front seat. The Element's elevated back seats aren't the best option for Gran and her limited mobility.

"I can drive us home," Mom offers, and I hand her the keys.

"Home," Gran repeats softly.

Home. Gran's mouth curves into a soft smile at the mention of her true home, of Volana. Her eyes, which are ageless and green and sharp, are watery with emotion.

Mom dabs at her eyes, mascara smearing, and my tears fall, heavy and fat.

Goddess above, the lot of us. Crying in front of the Volana County Airport.

When we take Volana's one highway exit into town, Gran straightens in her seat. By the time we turn into our long, dusty driveway, she's crying. The lavender-gray house. The electric-blue door. The oak trees swooping above in a canopy. Home.

Gran's silent as tears roll down her cheeks. Dripping from her chin into her lap. Mom doesn't say anything, so neither do I. It's been four years since Gran's been back in Volana, to the house she grew up in.

We park out front and Gran asks for her walker, which is in with their luggage, and I fumble setting it up. Then Mom and I lift Gran out of the car, and she leans onto her walker, shuffling forward.

"I'm so glad you brought her home," I tell Mom as Gran slowly makes her way to the porch, pauses at the stairs, and takes them one shaky step at a time.

Mom hangs back, gathering the luggage. "I'm surprised she said yes." Her mouth turns. "The past few weeks . . . they haven't been easy, Bug. She's having a good day, but they aren't all like this."

I grab the last suitcase. "I understand," I say, but worry flickers inside of me. If this is Gran at her best, what does her worst look like?

Mom pauses, smiling at me. Tucks my hair behind my ear. "Thank you," she says, before following Gran and unlocking the door for her. I hang behind, watching as Ford excitedly greets his owner.

When I join them inside, my throat catches. Memories of what life was like years ago—when Gran still lived with us—make my heart warm. Happy.

"Wow," Mom says, peeking inside the study. It still needs a few additions and a fresh coat of paint, but it's livable. "This is great! All that's left is putting together the hospital bed. It's supposed to be delivered this afternoon."

Gran's holding Ford, who licks her face with uncontainable enthusiasm. "He remembers me," she says, gleeful.

"Of course he does. Mom, don't let him lick your face. Ford!" she admonishes, and helps Gran with the wily old dog.

Once Ford's back on the ground—running between the three of us like he doesn't know how to split his attention—Gran walks over to the kitchen. To the patio door leading out to the backyard.

"Can I visit the bees?" Gran asks.

"Do you even have to ask?" my mom teases. "They're *your* bees."

Together we help Gran outside and down the hill to the sprawl of the apiary. I hold one of her arms, while Mom steadies the other. I had no idea she'd be this frail. Mom tried to warn me, but I didn't listen.

Gran sings quietly as she approaches the nearest hive—"Crimson and Clover" by Tommy James and the Shondells—and presses her cheek to the gabled metal roof on top of the highest honey super. Tears stream down her powdery cheeks.

"It's so good to be home," she says. "With all my girls."

My phone buzzes after dinner.

> **EZRA: Any chance you can sneak away tonight?**

I bite my bottom lip to stop the traitorous smile from forming, and shift back in my chair. We just finished dinner, and we're still gathered around the kitchen table. Gran's sleepy, and Mom will probably get her to bed soon. They're still three hours ahead on Florida time.

> **ME: I'll definitely try. They both might be going to bed soon? For once, jet lag isn't a bad thing.**

"Josie?" Mom says.

"Sorry? What?" I tuck my phone into my cardigan pocket and smile. The picture of innocence.

Mom doesn't comment on my odd behavior. "Mind cleaning up while I get Gran to bed?"

"Not at all." I push up from the table and collect the plates. I pause beside Gran, rest my hand on her shoulder. "I'm so glad you're home."

Gran peers up at me. "Me too, Button."

As Mom helps Gran get ready for bed, I load the dishwasher, my phone burning a proverbial hole in my pocket. And because I'm the tiniest bit guilty, I spray down the counters and wipe them clean until they sparkle. I'm wrapping up when Mom wanders into the kitchen and slumps into her seat with a weary sigh.

"I gotta say," she says, and glances sideways at me, "you've outdone yourself, Bug."

"Yeah?" I ask, twisting the damp rag between my hands.

Mom nods. "The house looks great, the yard and apiary are organized, clean. Your notes on all the hives are fantastic." She shrugs, smiling pridefully. "I'm impressed."

"Thank you." The smile pulls at my face. "I've loved helping out. It makes me happy."

"I can tell," she says, smiling wider. "This summer . . . you seem really happy."

My smile slips.

I'm *really happy* because of Ezra Blumstein-Abramo. Of course, beekeeping makes me happy and fulfilled. But the past few weeks with Ezra have been unparalleled. I never thought I could feel this way about another person—and have them feel the same. Being with Ezra is easy and fun and thrilling.

I want to tell her *everything*.

I open my mouth, then close it. What if she freaks out? Prevents me from seeing Ezra?

Mom, who must be exhausted because she doesn't notice me gaping like a fish, gestures out to the darkened backyard. "It means a lot to your gran that you love the bees. She was worried the tradition would die off with me."

"Why?" I ask, but I already know the answer. This was never the life my mom wanted. Someday, sure, but she didn't want to sacrifice college or travel to run the family business. I drape the rag over the faucet and slide into the seat beside her.

"Don't get me wrong, I enjoy this work. I love my life. But sometimes I wonder . . . well, I wonder what would've happened if I'd taken out a student loan, gone to UC Davis." Her gaze slides past me, unfocused. "I never loved the honeybees like you do. Like Gran does."

"I'm here if you need me, Mom." I choose my words carefully. "I'm happy to help out."

"I know, I know." Mom's smile is bittersweet. "Too bad I only have you for, what, another month and a half?"

A lump forms in my throat, an ache so raw it nearly silences me. "I'm glad you're both home. If you need my help while you get Gran settled, say the word."

"I might take you up on that." Mom squeezes my hand. "I'm going to start interviewing caretakers tomorrow." We're quiet for a spell, then she says, "You know what? It's only nine, but I'm going to take a bath, then pass out."

My heartbeat picks up. "I might hang out with Nan later, if that's okay?" The lie comes so easily it scares me. Nan leaves for her graduation trip tomorrow, and her absence is the perfect cover for finding moments with Ezra.

Mom yawns into her fist. "Oh sure. No problem."

The guilt is heavy in my chest, but I'm so, so conflicted. Excited to see Ezra, guilty over lying. My new normal. I say good night to Mom, then plop down on the couch with my phone.

> **ME: Sorry, I was with my mom. Meet you in like 15 min? (Also, I miss you too.)**

> **EZRA: Great! At the street corner?**

> **ME: See you there.**

I set my phone facedown on the couch, willing my chest to loosen. The anxiety is heavy, though. For someone who wasn't made for lying, I lie an awful lot, don't I? Above my head, the pipes groan as Mom begins running her bath.

I glance around the house, at the little signs of Mom being home. Her purse in the foyer. Sweater on the banister. The half-empty cup of tea on the counter. While I grew accustomed to the freedom of living alone the past few weeks, it's a relief she's here. It's an even bigger relief she knows how much I care about this place and our business. Like all the wrong I'm doing might be outbalanced by the good.

When I'm outside, I breathe easier. Maybe it's the fresh air or the fact I'm no longer physically confronted by those I'm lying to. But I take long, deep breaths as I walk the path beside the highway. My heart thumps faster in anticipation of seeing Ezra, and when I finally do, the muscle does a little hiccup inside my chest.

Ezra waits beneath the streetlamp on the corner where our two streets meet, leaning against the pole with his hands tucked into his pockets. I've decided it's his signature posture.

"Hey," I call out when I'm close enough.

Ezra grins, and when I reach him, he pulls me into a hug. Our bodies pressed together, our hearts beating in sync. "Hey yourself." Then he ducks down, kisses me full on the mouth.

I push onto my tiptoes and kiss him back. The kiss is slow, sleepy, and sweet. Not even an entire day has passed since he snuck out of my bedroom, but I've missed him.

And unlike how I felt after I slept with James, there's no awkwardness between me and Ezra. If anything, last night brought us closer together.

When we part, I link my hand through his. "Can we walk?"

"After you."

We find ourselves at Volana Vale Park, the site of our first date.

Instead of going off toward the fields or sitting at the picnic benches, Ezra leads me to the swings. He drops into one, and I take the other.

"So? How'd it go with your mom and grandma?" he asks, pumping his legs.

"Good. It's been a lot, but it's good." Then I recap the day as succinctly as I can as we swing, our bodies cutting through the cold night air. The airport. Gran's frailness. Mom's praise. "I want to tell her about us," I add, "and I almost did. But what if she freaks?"

"Josie, hold on," Ezra says, and he skids his heels into the wood chips. He twists his torso toward me, wrapping his hand around mine as it clutches to the chain link. I soak him in—cheeks reddened by the cold, the breeze ruffling his waves. "Telling your mom, well, I won't lie. It'd be great. But I understand why you can't."

"I just—this *sucks*." I hate how my voice breaks, a hairline fracture. "Sneaking around was fun at first, but I hate it now."

"I hate it too," he says softly, his hand squeezing mine. "But what did you expect? She would return from Florida with a brand-new outlook on life—grudges be damned?"

"Not when you put it that way. I hoped . . . I wouldn't have to keep lying. That she'd remember the important things in life now that Gran's back, not this ridiculous feud." My breath fogs between my parted lips from the cold.

"Are you . . ." Ezra hesitates. "This isn't too much for you. Is it?"

"No, no, that's *not* what I was saying." I tug him closer, kiss him. As if the press and heat of my mouth on his will speak louder than my words. When we part, I add, "I wish we didn't have to sneak around. But I'll figure something out, okay?"

"Okay." He knocks his legs into mine. "Because I'll do whatever I have to," he tells me, voice low, serious. "Even if that means stealing kisses at midnight and pretending like I don't know you when I see you around town."

I laugh softly. "You sure?"

"Never been more sure of anything in my life," Ezra says, and pulls my swing closer until his mouth catches on mine. And I try to believe him. Believe that we can do this.

Chapter Eighteen

HALFWAY THROUGH MY Tuesday shift at Waxing Poetic, my phone vibrates.

> **NAN: Wish you were here, mon amie!**

Below the message is a picture of Nan and her mom in front of the Louvre. While touched by her gift, I'm still irked by her selfish behavior on my birthday.

Other than my text thanking her for the gift and wishing her a happy vacation, I haven't reached out. She's texted me before this but hasn't broached the topic of my birthday. Hasn't apologized. But she has to know I'm upset, right?

Maybe she's hopeful I'll have moved on and forgiven her by the time she comes back from Europe. Self-preservation through avoidance. Honestly, I'm torn over what to do. I'm running out of time to tell her—and Mom—about my fictional college plans. It's almost *July*.

I love Nan, but what if things are too broken between us to try and maintain our friendship? We used to be so close. But we haven't been that way in years. When I tell her about LA, will our friendship be over?

Am I simply clinging to the past?

With a sigh, I lock my phone and turn it facedown beside the register. Nan won't be home until the first week of July, so I still have a few days until she'll even be back in town. But anxiety edges against my calm. The pressure of running out of time. I'll figure it out. When the time comes, I'll figure it out.

As for Mom . . . I'm less ready to tackle that particular situation. She and Gran have been back for less than a week, but it's been great, and I want to ride this out for a little longer. The goldenness of working beside her, the undercurrent of her pride. She'll have to accept my decision. Nothing will change when I tell her—hopefully. I just need to find the perfect moment to break the news.

And it's not my fault the perfect moment hasn't presented itself yet.

The bell above the door jangles, and I switch into customer service mode. All big smiles and small-town small talk. While I'm the opposite of my mom—I'd rather spend my time working in the apiary, not at Waxing Poetic—I don't mind the work. For one, it keeps my mind occupied. For another, it's nice to get out of the house and actually sit instead of lugging around forty-pound honey supers.

As I wrap up with a rush of customers, I catch sight of Mom outside on the sidewalk, headed my way. I wave with one hand, the other counting out change.

"Have a great day," I tell the customer, handing over their change, and swivel my attention toward Mom as she works her way to the back of the store.

"Hey, Bug," she says, and slides an iced coffee toward me. "Ready to call it quits?"

I check the clock; my shift is almost over. "Yeah, unless you need me to stick around?"

"Nah, I've got it under control." Mom shimmies behind the counter and gives my arm a squeeze. "Do me a favor when you get home? I left some frames in the office."

"Want me to put them in the fridge?"

"That'd be great." Mom chews on her iced coffee's paper straw, clearly preoccupied. Her sunburn is healing, but it's left her skin perpetually pink, flushed. "I totally blanked. Hopefully this jet lag–induced brain fog is almost over."

"I don't mind!" We're beginning to organize, pull, or note which hives we'll harvest from for the honey show. The event is creeping up on us. We're less than a month out from our most important event of the year—from our twenty-fifth ribbon. From the Royal Jelly.

My phone buzzes on the counter. Before Mom can see the name, I slide the phone off the counter and clear the notification. But not without reading it first.

EZRA: Any chance you're free?
My grandparents are in SF until
tonight and my mom's working.

"That Nan?" Mom asks.

I shove the phone into my purse and sling it over my shoulder. "Yeah," I lie, hating the way my stomach cramps in response. Nan's vacation, coupled with the fact that Mom doesn't know she's out of town, has made my best friend an unwitting alibi when I have plans with Ezra.

Oblivious, Mom ties her dark curls into a high ponytail. "Tell her I say hi."

"Will do." I shift out from behind the counter, forcing a smile on my face. "I'm heading out. See you tonight?"

Mom leans across the counter, smacking a kiss on my cheek. "I won't be home for dinner—Bev and I are taking Gran out—but we'll be back around eight. Movie night tonight? Gran's choice?"

"For sure." I lift my fingers in a wave before trekking out of the store. The heavy heat blisters on my pale shoulders, and I curse myself for forgetting sunscreen. The days have been long and hot, the usually temperate Northern California weather turning caustic, oppressive. Thanks, climate change.

Today, it's a high of ninety-five, and I have to walk home. The iced coffee in my hand is already sweating.

As I walk out of downtown Volana, I text Ezra back.

ME: When? Right now?

EZRA: Yeah!

Then,

EZRA: You could come over?

I pause at the crosswalk, rocking back on my heels. Bite the inside of my cheek.

Gran's out with Ford at the park and her new caretaker, a woman named Marilyn, so no one is expecting me home. My chances to spend time with Ezra are few and far between. And when we do hang out at the park, we don't exactly have privacy. With a shaky exhale, I type that I'll be over in fifteen minutes.

Who am I kidding?

I was always going to say yes.

I walk quickly out of town, turning onto Highway 10, and when I reach the corner where the highway and the street to the Blumsteins' meet, I turn right. It's weird, walking up their street in the light of day. Honestly, it feels wrong. Which, I guess it is.

Blumstein Farms is backed up onto undeveloped hills,

the outline of the single-story house casting shadows. The air is thick with manure and hay. Farther back are their hives. Stacks and stacks of boxes, towering Langstroths, partially obscured by their fence. It's a beautiful lot of land.

No cars are in the driveway, but I feel like an intruder as I walk up the groaning porch steps to the wraparound veranda. I hesitate at the front door. Do I knock? Text Ezra? But before I make a decision, the front door swings open.

"Hey!" Ezra grins at me, leaning against the doorframe. Dressed simply in jeans and a white T-shirt, barefoot, he makes my heart warm. Sends tiny goose bumps along my arms.

"Hi." I smile, vaguely aware I'm a sweaty mess. When I tossed on the nearest clothes I found this morning, I had no idea I'd be seeing Ezra. But he reaches out, his fingers curling around my wrist as he tugs me inside the house.

For a second I stand there in the Blumsteins' hallway. What the hell would Mom say if she knew I was here? She'd probably ask me to snoop and pry. But I can't bring myself to snoop. Yes, I'm behind enemy lines, but Ezra isn't my enemy. Far from it. The lights are off, the natural light dim. The AC is on full blast, and the sweat on the backs of my legs chills.

The entry hall is small, but everything is nice and organized, unlike our chronically sloppy house. It's as if the Blumsteins preserved their house in time. The wooden floors gleam, the fruit-printed wallpaper is 1950s classic.

The knickknacks are vintage, lining the shelves and window-sills. Cross-stitch patterns are framed on the walls.

"What're you doing?" Ezra asks with a bemused smirk.

"Just . . ." I break off. "I've never been in this house before. It's so weird."

He laughs and leads me into the kitchen.

The room is bright and sunny, smelling strongly of lemon cleaning spray. "So your grandparents are in the city?" I ask, tossing my iced coffee cup in their recycling bin.

Ezra drums his knuckles on the counter. "Yeah, doctor's appointment."

"And your mom?"

"Working late." Ezra pauses before adding, "We can watch TV? Or I can show you around the yard?" He drags his fingers through his hair. "No pressure. Seriously."

I step around the counter and reach onto my tiptoes to wrap my arms around his neck. Ezra's mouth is on mine within seconds, and he backs me up against the counter, his hands in my hair. I sink into it, anticipation and nerves filling my chest. Because while the other night in my bedroom was pretty damn great, I've worried we'd never get a second chance.

After the time I slept with James, I never wanted him to touch me again. Beyond the overall awkwardness and disappointment, I didn't leave that experience feeling good about myself or my body.

But with Ezra, it's different. With him I finally get what all the fuss is about.

After a moment, Ezra takes me by the hand and leads me down the hallway, through a door on the left. "This is my room," he says, and gestures to the plain bedroom. It's clearly a guest room, with a bulky suitcase on the floor and vintage lace curtains. Small signs of Ezra are around the room—stacks of comics, a laptop, the unmade bed—but seeing this? It's an oddly stinging reminder that he's temporary.

Rather than humor those thoughts, I shut his bedroom door and pull him to the bed.

◇ ◇ ◇

"Josie."

I groan, rolling onto my stomach and flinging my arm over my head.

"Josie!"

"What?" I murmur, not bothering to open my eyes.

Someone gently shakes me. "We fell asleep. It's seven thirty."

My eyes shoot open. "Wait, what?"

The demure guest bedroom. The overly soft king-size bed. The lace curtains fluttering with the air-conditioning. The heat of Ezra's body curled behind mine. *Shit.*

I push upright, the sheets pooling around my waist, and yep, I'm naked. Face hot, I lean over the side of the bed and grab my tank top and bra off the floor. I pull them on quickly before turning to face Ezra. He's clearly unconcerned that we fell asleep and it's past seven at night. He's propped up on one arm, hair a mess, expression soft and sleepy. My heart tightens at the sight of him.

"I should go," I tell him, my voice lacking the conviction it needs. "My mom's supposed to be home by eight."

Ezra flops onto his back, then turns his head and grins. "You snore."

I roll my eyes, trying not to laugh. "I do not."

"I beg to differ." He playfully tugs on my arm, and I give in, curling against him with my cheek on his chest. He kisses the top of my head and adds, "I like that I know that."

Something painful tugs at my breastbone, but I tamp it down. Listen to the steady thud of his heart instead. "I should probably leave."

"Probably."

But we lie there for another moment, neither of us quite willing to let go. I'm the first to move, rolling off the bed and grabbing my underwear and skirt from the floor. After tugging them on ungracefully, I slip on my shoes.

"See you tomorrow?" I ask, slinging my purse over my shoulder.

Ezra swings his legs over the edge of the bed and pulls on his clothes. "For sure."

I step closer and lean down, pressing my mouth to his. The kiss is slow, sweet. The perfect end to this evening. Something slams outside—in the house or their front yard, I can't tell— and Ezra stills against me. Then, unmistakable: the front door opening.

"Ezra?" a voice calls. "Penny?"

I shift back from Ezra, eyes wide.

"That's my grandma," he whispers.

"I figured." If Mrs. Blumstein called me a slut for seeing me make out with James, what would she call *this*? "What am I going to do?"

Ezra hops off the bed and laces his hands behind his head. "Um, well, we can wait them out until they go to bed . . . maybe an hour or two? Or you can climb out the window?"

There's no decision to be made. I'm *not* waiting around here until they go to bed. For one, Mom's going to wonder where I am—I told her I was going home. We're going to watch a movie! I can't bail without raising serious suspicion. The window it is.

Ezra removes the screen and helps hoist me up over the frame. I lower myself down into the itchy shrub beneath the bedroom window.

"I'm sorry about this," he says, voice low, and leans outside with his hands braced on the frame. Concern wrinkles his brow.

I lift onto my tiptoes to kiss him. "I'm glad you live in a single story," I joke, because it does suck. But I don't want to think about that right now.

The worry lessens, slightly. And he smiles—dimples and all. "Text me when you get home?"

"Worried I'll be eaten by coyotes?"

He laughs softly and ducks back into the bedroom.

"Let me know when you're home safe, okay?"

"I will," I promise, hoisting my purse over my shoulder. "Good night."

Ezra flashes those dimples once more as he waves. "Night."

I back away from the house and follow his instructions on how to escape his backyard without being seen. I circle all the way behind the big red barn, walk through a field for a few minutes, then turn left and cut down to Highway 10. From there, I sprint home, my purse smacking into my hip.

The house is quiet when I arrive, and I let myself inside. Sink into a chair at the kitchen table. Ezra and I need to be more careful, but how? We're already careful! If we're even more careful, we'll never see each other. I shoot a quick text off to Ezra, letting him know I successfully avoided any coyotes on the short walk home, then drop my forehead onto the table. Too many different emotions make my chest ache.

Not even five minutes pass before the front door opens, and Mom, Gran, and Ford walk inside. Mom helps Gran onto the couch, and I straighten up before they catch me moping. I also smooth down my curls because there's a 90 percent chance I have sex hair.

"Hey, Bug," Mom says as she enters the kitchen. "I brought leftovers. You hungry?"

"Starving, actually," I say, which is the truth. "Hey, Gran. How was the park?"

"Lovely." She primly sits, shakily picking up the remote and turning on the TV. "Marilyn and I fed the birds."

Mom hands me the leftovers and adds, "You need to eat dinner sooner, Josie."

"I—"

"You lose track of time in the apiary again?" she guesses with a wink.

"Yeah," I lie. And I remember a second too late: I was supposed to put the frames away. I *forgot*. Panic tightens my chest, but I school my expression to soften. I take the plate of Italian leftovers and head to the couch to watch *Moonstruck*, Gran's pick. She doesn't quite get our movie tradition. Obviously *Moonstruck* is cinema gold.

As I eat, I kick myself for being so careless. If I'm going to survive the rest of this summer, I need to be more careful. Because I can't fuck up. Not when things have been going so well.

I barely pay attention to the movie and Nicolas Cage's prosthetic hand, not even tasting the cannoli Mom brought home. After the credits roll, Mom and Gran go to bed. I sneak outside and put all the frames away, sticky from being left in the warm office. Since the days are hot, it's best to keep them cool until extraction. I didn't cause any damage to the frames by leaving them out, but I feel awful.

I slump into the velvet chair in the corner and breathe for the first time in what feels like hours. My heart pounds its familiar anxious drumbeat and my hands shake. *You've got this under control*, I tell myself, pressing my eyes shut, but something edged weighs heavily on my chest.

The mistake we both made today—and nearly got found out.

The mistake *I* made today because I was too wrapped up in my summer romance.

The suitcase in Ezra's bedroom.

The undeniable, heavy feeling that I'm running out of time.

Chapter Nineteen

NAN RETURNS HOME from Europe, and her first order of business is inviting me to sleep over.

A week and a half has passed since my birthday, and the distance has faded some of my more negative emotions toward Nan. The snow globe sits on my bedside table, a teeny tiny reminder that she isn't completely oblivious. But I still want an apology—or her to acknowledge that using my birthday to hook up with Nick was seriously selfish. Something to show that she *does* know me.

Duffel bag packed for the night, I drive Mom's car into the Volana foothills. The windows are rolled down, the stereo's on, and I try my very best to psych myself up to see Nan. Ezra's busy helping his mom out at the veterinary clinic tonight, which factored into why I said yes. If Ezra were free, I would've turned down the invite.

When I pull into the Johansens' large driveway, I take out my phone.

> **ME: At Nan's. Wish me luck and sanity**

> **EZRA: It's going to be GREAT!**

> **ME: You and your positivity** 🙄

> **EZRA: You know you love it**

I smile at my phone as I lock it, then climb out of the car. I follow the driveway to the front porch, but as I reach for the bell, the heavy glass door wrenches open.

"Hey, lady!" Nan motions me inside before hugging me tight, my hands hanging limp at my sides. Her long blond hair is pin straight, her makeup clearly Parisian-inspired, with a bold red lip and winged eyeliner. "I have so much to fill you in on. The trip was *amazing!*"

I open, then close, my mouth. Let the duffel bag slide down my arm and land with a *thunk* beside the front door. "Can't wait to hear about it," I say, forcing a smile onto my face.

In the den, Charles plays some action video game on the giant flat screen, and their parents are nowhere to be found. Normal fare for a Friday afternoon.

"We're going swimming," Nan announces to her brother. "Order dinner at five?"

Charles, not taking his eyes off the screen, gives us a thumbs-up. Nan and her brother are a meager thirteen months apart, and for siblings, they get along. Nan's older, but Charles is protective of her. He even beat up Nan's ex-boyfriend who had the, and I quote, "audacity to cheat on her." As an only child, I can't even bother relating to their dynamic.

I wave at Charles before following Nan outside to their deck, which wraps around the back of the house. Since their house is built into a hill, their backyard is mostly deck, the grade of the foothill dropping off. But the view is killer. At night, all of Volana is lit up and spread out below them. Their infinity pool glistens beneath the hot summer sun.

Nan instructed me to bring my bathing suit, which I'm wearing beneath the novelty *Arrested Development* shirt she got me, and shorts. After ditching my clothes, I cannonball into the water. Nan glides an inflatable pool lounge shaped like a unicorn onto the water and crawls on top, stretching out beneath the sun. But I let myself sink. Become weightless. When my lungs tighten, I push upward through the saltwater pool and reach the surface, taking a gulp of fresh air.

"You're lucky you don't straighten your hair," she says when I swim over to her. My curls are plastered to my face and neck, but Nan's hair is pulled into a bun atop her head.

A pair of sunglasses perches on her upturned nose.

"Is it luck when it's a choice?" I joke, and float onto my back. There was a hot second in freshman year when Nan convinced me to straighten my hair, but it was too much work, in my opinion.

Nan flicks some water at me, then launches into telling me about every little detail of her European trip. I float, trying to pay attention, but I care little about her shopping excursions or what Parisian boys she made out with—once Nan landed Nick, she lost all interest in him. Truth be told, my mind keeps wandering toward Ezra.

We've seen each other only at night the last few days, my daylight hours too busy with Mom, and Ezra's with his own responsibilities. I didn't tell him how close I came to messing up with Mom the other night. I still can't believe I completely blanked on the favor she asked of me. It's so unlike me to forget. But Ezra has proved to be . . . distracting.

Water sprinkles my face and I flinch. "What?"

Nan pouts in my direction. "I asked what you've been up to! We've barely hung out this summer." She drags her fingers through the water, the intricate buckles on her bikini glinting in the sunlight. Expression unreadable behind her sunglasses. "I know you've been busy with lover boy, but you could've at least returned my texts."

"Didn't we already have this conversation?" I dislike where this is headed. "*Lover boy* is the creepiest term of all time. He has a name, and it's Ezra."

"Whatever." She sighs. "My point still stands. You've been a shitty friend lately. I've barely heard from you since your birthday."

I force myself to take a deep, calming breath. "I've been busy."

"Thanks for fitting me in."

I wait to speak until I no longer feel like reaching over and capsizing her unicorn floaty. Passive aggression is one of Nan's hidden superpowers. "It's not just Ezra," I say, which is the truth. "I had to cover for my mom when she was in Florida. It was a ton of work. Summer is always busy, especially in the weeks leading to the honey show."

"Yeah, yeah." Another sigh. "Your mom should ease up. This is your last summer before college! Just you wait. Bee-keeping will be the last thing on your mind when we're in LA."

At that, I say nothing. Close my eyes against the blinding sun and let myself float.

Not long after, Nan decrees we're done swimming, and we towel off by the pool house. The silence between us isn't easy. Rather, it's barbed. Full of unsaid things.

Nan pulls on her cover-up and stretches out on one of the lounge chairs. "So. How are things with *Ezra?*" she asks, and gives me this look—like she wants me to acknowledge that she used his real name.

I hesitate, feeling out this neutral, safe ground. Then I sit on the chair closest to her and say, "Really good."

Nan cocks her head at me, brows raised. "Yeah? Do tell."

I laugh, and normally I'd happily spill everything. That's what I did with James. We even broke down the entire night when I slept with him—disappointments and all. But Ezra isn't something I want to share or expose. I want to hold the moments he and I have had close to my chest and never let them go. Or let Nan scrutinize them.

"Nothing to tell. He's . . . great."

Nan stares at me behind her amber-tinted sunglasses. "You slept with him, didn't you?" she asks, her voice faux scandalized. She even presses her hand to her chest, as if clutching imaginary pearls.

My red cheeks give me away. "I like him, okay?" I wring my hair out over my shoulder before towel-drying it. "Ezra's different. He's sweet and fun to be around."

"Hey, no judgment here. You seem happy, Jos."

The tightness in my chest relaxes. "I am."

"Good thing you two have an understanding."

I pause my hair-drying. "What do you mean?"

She shrugs one shoulder. "That it's just for the summer. I mean, you'll both be on to bigger and better things come next month."

Something icy passes over me. Because of all the conversations Ezra and I have had, we haven't had that one. I've done my best to avoid thinking about what happens when Ezra leaves for UC Berkeley. I've focused on more immediate threats to our relationship—like Mom coming home—and keep telling myself we'll figure it out later. Except we're running out of time.

All I say is, "Right."

"Ezra's cute, don't get me wrong," Nan continues, unfazed, "but you don't want to bring a boyfriend to college. Just like he doesn't want to bring a girlfriend to college."

I flinch internally. Is Nan right? I try to squash the thought down, but it buzzes around my brain. Taunting me. I rub my hand up and down my arm nervously. I don't want whatever I have with Ezra to end. But I'm not the one moving on. I'm not the one who was temporary in our situation. I swallow hard, my throat oddly thick.

When I try to breathe, my lungs refuse to fill, my chest tight. Knowingly or not, Nan is pushing every single one of my buttons today. I try again, but I can't muster a deep breath. Sweat pricks against my palms, the undersides of my legs. Everything—my lying, all the sneaking around, my complicated feelings for Ezra—overwhelms me. The panic multiplies.

"Hey," she says softly, picking up on my spiraling, "don't worry. I have it on good authority that LA has no shortage of cute guys."

Nan's lack of understanding cracks me. I'm not panicking over whether or not I'll find another cute guy to date. I'm worrying because I have shitty anxiety and the boy I really, really like is going to leave me next month. Is it that wrong of me to want Nan on my side—for once? To fucking understand me, her best friend?

Softly, with my fingers curled around the edge of my lounge chair, I say, "I'm not going to LA."

On the chaise beside me, she snorts. "Funny."

The anxiety abates, slightly, and I chase the relief. "I never accepted my spot at GSU."

Nan pushes her sunglasses onto the top of her head, swiveling to face me. "What're you talking about? Did you get into Charles's weed?"

I don't laugh at her joke, staring at the tiny cracks in the cement by my feet. "I've been waiting for a good time to tell you—"

"Are you serious?" she asks, voice sharp.

I force myself to look her in the eye; steely blue stares back. "Yeah."

Nan blinks several times, mouth pursing. "Okay. What the fuck?"

"My mom *made* me apply to college. I never wanted to go—you knew that. I want to stay in Volana and work at Hazeldine Honey. I love it here. This is my home." My hands are shaking now; I tuck my palms beneath my armpits.

"Josie, you only love Volana because you've never *been* anywhere else," she says. Adjusting her sunglasses, she adds, "We'll figure something out. There're community colleges in Los Angeles—"

"I'm not going. I'm sorry, but I'm not." The words are hoarse. I try to smile, a peace offering, but her incredulous expression shifts into a scowl. "Nan—"

"Is this about Ezra?" She lifts her chin. "Sure, Volana is closer to Berkeley than LA, but c'mon! You're his summer fling. Whatever you think you have, it isn't real. Don't be that girl."

"I'm not!" A flash of anger worms its way into my system. "I turned it down before I even met Ezra."

Nan rolls her eyes. "You want me to believe you turned down college—you turned down LA—so you can stay here and take over the family business?"

"Yes." I stare, willing her to finally understand. This is what I've *always* wanted.

Nan cocks her head to one side. "What does Emma think of this? Is she on board with you flaking out on college?" Her voice is laced heavily with sarcasm. I wince, and understanding crosses Nan's face—but not the understanding I need. "You haven't told her, have you?"

"I'm going to." I release a shaky breath. "Soon. I'm going to tell her soon."

"So, what?" Nan tosses her hands in the air. "You've been lying to everyone this summer? What about Ezra? Does he know?"

The cut of her words hurts, aches. "Yeah, he does, and he supports me."

I expect another biting remark, but Nan stares, something shifting in her eyes. I realize a second too late what that emotion is: betrayal. "You told Ezra about GSU? Some guy you've known for, what, a month?"

I open my mouth to explain, but she shakes her head. Pushes up from the chaise lounge and stares down at me, her arms hanging loosely against her body. "You lying about GSU is fucking shitty. But the fact you told Ezra is way worse. I'm supposed to be your best friend!"

"I didn't tell Ezra to slight you; it just happened." I stand up on wobbly legs. Even standing, I shrink in Nan's shadow. "And you haven't acted like my best friend in a long time. I'm not going to apologize for talking to someone who listened to me instead of making me feel bad about myself."

Nan crosses her arms, but hurt flickers across her face. "If what I say makes you feel bad, that's not my fault. You've always had thin skin." Her nostrils flare. "All I've wanted is for you to move on. Get out of this town. I love your mom, but don't you want better than her?"

"Fuck you," I whisper.

Nan's eyes widen, incredulous and glassy. "Fuck me?" she repeats with a bitter laugh. "Sure. I'm at fault here. You're the one who lied—"

"Because you don't support me," I interject, done with being trampled over. "If we were really best friends, you would've known college is the last place I want to be. That throwing me a surprise birthday party—just so you could hook up with the White Whale—would give me a panic attack. You're selfish."

Nan winces as I hit a nerve. But she says evenly, "You're the selfish one. You're the one who lied. Who acts so sweet and innocent. But you know what you are? A joke. A girl so scared of living that she won't even leave her mom's side. You need to grow up, Josie. Grow the fuck up."

I open my mouth to reply, but nothing surfaces, and my eyes are watering. Before any tears fall, I turn on my heel and run back inside the house. Past Charles, who yells at me for walking in front of the TV. I grab my duffel off the floor in the entry, shove on my sandals, and storm outside.

Inside Mom's car, I pull out of the Johansens' elegant driveway and stop at the base of the hill so I can wipe my eyes. Folding up a loose napkin, I try to dry my tears, but they keep on coming. I almost laugh at the thought of Nan ever understanding where I was coming from. Nan's never understood me, and she certainly isn't starting now.

At least the truth is out there. At least I'm keeping one less lie.

⬡⬡⬡

Penelope Blumstein-Abramo works at Volana Vet, the veterinary clinic that treats everything from hamsters to horses. Literally. That's their motto. Ezra's helping his mom out, since their receptionist called in sick, and after the disaster with Nan, he's the only person I can talk to. The only person I *want* to talk to.

I pass the ridiculous sign—VOLANA VET, FROM HAMSTERS TO HORSES FOR OVER FIFTY YEARS!—on my way into the squat, old building. Ezra's behind the front desk, and he doesn't see me at first. He's on the phone, studying something out of sight. Head bent down, brown waves flopping into his eyes. The button-down he's wearing has tiny paw prints all over it.

"One second," he says automatically, then looks up. A smile blossoms across his face. "Hey!"

I walk up to the counter, force a smile. But it takes effort, feels unnatural. "Hi."

"Can I call you right back?" he says into the phone, and hangs up before the person on the other end can respond. "What's wrong?"

I shake my head. "Can you take a quick break?"

"I'm just answering the phones. Let me forward them to voice mail," he says, and fiddles with the old landline on the counter. "There we go." Hand in hand, he leads me outside to the back of the building, where there's a tiny dog park. We perch on a low brick wall encasing the grass.

"What happened?" Ezra asks after I don't explain. I'm too busy trying not to cry. "Is your gran okay?"

I laugh, but it's watery, choked. "Yeah, she's fine. Um, I got into a huge fight with Nan."

"Shit," he says quietly, rubbing the small of my back. "What happened?"

Nan's words haunt me. The fact Ezra won't want to bring a girlfriend to college. That I'm selfish. That I'm a joke. That I'm too scared to live my life. But all I say is, "We were arguing. One thing led to another, and I ended up telling her about GSU."

"She didn't take it well?" Ezra stops soothing my back and pulls me to his side instead.

"Nope," I say, my voice tired. "And it spiraled from there. It was . . . bad. It was really bad."

"You think she'll tell your mom?"

I groan. "I didn't even consider that. But I hope not? She knows about you, about us. She knows I've been lying to my mom. Seems foolish, telling one person all your secrets."

"Nan's your best friend. That's normal."

Ezra's probably right, but from where I'm standing right now, it feels pretty foolish. "I don't know if she's my best friend anymore. Or if she's even my friend."

"Everything will work itself out," he says soothingly, rubbing my arm up and down, his palm hot against my bare skin.

Ezra's comfort—his mere presence—springs fresh tears to my eyes, and I press them shut. Ever since I left Nan's, a stinging pain has bounced between my rib cage, weighing down my chest with anxiety. But now that I'm beside Ezra, the heaviness lifts. It doesn't disappear, but he makes me steady. Like it's okay to fall apart a tiny bit because he'll be there to put me back together.

"Thank you." Part of me wants to voice my other concerns, the ones I wasn't even worried about until Nan used them to hurt me. That Ezra might be temporary. But I'm so tired, and sitting beside him is so nice. I want to hold on to this for as long as possible.

"Look on the bright side. The VCBA potluck is tomorrow—not like we'll spend it together, but we'll both be there! And the honey show is in three weeks. I know how excited you are." At that, he nudges me.

"No, you're right. I *am* excited." Or I will be, when this stops hurting so much.

"There's a lot of good on the horizon."

Opening my eyes, I smile up at Ezra, his body warm and solid beside me. I might not be able to let go of today's hurt yet, but I can fake it until I make it. Right now, I'll let Ezra cheer me up, and push Nan's words from my mind.

Sniffing back my tears, I ask, "So, is your family ready?"

"For what?"

"To have your asses handed to you at the honey show?" I joke.

Ezra scoffs, unraveling his arm from around me. "Whoa, where is this coming from?"

"I just call 'em as I see 'em."

He ducks his head so his lips hover above mine. "Bring it on, Hazeldine," he says, and kisses me.

Chapter Twenty

THIS YEAR, THE VCBA's annual Fourth of July potluck is held at Anderson Farms. Not only do they have sprawling acres of lush land, but there's a spiral-patterned maze made of their tallest sunflowers. They're our closest neighbors off Highway 10, but we're driving over instead of cutting through our property. Mainly because Gran's coming with us—her first official appearance into the Volana beek scene since she returned home.

For the first time in four years, three generations of Hazeldine women are going to the VCBA potluck. It feels good. *Right.*

As Mom finishes getting ready, I fetch Gran, who sits at her vanity in the converted study.

"Hey, Gran." I rap my knuckles on the door. Over the past week, Mom and I transformed the room from home study into cozy bedroom. It has its own little half bath, and we've decorated the walls with all of Gran's old pictures Rosa sent from Florida. Lined the windowsills and bookshelves with her favorite knickknacks.

"Can you help me, Josephine?"

I pull up the extra chair beside the vanity. "Sure. With what?"

Gran takes her time, trembling, to extend her hand out. A long silver tube of lipstick rests in her palm. If Gran had a signature color, it'd be Clinique's Black Honey.

Since Gran's only been home a week, I haven't spent much time with her yet. Honestly, I've avoided any one-on-one time. Looking at Gran and reconciling that the same woman we brought home from Florida is the one who made Hazeldine Honey what it is today is painful. For so long, I've held an immovable image of my grandmother—strong, sharp-tongued, witty—and I don't want to accept that that version of Gran is forever gone. But I know it isn't the way to approach this situation. I should be thankful for this extra time with her, even if her moments of lucidity wax and wane.

I take the tube and pop open the cap. The rich red-brown color looks intense, but it goes on smooth and sheer. "How's that?" I ask after applying the lipstick to Gran's mouth.

She turns and purses her lips; an image that almost makes me laugh because it's so quintessentially Gran. "Perfect.

Thank you, Josephine." Her tremor makes all her movements jerky, but she clearly nods. "Give it a try. We have similar coloring. Believe it or not"—Gran pauses to pet her sleek gray hair—"all of this used to be red."

"Thanks." My stomach tightens because Gran forgot I used to braid that red hair for her every night until she moved to Florida. But I humor her, swiping the lipstick on before handing it back.

Gran folds my fingers over the lipstick. "Keep it."

We smile at our reflections.

"Girls?" Mom calls from upstairs. "You ready to go?"

Shuttling Gran to and from the car is a small ordeal, but it's worth it. Anderson Farms is sprawling, the perfect amount of busy. We park in a dirt lot and unload the car. The potluck is our biggest event of the year; we invite family of all the members, plus regular townsfolk as well. We get anywhere from fifty to one hundred people. A local band set up their instruments on the Andersons' second-story deck. Immediately my lingering stresses over my fight with Nan, my worries about my whatever future with Ezra, fall to the wayside. The energy here—floaty and summery—is what I need.

Mom and Gran claim a table underneath the sunshade beside the sunflower maze, and I plop down into an empty lawn chair. I scan the crowd, but no Ezra. He and the other Blumsteins are supposed to attend. Not like he and I can talk—let alone do anything else—in this setting, but it'll be nice just to be near him.

Mom fusses over Gran and rubs sunscreen onto her arms. "Who're you looking for, Bug?"

"No one. It's just . . . super busy!" I slouch deeper into my chair and internally cringe. Am I *that* obvious?

The Andersons' deck overlooks the backyard, and the band launches into a Roy Orbison cover. Mom gets a glass of white wine, and we sink into the afternoon. Enjoying ourselves. Bev and Antonia show up, and we're all gathered in the shade. Dipping chips into fresh guacamole. Talking about honeybees, the pros and cons of mite treatment, and suddenly, *me*.

"Josie did such a good job when I was in Florida with Mom," my mom's saying to the small group gathered around us. Other than Bev and Antonia, the Millers are here. "What did I do to deserve such a good kid?"

"Mom," I mutter, face flushed. "It was nothing." While I'm embarrassed, I'm also the tiniest bit guilty for abusing her trust during those few weeks. But Mom's praise is so rare that it eclipses the lingering negativity.

Mom is slightly tipsy. She rarely drinks and is a total lightweight. Smart move going for the wine when another family brought mead moonshine. Bev let me have a sip of hers and it nearly burned a hole through my esophagus.

"It was everything." Mom pulls me into a hug. "I'm going to miss you so much next month. So fucking much."

I tuck myself against Mom, insides aglow. But I have no response for her. Our friends watch on with admiration, and while I hate being the center of attention, this moment is pure. Mom's love radiating a warmth, tangible and real. The music and the laughter. The camaraderie of so many bee-keepers in one place. This is how it should be—no silly feuds, no hatred. Just happiness.

Mom kisses my forehead. Voice dropping so only I hear, she says, "I'm worried."

I inch out of her hug. Our lawn chairs are pushed next to each other, and I lean against the armrest on her chair, chin in my upturned palm. "About what?"

Mom glances upward, mouth tight. "Forcing you out of the house. You told me last year you wanted to stay, and I don't know, maybe I should've listened."

I swear, my heart does a full-on stop. One second. Two. Three. Then it kick-starts back to life. How much has Mom had to drink? Is this how she really feels? If so, for how long? I blink at her, grappling around for the right thing to say. Difficult to do when my mind is buzzing with a million questions. "Mom, I love it here. And now that Gran's home, doesn't it feel right? All of us here together?"

Mom's smile is sweetly sad. "Yeah, it does."

Before I can say anything else: "Annalyse!"

I twist in my seat—and find myself face-to-face with the entire Blumstein family. The elderly Blumsteins are closest, with Penelope and Ezra standing behind them. Mr. Blumstein was the one who spoke. Dressed in tan pants, suspenders, and a white T-shirt, he doesn't scream intimidating, but his eyes are beady and his mouth is etched in a permanent frown.

"You're back," he says, his voice a grunt.

"My mom's—" Mom starts, but Gran cuts her off.

"Emmaline, please." Gran shifts in her lawn chair. Her walker rests beside it, but she can't get up without our help. I can tell it kills her to be unable to physically stand up for herself. "Daniel," she says to Mr. Blumstein. "Viveca," to Mrs. Blumstein. "I've returned to Volana to be with my daughter and granddaughter." Her green eyes—the only thing about her not dulled with age—glance between them. She has Vivien Leigh eyes. "Can't we all act civil?"

I sneak a glimpse at Ezra. His arms are crossed and his brow's drawn. We briefly make eye contact, and my whole body goes numb. He looks so good—he's all layered up, wearing a T-shirt, a flannel tied around his waist, corduroy pants.

Mr. Blumstein harrumphs. "We've never been civil, Annalyse. Why start now?" And with that, he totters off toward the house. Mrs. Blumstein follows.

Penelope hangs back with Ezra.

"I'm sorry, Emma," Penelope says, stepping forward. "My parents—"

"Your parents are right," Mom interrupts, and tips the rest of her wine back. Gone in one gulp. "Why start now?"

Frowning, I shrug subtly at Penelope. "Sorry," I mouth as Mom turns toward Gran and puts her back toward the remaining Blumsteins. Penelope mirrors my shrug, bumping her shoulder into Ezra's. They both head off, and Ezra's hand brushes up against my arm as he passes.

Today we have to take sides and pretend like we're strangers. I hate it.

Also, I'm silently seething that their rudeness jolted Mom out of her good mood. Our conversation was going somewhere. I almost want to tell Mom about Golden State right now, but I missed my moment. Mom's no longer focused on the good; her mood has soured. But I never knew Mom had doubts about her college-or-bust decision last November, and that gives me hope.

Sighing, I sit back in my chair and fiddle with the tab on my soda. I search out Ezra in the small crowd. We've never had to experience our fighting families in person before, and I'm left unsettled by it. I get that same guilty feeling when I lie, but it's somehow *worse*.

"I'm going to grab something to eat," I say, wanting to run away from this feeling.

Mom pats my hand and launches into a conversation with Antonia about how well her soaps have been selling. Hands tucked deep into my yellow sundress pockets, I walk up the steep slope to the house, forcing a smile whenever someone from town or the VCBA calls my name.

Upstairs on the deck, I pass the band and stuff a dollar in their tip jar on my way inside. The Andersons' living room is packed, and I maneuver my way to the potluck table in the back.

"Well, that was awkward," says a familiar voice beside me in line.

I glance up at Ezra, who's shoveling potato salad onto his already buckling paper plate. He catches my attention, giving me a boyish, dimpled smile. The very smile that first reeled me in. Teeny tiny goose bumps prick my skin.

"Yeah," I say slowly, drawing the word out. "It's like they hate one another or something?"

Ezra huffs a laugh, and we shift down the line. "Sorry about my grandpa." His hand covers mine, briefly, where it rests on the table. Fingers curling around mine, giving them a swift and almost accidental squeeze. I bump my shoulder into his—a silent *no worries*—grateful for the busyness of the potluck, all the people. Ezra tips his head at me in acknowledgment before exiting the line and disappearing outside.

After my plate is piled with pot roast, seven-layer bean dip, and seventies-style potato-chip salad, I work my way through the crowd. On the patio, someone calls my name. I pause long enough for Bev to bustle up to me, carrying a mason jar with topped-off moonshine.

"Hey, hon," she says with a strained smile. Her short, graying hair is artfully mussed, her eggplant lipstick flawless. Despite the smile, her eyes are hardened.

"Headed back down?" I ask.

"Let's talk real quick." She adjusts her cream pashmina and tilts her chin toward the side of the house, where the crowd's thinned out. I hesitate, something heavy forming in the pit of my stomach. But I follow her—partially because I don't have a choice, partially because I'm curious.

When we're somewhat alone and standing beside the Andersons' compost bin, I force a big, carefree grin. "What's up?"

Bev purses her lips to one side. "You have to stop, Josie."

My stomach swoops. "Stop what?"

Sighing wearily—like she'd rather be anywhere else in the world—she says, "You and Penelope's son. You should be thanking your lucky stars that your mom's been so distracted this summer."

No. There's no way Bev knows about me and Ezra. "I don't know what you're talking about."

Bev gives me a look. "I might not have as big of a stake in this feud, and personally? I like Penelope. But I know your mom—she's my best friend. And if she ever finds out about this, it'll gut her. I'm not sure what's worse. That you're lying to your mom or you're sneaking around with a Blumstein."

My bottom lip trembles, and I steel myself. "How'd you know?"

Bev's hardened expression softens. "I didn't, not until today. I had a hunch, though. At the last VCBA meeting, I noticed he followed you outside. Didn't think much of it." She sips her moonshine. "But you've been acting, well, not like yourself the past month. And I saw you two in there. . . . There's something going on, isn't there?"

My eyes are hot, my breath tight. But I nod. "Please don't tell my mom."

She sighs again. "I like seeing you happy, Josie, but I can't keep secrets from your mom. I'll keep quiet for now. But here's my free advice: Put an end to this before it spirals out of control. I'm much more forgiving than your mom."

I nod, my legs jelly beneath me. Afraid to speak, to open my mouth.

Bev squeezes my arm before she turns around and slips through the crowd.

Leaving me alone with a lie I'm not sure I can afford to keep up anymore.

⬡ ⬡ ⬡

The fireworks pop and crackle in the sky, and I don't feel any better about my altercation with Bev. Have I been that transparent the past month? That *careless*? First Penelope. Now Bev. It's laughable: I'm a mess! This whole twisted situation is a mess. And I'm in the middle of it.

Ezra leaves next month. Right around the time I'm supposed to pack up my life and head to Southern California. I always knew he was leaving, and I refused to think about it. But Nan's words, however cruel, hold a nugget of truth. Ezra's not going to drag his summer fling into college. Mom will already be upset with me when I tell her about Golden State, and if I kept up a relationship with Ezra, that truth would eventually come out too.

All of it makes me panicky with dread.

Up in the sky, the fireworks shatter across the darkness. But I can't summon myself to join in with all the oohing, the aahing. Instead I tell Mom I'm getting dessert, and push up from my lawn chair. I pull my cardigan tighter around my body and head toward the sunflower maze.

Unlike dinner, all the desserts are laid out by the stairs to the house, in front of the maze. The band has long since packed up, the only noise the crackle of firecrackers. As I stand there, staring at the picked-over cookies and soggy slices of pie, my chest continues to tighten with anxiety. With panic.

My therapist told me anxiety is different for everyone. Oftentimes it's like I'm exposed, stripped naked with an anvil on my chest, threatening to snap my sternum in two. Or like tonight, anxiety is being trapped in a human centrifuge. Fighting for every breath, straining against every movement.

Tears well. I'm so fucking overwhelmed.

I want Ezra.

I want Hazeldine Honey.

I want to go home, crawl beneath the covers, and wait for this to pass.

"*Psst,*" someone says.

I look up from the dessert. A camping lantern illuminates the table, but its glow barely lights anything beyond a few feet. I step tentatively toward the sunflower maze, and a hand shoots out, pulling me in. Ezra grins down at me, lacing his fingers through mine as he leads me farther into the maze.

We stop in the center of the empty, quiet ring of sunflowers.

My heart hammers—a conflicted mixture of warm, effusive, and anxious. "What're you doing?"

"I wanted to see you." He beams and rocks back on his heels. "I knew you wouldn't be able to resist the dessert table."

All I want is to step closer and closer until my cheek presses against Ezra's chest and his arms wrap around my waist. But I stand still, fighting with myself, my hand limp in his.

Bev warned me to not let this spiral out of control, but I'm afraid I already have.

"We shouldn't—I need to get back to my mom, okay?" I take a step toward the maze's exit. But he grabs the sleeve of my cardigan and swings me to a stop.

"Josie, wait."

"Ezra." I exhale shakily. "I can't—"

"No one's around," he says, and reaches out to trace my jawline. "Don't worry, I checked."

I recognize the look in his eye: the dopey sweet one. My self-control around Ezra has always been iffy at best, and when he kisses me, I kiss him back. Ironically, kissing Ezra undoes some of the anxiety knotting up my chest. The press of his mouth to mine, the tightness of his fingers in my hair . . . I almost forget why this is the *worst* idea. Completely inadvisable.

Outside the maze, someone shrieks in laughter. Conversations growing closer, then fading.

And I do something I've never done before: I push Ezra away. If Bev saw us, half-drunk on moonshine, then so can anyone else. If they haven't already. We're not being as careful as we pretend.

"What's wrong?" Ezra stumbles back, his eyes wide.

My throat tightens, and I scramble for the right words. "Someone could've seen us."

He glances around the empty clearing. "Uh. *Who?*"

"What happened to playing it down in public? You said you didn't care if you had to pretend like you didn't even know me," I say, my words tumbling out fast.

"Sorry, I thought . . ." He draws a hand over his mouth. "I'm sorry, okay?"

I want to accept his apology, press my mouth to his, and ignore everything and everyone else. Except I've been doing that all summer, and reality is finally catching up with me. "I should go."

"Wait." Ezra's fingers loop around my wrist, trailing down until they lace with mine. In the near darkness, he studies my face. "Something happened." A statement, not a question.

I pull my hand from Ezra's—he flinches—and I cross my arms tight over my chest. "Bev saw us, okay? Earlier, in the potluck line. And last month."

"Wait, what?"

"Yeah, she knows, Ezra. This is too risky." My breaths turn sharp and pointy, stabbing at my lungs. The enormity of everything I'm putting at risk for a boy who'll leave my life without a trace next month slams into my heart, my brain. *Deep breaths*, I coach myself, but it doesn't work.

"Josie, it'll be okay," he says in earnest. "What else did Bev say?"

"I can't . . ." I shake my head. "I need to go."

"You can't *what?*" Ezra sighs his frustration. "Talk to me. Please."

I rock back onto my heels. One arm pressed against my stomach—as if holding myself tight will keep me from falling apart. "I don't think I can do this," I whisper.

"What can't you do?" His voice pitches in panic. When I don't respond, he adds, "Josie? What can't you do?"

"You deserve someone who doesn't have to hide you, okay?" I whisper the words, but they're fervent and real. A truth I haven't wanted to acknowledge. "You deserve way better than this. Than me."

Ezra takes a half step closer. Up in the sky, firecrackers pop, trails of light streaking as they fade. "You don't decide what I deserve," he says, his voice a low growl. "I make that decision, Josie, not you. And I want you. I choose *you*."

"I'm sorry—"

Ezra grabs my forearm gently, even if his words are heated. "I thought we were good! Better than good."

That's the problem, isn't it? Ezra's great. The kind of great that will get me into serious trouble with my mom. If he weren't going anywhere next month or if Mom didn't care so much about the feud, then I'd roll the dice. Gamble. But I'm not *that* girl.

I'm not the girl who risks her future on a boy who will leave her in a matter of weeks.

"What do you want me to say?" My eyes are hot and burning as I fight back tears. "You're leaving next month anyway. Why prolong the inevitable?"

Ezra blinks at me, like he's confused. "I don't know what Berkeley has to do with this, but wow. Okay. You're breaking up with me." He says this slowly, and his hand slides from my forearm.

Tears blur my vision. Ezra, the sunflowers, the fireworks—they all merge. Sniffling, I shrug and try to play my pain off as indifference. "We've always been temporary."

"You didn't even consider . . . ," he starts to say, then stops himself. Takes a deep breath. "Nope. Forget it. Clearly I had a very different idea of what this summer meant. But you're right about one thing. I deserve someone who doesn't take my heart only to break it."

The words land like a blow to my solar plexus. Big, hot tears roll down my cheeks, catching on the bow of my lips. He brushes past me, and I'm tempted to reach out to him, to apologize, to somehow fix this. But my arms fall limp at my sides.

Before leaving the maze, Ezra wipes his eyes with his fist and says, "I thought you were brave, Josie. But this? It's fucking cowardly." Then he's gone.

I try breathing, but my chest is too tight. I lean forward and brace my hands on my knees, suddenly nauseous.

I had to do it. Before I ruined my relationship with my mom. Before I ruined my chances at having a shot within Hazeldine Honey. Maybe if I keep telling myself that, I'll believe it.

I sink onto the ground and bury my tear-streaked face against my knees.

This summer, I've lost my best friend and now my boyfriend.

I couldn't let my future be another casualty too.

Chapter Twenty-One

THE MORNING AFTER the potluck, I wake up to the worst type of chaos.

Mom's fist is banging on my bedroom door like an endless riot. Throwing off the covers, I'm immediately thrust into survival mode. Heart hammering a cacophony inside my chest, I stumble out of bed on weak legs and wrench the door open.

"What?" I ask, wiping the sleep away from my eyes with my thumbs. "It's, like, five in the morning!"

Mom's wild-eyed, dressed in her robe. "Outside," is all she says, so I follow her downstairs, grabbing my robe from the hallway bathroom, feet shoved in slippers.

Mom loops her arm through mine, dragging me until

we stand on the crest of the hill overlooking the apiary. Every attempt at asking what's wrong has been answered with silence. Mom points to the apiary. It's quiet, but that's not unusual. Honeybees usually don't stir until eight or nine.

"What?" My brain's still half-asleep. I didn't drink last night, but I might as well be hungover. My eyes are swollen, my stomach upturned. I'm depressed as fuck. Doubting all my decisions from last night. "Am I missing something?"

"Look closer." Mom's trembling. But not from this morning's cold front.

At first, I don't quite realize what's different. Like I'm so used to seeing the exact same thing when I stare out onto the apiary, the change isn't as obvious as it should be. My mind filling in the blanks. Then it becomes obvious.

The hives. Some are toppled over. Partially, or all the way off their stands or cinder blocks. Frames flung across the grass. Every hive is missing its telescoping lid and inner cover.

What the hell happened?

"They vandalized them," Mom says, clinging to me so hard her nails bite into my skin.

I shake Mom off and approach the ruined apiary. I'm still, holding my breath as I listen for the telltale buzzing. The sound that'll let me know everything's going to be okay. But the backyard is deathly quiet. The first hive rests on its side. The honey frames on the grass are smashed.

Cracked open. Layered on the grass and along the bottom boards of the hives are thousands upon thousands of dead honeybees.

"How?" is the only question I can ask.

"It was down to forty degrees last night. They must've knocked the hives over or removed their lids."

Honeybees can survive the cold—but only if they're in a hive—and the mix of the cold weather and the dismantling of their home is fatal. Numbly, I remember a fact Gran told me years ago: Honeybees can't fly at forty-two degrees and lower.

Thousands of our girls.

Dead.

A worker bee will only live up to six weeks in summer, shorter if she works herself harder and faster, but this loss is heavy inside my chest. Thousands of small deaths, piling into my heart.

My entire future, my family's legacy, *gone*.

I push away from the hive, moving on to the next-closest one, inspecting it. Dead. To the next—dead. And to the next—empty. Dead and empty. Mom wraps her arms around me and pulls me away from the hives to the back patio. My slippers crunch over the dead bee bodies in the grass.

"Who would do something like this?" I slump onto the swinging love seat. Tears cold on my cheeks. Fingers stiff.

Mom kneels before me, her cheeks flushed and eyes glassy. "There's only one person, one *family*, Josie."

I meet Mom's gaze, her saddened expression replaced by one of rage. A visible change, the tears drying on her cheeks. A sinking drags my gut down. Because she can't believe the Blumsteins are responsible.

"Mom, the Blumsteins didn't do this," I say, forcing my voice to say neutral. Penelope doesn't give two shits about the feud and neither does Ezra. The elderly Blumsteins are too old to pull something like this off. And why would they bother now? After so many years of bitter coexisting?

"If they didn't," Mom says, "then who did?"

I open my mouth, but nothing comes out. Because I don't have an answer.

Mom's slanted green eyes are full of rage. "Exactly. Do you think this is a coincidence? Weeks before the honey show?" Standing up, she adds, "I'm going over there."

Before I can argue against this awful idea, she heads inside.

I slump forward, my mind swirling. A dark sinking overtaking me. Those hives were our livelihood. The reason I turned down GSU. The reason I broke up with Ezra. Gone, in an act I can't wrap my mind around. As much as I want to band behind Mom, I can't reconcile my image of the Blumstein-Abramos with the massacre in our backyard.

I drag my fingers through my tangled hair, cursing silently. There's one thing for sure: Mom *cannot* find out about Ezra and me. If she believes they did this, she might blame me, too. I'm screwed. I am so epically screwed.

Actually.

What does it matter? There aren't any hives left.

All my plans, all my lies, have come tumbling down around me in a spectacular fashion.

I hurry into the house and swap my pajamas for jeans and a sweater. Then I run the entire way to Blumstein Farms, fueled by grief and adrenaline. As I crest the hill, spikes of yelling pierce the morning air. Sharp words. Raised voices.

The morning is foggy, making the scene even more eerie. The porch lights glow a buttery yellow, and two people face off on the veranda. Mom and Penelope. Ezra's nowhere to be seen, which disappoints me in a way I don't want to examine.

As I approach the porch steps, out of breath, Mom's saying, "This is like UC Davis all over again. You can't help yourself, can you, Penny? You take, take, take."

Penny? I pause behind Mom, my brows scrunched together. "What're you talking about?"

Penelope's eyes are red-rimmed, her arms crossed. She's in overalls, a sweater, muck boots on her feet, clearly pulled away from morning farmwork. "That was twenty years ago, Emma. Let it go."

"Let what go?" I ask, so terribly lost in this conversation. "What does this have to do with our hives being vandalized?"

"Your hives were vandalized?" a voice asks behind me.

I turn. Ezra stands on the porch. He's carrying a basket

with fresh eggs, wearing his hoodie. My heart aches at the sight of him, and I make myself turn away. I'm not sure how to be around Ezra now that he's no longer mine. Not mine to look at, not mine to touch.

Penelope turns toward me and says, "Your mom is still upset I got the scholarship she applied for to UC Davis when we were in high school." Her tone is flippant—incredulous, even—like she's struggling to believe my mom has held on to this hurt for so long.

Ezra comes up beside me. "What's going on?"

I shake my head. Completely at a loss.

"This isn't about what happened then. It's about what happened now," Mom says, teary-eyed. "You vandalized our hives last night. And if you didn't, your parents did."

"Emma, I didn't vandalize your hives. And my parents definitely didn't vandalize—"

Mr. Blumstein walks out the open front door. "What is going on out here?"

A new target spotted, Mom rounds on Daniel Blumstein. "What's going on?" she repeats. "You vandalized our hives. You petty little man."

Mr. Blumstein laughs. "Excuse me?"

"This morning, I found our entire apiary vandalized," Mom says. "And I asked myself, who would do such a thing? The Blumsteins, of course. Right when we were about to take your precious Royal Jelly award from you."

Penelope looks aghast. "You don't think we'd kill your bees

over the *honey show*, do you? We didn't hurt you or your business. We would never."

Mrs. Blumstein joins the party on the porch, and the conversation dissolves into yelling and bickering. I stand there, clutching the column next to me, wondering what's next. My mind keeps hitting a wall. How are we supposed to move on? It took us decades to build up our bee farm, starting with my great-grandmother. And it was felled in one night.

"We should be calling the cops," Mom says, crossing her arms tightly over her chest. She looks to me for confirmation, to egg her on, but my eyes fill with tears. Because I'm *done*.

I don't want any part of this.

My heart will burst if I stand here any longer, so I leave Mom and the Blumsteins, and return home. I walk around to the side gate, letting myself into the apiary.

For a hot second, I hope I exaggerated how bad it was inside my head.

But no. This isn't just vandalism. This is the end of an era.

"Josie?"

I startle, and turn to find Ezra lingering by the gate.

Then I sigh heavily. I can't deal with him right now. The tiredness hits me. So tired.

"Holy shit," he says, glancing around. His entire face is pale, losing its usual luster. "I'm so sorry. This is awful."

I steel myself, not wanting to cry in front of Ezra. "Yeah. That's one word for it."

Ezra hesitates beside the gate before stepping into the

backyard. "You don't agree with your mom, do you?" he asks, voice pleading. "Tell me you don't think we did this."

"I—I don't know what to believe." My eyes glaze over as I stare at the mess of broken hives.

Ezra walks over to me, his fingers wrapping around my elbow. The softness of his fingers lingers along my inner arm. The heat of his body, a foot away. "Is there anything I can do?"

I drag my shaky hand through my hair. Unable to tear my gaze from our mess of an apiary. A sob catches in my throat because *it's all over*. Everything. This summer, I had everything. And I don't know how I lost it all. Hot tears turn my vision blurry and I tilt my head back. As if gravity can keep my emotions in check.

"No," I say, my voice cracking. "I don't know."

After a moment, Ezra shifts closer and wraps an arm around my shoulders. "Hey," he says gently, soothingly. "It's okay. Cry, let it all out. But everything's going to be okay."

I curl into Ezra's chest, my tears soaking his hoodie. Give in to the feel of his body comforting mine. The solidness of his arms, the thump of his heart. And I cry for all the things I've lost recently. Whether willingly or not, I've lost so much.

But when my tears slow, my hiccupping breath calming, I pull away from Ezra. Wipe my eyes with the sleeve of my sweater. "Um, thanks for checking on me," I say, "but my grandma's inside. You really shouldn't be here."

His face falls. "Seriously?" he asks, not angrily, but like he can't believe my request.

I shrug, grasping my elbow with one hand.

Ezra searches my face for one long moment before turning his back to me. Then he walks out of the backyard without another word.

The gate falls into place, leaving me all alone in a grave-yard of honeybees.

Chapter Twenty-Two

WITHOUT MY HONEYBEES, summer turns dull and muted, fuzzy around the edges.

Without a plan—without a *future*—I turn part desperate, part hopeless.

Desperate enough to reach out to Nan, which I did a few days after the vandalism. My text was both a peace offering and an apology. One she accepted. Because without Ezra, I had no one to turn to about my life plans falling to pieces.

Not unless I come clean to Mom, which I'm hopeful I can avoid altogether.

Today I'm going to call Golden State University's admissions office and beg them for my spot back. It was Nan's idea, but if I convince GSU to reinstate my admission, I won't have to tell Mom about turning them down in the first place. Also, I'm itching for a plan—and fast. In one night, I lost my future, and anxiety *does not* do well with the unknown.

Rebuilding Hazeldine Honey would take the money and resources we don't have. In the past week and a half since the vandalism, Mom has expressed zero interest in rebuilding. A few VCBA members have reached out and shown their support—offering to help us rebuild in the spring—but Mom turned them down. It's not financially viable, and Mom says it's too much work. Our beehives weren't insured. Most companies consider them a huge liability. Generally speaking, it's not worth it, considering how rare vandalisms are out in the country. In urban areas and cities, vandalisms and thefts occur quite frequently.

Without Hazeldine Honey, there isn't as much left in Volana for me. Maybe it's the universe telling me it's time I get over my anxiety and leave home. But every time I try making sense of the vandalism, I come up short. Nothing makes sense anymore. The pain still lingers like a thousand phantom limbs with wings.

After eating lunch, I hop on my bike and pedal down Highway 10, headed to Nan's. I'm grateful to get out of the house. Gran took our loss in stride, but Mom's struggling. If she's not busying herself by cleaning the house, then she's trying to find a way to keep Waxing Poetic afloat. Without our hives, we don't have the supplies to make the products we sell.

I bike past the Blumsteins' street—and the corner where I used to meet Ezra—and my chest aches. Mom contacted the police and reported the vandalism. But the police concluded there wasn't enough evidence to charge any of the Blumsteins. Apparently, a near-century-old feud wasn't enough for them. And honestly, it's not enough for me, either.

Even Gran thinks it wasn't a beekeeper, rather a random vandalism. Mom still believes the Blumsteins did it, since the honey show is coming up. The vandalism knocked us out of the competition. We have honey frames stored in the cooler, but not enough to enter. Any honey shown must be from your personal hives from this year's harvest. No hives equals no harvest.

Sure, the Blumsteins were the only ones with a motive, but it doesn't sit right with me.

I slow to a stop in front of the Johansens' house, dragging the toes of my jelly sandals against the pavers, and I rest my bike against their garage.

"Josie!" Nan leans out the front door and motions me to hurry up.

I wave, hoisting my messenger bag out of the basket and slinging it over my body. Nan's acted cautious and overly friendly since our reconciliation. As if she actually listened to what I said during our fight, and she's trying to do better. We might not ever be as good of friends as we once were, but she's all I have left.

"Hey," I say once I reach the porch, and hug Nan. She